Also by Wendi Nunnery

The Best Kept Secret Series
The Best Kept Secret (#1)
The Next Best Thing (#2)

Good Enough: Learning to Let Go of Perfect

THE BLUESTOCKINGS

WENDI NUNNERY

The Nunn Press

Published by The Nook Press
Atlanta, Georgia

Cover design: Wendi Nunnery
Cover images: Canva

First Printing, 2025

THE BLUESTOCKINGS

For every girl who has ever found hope inside a book.

Contents

1

Prologue

Everyone in Hawthorn, Georgia, believed that Eleanor Black's mother was dead.

Everyone, that is, *except Eleanor.*

It had been six long years. *Six.* Two-thousand-and-ninety-one days, give or take a few. Fifty-two-thousand-five-hundred-and-sixty hours. Enough time that Eleanor knew now, even if she hadn't at first, that her mother wasn't coming home.

A missing persons case that had gone cold almost as soon as the first police report was filed, the strange disappearance of Vera Black—beloved mother, wife, and owner of the local bookshop, Bluestocking Books—could only be labeled as such:

Strange.

Six-year-old Eleanor and her grandmother, whom Eleanor called Poppy, had come home from Eleanor's gymnastics class that night to the horrifying news that Vera was missing. In the days following her disappearance, everyone in Hawthorn was baffled. Multiple witnesses had seen Vera enter the bookstore that morning. Nothing had seemed amiss, and Vera had appeared her typically friendly, if quiet, self.

She had never returned home that evening.

Eleanor understood how her mother would sometimes disappear into herself, how her thoughts sometimes took up more space in her head than there was room. Eleanor's brain was like that, too, except she wasn't quiet like her mother. Eleanor *talked*. She didn't have a choice. She had to get the words out in some logical order, or they would spill out on their own and ruin everything. Eleanor's memories were littered with the messes her words had made. Birthday parties. Crushes. That one time she got sent to the principal's office for repeatedly correcting her English teacher when he said "agreeance" wasn't a word.

But there was one thing Eleanor had long ago decided she would keep to herself.

In the weeks after her mother's disappearance, Eleanor's family had little to offer anyone who asked them questions. There was no evidence of foul play. No evidence of *anything*. All anyone had to go on was a missing mother and an otherwise ordinary day in an otherwise ordinary place. Only the lack of Vera's presence was proof of something gone wrong.

Eleanor remembered police officers murmuring in low voices and the quiet house her mother had left behind. A tomb, with its inhabitants still alive, but only just. She remembered standing in the bookstore her mother had named, her family's bookstore, running her small fingers over the spines of the books they'd read together, a quiet knowing settled over her.

Eleanor's mother hadn't been harmed. She had *left*.

Eleanor believed that deep in her bones, even if she had no way of explaining it to others. She still felt her mother's presence in the world—a tether, an umbilical cord still connected to both of their bodies. Invisible, yet strong. But how could Eleanor ever put those thoughts into words? She had never even tried because, honestly, who would listen?

It was a secret tucked into a corner of Eleanor's heart, where it would remain. Hidden, but never forgotten.

A story within a story.

2

Eleanor

With his hand frozen above the touchscreen register, Eleanor's dad fixed his face into a pleasant smile as their neighbor, Agatha, droned on about her broken ankle. It was an expression Eleanor knew well, a smile that said, "Please stop talking," even though James would never be so rude as to speak the words aloud. It was the only smile Eleanor had ever seen on her father's face.

"Marty told me not to step up on that ladder, but I really didn't think it was gonna hurt anything," Agatha said, leaning on the mahogany counter. Her thick arms jiggled as she settled onto her elbows. Eleanor resisted the urge to reach out and squeeze them. She wondered if they felt the way her grandmother's had, pillowy and smooth, like the dough in her homemade biscuits.

"Well, I'm glad it's not too serious," James replied with a wink at Eleanor. She turned her back to swallow the giggle that threatened to bubble up in her throat. "It's a good thing you're right next door. I don't have to worry about missing my morning coffee."

Agatha pouted, her face reminiscent of an overgrown toddler. "I hate being stuck," she said, sticking out her foot to scowl at the orange cast. "I've never broken a bone before now if you can believe it."

"Never?" asked James, still smiling with polite interest.

"Neither have I!" interjected Eleanor as she whipped back around to face Agatha. She couldn't resist a chance to join the conversation, even if Agatha was the sort who talked a whole lot but never said much of anything. "I got a concussion once when I fell off my skateboard, but that wasn't so bad."

Agatha's face brightened. "Say, that's an idea!" she said with a finger pointed at Eleanor, who stopped shuffling bookmarks and frowned in confusion. Adults who pointed fingers at kids rarely had much good on their minds. "How about you do some deliveries for me while I've got this blasted thing on my foot? Maybe leave the skateboard at home, though." When Eleanor hesitated, Agatha added, "I'll pay you."

Eleanor changed her mind about pointed fingers. "Really?" She glanced at her dad, who sighed.

"If you want," he said. "Just as long as you don't go too far."

"Oh, don't you worry about that," Agatha said with a conspiratorial grin at Eleanor. "Most customers are right here in town, and, besides, everyone in Hawthorn knows our girl. She'll be fine."

Eleanor chose to forgive the "our girl" in favor of Agatha's confidence in her. "Thanks!"

She pictured herself, messenger bag over one shoulder, strolling around the square from the hair salon to the antique store, dropping off coffees and baked goods to the adults who worked there. She'd hold her head high, long dark curls in a ponytail down her back, and call out names from the list of customers. She would never mispronounce them since she had known almost everyone in Hawthorn her entire life, and she would never, *ever* give them the wrong order.

Eleanor Black, Coffee Messenger. It had a nice ring to it.

"I'm already helping out here with Dad while we're on winter break," Eleanor added, her eyes bright with excitement. "But he doesn't pay me, so this is way better."

James scoffed and eyed Eleanor over his thin reading glasses. "Oh, thanks a lot."

"You know what I mean, Dad," Eleanor said, lifting her chin. "I love the bookstore, but a young girl needs to learn some fiscal responsibility."

Agatha hooted and slapped the counter. "Got yourself a real smart kid there, Jimmy," she said, pushing off with some effort. She pointed at Eleanor again, but this time Eleanor didn't mind. "Come by and see me first thing when y'all open, and I'll get you started on the morning orders."

Eleanor nodded, bouncing on her toes. "I'll be there."

After Agatha made her clumsy way next door to the bakery she'd opened with her husband thirty years ago, James swiveled on his old, faded Converse and gazed at his daughter, lips pressed into a tight line. "You sure you want to work for Agatha?" he asked. "She's a handful."

"Of course, I'm sure," Eleanor replied with more confidence than she felt. "I can handle her. It'll be great."

It had to be great. Eleanor was, quite literally, counting on it.

Two weeks ago, she had gone into her dad's office to grab the stapler from his desk drawer and had found herself staring at a document with large, foreboding letters, the sort of words Eleanor had only ever seen in movies and had thought, until that moment, was the stuff of sets and scriptwriters. Her heart had pounded against her rib cage as she read the lengthy notice and felt sick enough to puke. She hadn't understood much of what was written there, but she'd understood enough.

Unless Eleanor's dad came up with more money than she'd ever seen in her life, they were going to lose Bluestocking Books.

The shop had been her parents' dream even before Eleanor was born. Her mother had named it to honor all the women throughout history who had been scorned and punished for their love of learning, and now it was in danger of becoming a memory.

Just like Vera.

This was Eleanor's chance to help. Surely, Agatha would pay her as much as any other employee. Maybe with that kind of cash, Eleanor could make a dent in what they owed and keep them safe for a little longer. After all, people in Hawthorn had been generous to the Blacks over the years. Eleanor thought back to times when the shop was filled with customers, back when she would run between shelves and giggle in delight as people called out to her. Bluestocking Books had been her haven. Her palace of dreams and magical wishes that always came true.

As she peered around at the quiet space now, Eleanor wondered for the first time if perhaps she was mistaken. Maybe the shop had only seemed that way because she'd been so small. Maybe the trouble had started a long time ago.

How Eleanor loved Bluestocking Books. She loved the way it smelled like dust and sea air, no matter the season. She loved how the old pine floors creaked and popped as they settled. She loved how she needed a ladder to reach the top of the bookshelves, as though she were a character in one of her favorite novels. The shop was dreadfully romantic, and Eleanor was determined to save it. She needed—*they* needed—a miracle.

Two miracles. And each one seemed as impossible as the other.

Eleanor shuffled papers on the counter into a stack and cleared off the crumbs from her breakfast bagel. "I can still help out here, though, so don't worry about that."

"I'm not worried," James said. He removed his glasses and peered at Eleanor. "But you're *twelve*. You need to have some fun on your school break."

Eleanor shrugged, feigning indifference. "Work *is* fun."

James shook his head and offered a weak chuckle. "I've ruined you. I've taken my lovely, bookish daughter and turned her into a workaholic. Profit is king. All is lost."

Eleanor laughed, but his words made her stomach twist. She peered out the front window and took a deep breath in her nose to settle the anxiety that bloomed hot in her chest. She breathed out slowly through her mouth, just like she'd been taught, and pictured her fears disappearing into the air around them, swallowed by the cozy atmosphere of the bookshop. Her plan would work. It *had* to work. It was only three weeks until Christmas. Nobody would be terrible enough to close a family bookstore before Christmas. *Right?*

Eleanor watched her dad shuffle back to his office, his broad shoulders eternally slumped, and let out a heavy sigh. The clock on the wall behind her ticked away the seconds, a cruel reminder of every moment spent without the money they needed to keep Bluestocking Books in business. The multicolored lights Eleanor and James had draped on the bookshelves last week twinkled with a prism of warmth, but she only felt cold. Fingering the oval brass locket she always wore—a gift passed down first from her grandmother to her mother and then to her—Eleanor pushed her worries into the metal through her fingertips. A talisman to capture her anxious thoughts.

Everywhere she looked, Eleanor was reminded of her mom, no matter how they rearranged the layout or changed the decor. Vera had been the storyteller, the one who'd taught Eleanor to love words, and her stories were all around them. The bookstore was all they had left of her. Abandoned daughter or not, Eleanor couldn't bear to lose it, too.

As a small handful of customers trickled in and out of the store, Eleanor cranked up the holiday tunes and worked to finish the new window display: a large book tree draped with white lights that blinked in time to the music. Regardless of what people might say about Eleanor's mother, no one could ever say that Bluestocking Books wasn't a delightful place to spend an afternoon. The walls were lined with shelves of books, some new and some used, in every genre. A soft, leather couch sat in the center of the store, encircled by shelves, with a worn wooden coffee table and a threadbare rug where Willoughby, the stray tomcat who wandered in and out of stores all over Hawthorn, seeking snacks and chin scratches alike, would sometimes curl up and sleep for hours. Origami birds Eleanor had made from the pages of re-cycled books spun in lazy circles above her head. Her mother had even set up a little free library by the front door so they could cycle out old inventory for people who came into the shop but weren't able to buy anything.

"Everyone deserves books," she'd said to Eleanor as they filled it to the brim with paperbacks and old advanced reader copies.

Bluestocking Books was a place that allowed Eleanor to escape. If she didn't want to be reminded of her past, if the grief threatened to pull her under until Eleanor couldn't bear the sight of the store for another minute, she would simply open the cover of a book and dis-appear.

At least her disappearances were temporary.

Back at the house that night, after James had closed the shop and they'd walked home, Eleanor set her grandmother's old tea kettle on the stove and waited for the water to boil. James' mom and dad had owned their house for years before Vera and James married, and the whole family lived in it together until both of Eleanor's grandparents got sick and moved into the nursing home. Eleanor was ten years old the year they passed away, just months apart from each other, and she still missed them every single day.

Inside, the Black house was frozen in time. Floral wallpaper in every room of varying shades of rose or lilac. Wonky cabinet doors that didn't fully shut after decades of Georgia's coastal humidity had warped them. A poky fireplace that sometimes smoked. But the kitchen table was the same one where Eleanor's grandmother had taught her to make biscuits from scratch, its surface marred by thou-sands of meals. And the fenced garden out back, her grandfather's shed still standing sentry, bloomed in springtime with enough color and fragrance to make even the most skilled gardener pluck his beard with envy.

While Eleanor waited for the kettle to heat up, she peeked out the kitchen window into the garden. She giggled at the ancient porcelain

Santa her dad had perched in the center of the stone path, his rosy cheeks weather-beaten and faded. The kettle whistled, and Eleanor prepared their drinks, careful to measure the cocoa powder for her hot chocolate in precise spoonfuls. She topped it with a dollop of whipped cream and then carried the mugs into the living room. James sat on the edge of the couch, glasses perched at the end of his long nose. A folder of paperwork was open on the table in front of him, and the furrowed line between her dad's eyebrows as he scanned the papers appeared to grow deeper with each moment. He looked up at Eleanor and blinked as if to come back to himself from some other place. Then he smiled a weary smile.

"Tea?" he asked, taking a mug from Eleanor.

"Earl Gray for you," she said and pretended to gag. "Hot chocolate for me." Eleanor cast a glance over the papers, but her dad tidied them away before she could see what they were.

"One day, you will love tea, too," James replied with a clink of his mug to hers.

"Unless it's ice cold and sweet enough to make my teeth rot, no thank you." Eleanor turned on the television and browsed for a Christmas movie. James wrinkled his nose like he smelled something sour.

"I think I'll head to bed now," he said, moving to get up from the couch.

Eleanor huffed. "C'mon, Dad," she pleaded. "Don't you want to see another small-town artist slash bakery owner slash dog lover fall in love with the big-city bad boy determined to open a chain store and shut down her business?"

James laughed then, and the sound of it was a warm blanket on Eleanor's skin. "Maybe you should write those movie scripts, Elle," he said. "You'd probably do a better job."

"But then we wouldn't be able to hate on them," Eleanor replied, matter-of-fact. "Mine would be much better, *obviously*, and the cheese factor is what makes this so fun. I wouldn't want to let anyone down with my clever wit and stunning dialogue."

Besides, she thought, *I've got my own bookstore to save.*

James looked down into his mug, resigned to his fate.

"If you're looking for an answer in there," Eleanor chirped, "it's 'Yes.'"

Her dad sighed and sat back down next to Eleanor. Then he eyed his daughter with a raised brow. "I do this because I love you, young lady, and for no other reason."

Eleanor gathered her feet up under the blanket and scooted close to his side. The Christmas tree twinkled at them from across the room, and Eleanor watched it with a tender ache in her chest, a bruise that wouldn't heal.

"I know you do," she said and pressed play.

3

Ruby

Ruby stirred from her catnap by the fire, the cobalt blue afghan on her lap a closed oven door against her body. Her chest was damp with sweat, and with a grunt of displeasure, she cast the afghan onto the floor by her feet. Ruby stared at the blanket, one she had knit long ago before arthritis set in, and frowned. Like her, it was ancient. And, rumpled on the floor that way, nearly as useless.

She set her chin forward and stood, palms pressed against the arms of the chair for support. Ruby Hurst was eighty years old, but she was not, nor would she ever be, an invalid. Though she had no family or friends to speak of, except for Benjamin, her gardener, and Marianne, her housekeeper—if one could call employees such things—Ruby was of strong stock. She had survived greater hardships than that of a tired body, and useless though she may be, she would die before she lost all her mental and physical faculties. It was a decision she'd come to many years before, and once Ruby Hurst made a decision, it was etched in stone.

The clanking of pans in the kitchen drew Ruby to the door of the library, where she searched her pocket for a handkerchief and pressed it against her damp skin. If it didn't draw Marianne's noble nitpicking, Ruby would throw open the front door and stand, delighted, in the fresh, cold air. She could just imagine the prickle of her skin against the chill as it cooled down. Ruby could do without the manufactured holiday nonsense at this time of year, but she loved winter. She felt understood by the landscape, the way it turned quiet and still as life settled down to rest for a few months. Ruby thought more people should take their cues from nature.

Down the long hallway, past the front staircase, Marianne was hard at work on lunch. The woman was a sensational cook, and she prepared Ruby's meals with as much joy as if she were cooking for royalty. A delicious meal was as necessary to Marianne's peace of mind as a good book was to Ruby's, and they shared a mutual respect over their love of the stories each could tell.

A bowl of chicken salad in front of her, Marianne turned at the sound of Ruby's footsteps and smiled. "Hey, honey," she said in a gentle lilting accent. "Have a good rest?"

Ruby raised an eyebrow at the pet name but nodded. "The heat woke me."

"Oh, that's my fault," Marianne replied as she tossed a sprinkle of chopped almonds into the bowl and stirred. "It gets chilly in that front room, so I covered you with the afghan."

"I like the cold," Ruby said.

Marianne huffed. "Only God knows why."

Ruby ignored the comment and poured a glass of sweet tea for herself. It tasted of sunshine, of memories long past and a childhood spent exploring the house on her own, the library her sanctuary even then.

"Are you looking forward to seeing Maggie again?" Marianne asked. She set a plate of chicken salad and fruit in front of Ruby, who glanced up sharply. "It's been a long time since there have been any children in this house."

Ruby froze. "I forgot about Maggie," she said after a beat.

Marianne snorted. "How could you forget about your niece coming to stay with you?"

Ruby sniffed. "It's not as though I know the child. She's my brother's youngest granddaughter. I haven't seen her since she was three."

Marianne laughed, and her entire body shook with it. "Good gracious, woman! I don't know how that makes a bit of difference. If my great-niece was coming to visit with me for a month, I think I'd keel over from the joy of it."

"I have no doubt."

"Well, lucky for you, I've already taken the liberty of getting the guest bedroom ready upstairs." The room that had been Ruby's as a child, long before her life became a shadow of what she had hoped it would be.

There was no use in hope anymore. Ruby knew that now.

"Fine. She's welcome to stay wherever she wants as long as she doesn't act like a fool in my house," Ruby replied. "I don't know much about young people anymore, and I certainly don't know why I agreed to this. I must have been drunk."

Marianne eyed her employer with a twinkle of amusement in her eyes. "Oh, what I wouldn't give to see that. But anyway, you agreed because she's your *family*."

"Hmm. Well. Don't let her treat you like the maid."

Marianne laughed again. "Ruby, I *am* your maid."

"You're my *housekeeper,* and I pay you handsomely," Ruby corrected her.

"Shush and eat your food."

Nearly a decade had passed since Ruby had last seen Maggie. Ruby's younger brother, Edward, had once hosted a family reunion here at the Hurst family homestead, and Ruby had been anxious for everyone to leave before they even arrived. It had been painful to have family gathered together in this house when so many others were gone by that point. Their father. Their younger sister, Caroline. Ruby's mother.

A few years later, Edward died, too, and Ruby was left well and truly alone in the world. No one she'd ever loved had survived long enough to share in the blessing of growing old with her, and so she hated growing old. She hated feeling useless.

She couldn't wait for it all to end. She would only miss her books.

By eight o'clock that evening, Ruby's stomach was twisted into knots. Maggie's plane would have arrived at Savannah International Airport at six, but dinner had come and gone, and still no Maggie. It didn't take but fifteen minutes to get to Hawthorn from Savannah. Even with baggage claim and traffic in the city, the girl should have been here by seven at least. Ruby paced the foyer.

She was nervous. Ruby preferred to keep to herself over the hassle of getting to know anyone new, and Maggie was new, family or not. When Maggie's mother, Janet, had phoned a month ago and asked if the girl could come to visit for a while, Ruby had bristled at the idea of a child living in her house. She was thirteen, the age when one is too young to know just how young she still is, and Ruby could think of plenty of other things she'd like to do than deal with a bratty teenager for a month.

It turned out that Maggie—Margaret—was about to become a child of divorce, and Janet was well on her way to single motherhood. She needed a few weeks to set up house and wanted Maggie to have somewhere nice to stay for the holidays, somewhere free from the stress of her parent's separation. "Somewhere with family," Janet had said on the phone, which was quite a statement considering how irregular her contact with Ruby had been over the years. In the end, Ruby had agreed to let her great-niece travel down here from Virginia to a secluded house in a secluded town she had only visited once as a toddler and live with her until January.

In truth, Ruby had hoped Janet would forget the whole thing. She certainly had.

Half an hour later, as Ruby sat in the library reading, there was a sharp rap at the front door. Ruby glanced up from her book as Marianne crossed the hall to greet their new arrival. As the door swung open, Ruby stood to take in the couple on the threshold before them. Janet was a petite woman with blond, wavy hair and wide, blue eyes. Even though Ruby hadn't seen her in almost ten years, she hadn't changed much. To Janet's right, swallowed in a pair of jeans and a sweater that must have once belonged to a man, was Maggie.

"Oh my goodness, hi!" Janet exclaimed as she pushed forward into the foyer and threw her arms around Ruby, who stiffened at the touch. "It's so good to see you, Aunt Ruby. Thank you so much for letting Maggie come and stay with you for Christmas. I just know she's thrilled about it."

Ruby and Maggie eyed one another with skepticism. "Yes," Ruby said. "Thrilled."

Maggie stepped into the hall and peered at her surroundings. Ruby imagined she had never stayed inside a home as grand as this one. Her face was open and curious, intrigued rather than anxious, and Ruby recognized the small child she had once been. Maggie's cropped, messy haircut framed her pointed chin, and while she wasn't short like her mother, her delicate features gave one a certain elfish impression. Ruby scanned the girl's appearance with disdain. It looked like she had rolled around in a donation bin.

"Maggie!" exclaimed Marianne, coming up behind Ruby. "Come on in, honey, we're so excited to see you!"

Ruby pursed her lips together but nodded. "Welcome, Margaret. I'm pleased you're here." With a turn to Janet, she added, "We had begun to wonder when you'd arrive."

Maggie moved further into the room and dropped her backpack on the floor. Ruby stared at it as though it were a dirty dish rag. "It's Maggie," she corrected Ruby, who merely blinked.

"I should have called, I know," said Janet, talking a mile a minute. "But I met this fantastic woman on the plane who was on the third leg of her trip home from India, and I had so many questions for her. I've always wanted to visit, so after the plane landed, we grabbed coffee. Before I knew it, we'd talked for an hour!"

"How lovely," Ruby said, though she had no idea why anyone would want to spend an hour talking to a stranger she'd just met on a plane. Ruby didn't like talking to anyone except Marianne and Ben, and even that was a stretch. Talking got one into trouble.

Maggie cast a sideways glance at her mother and rolled her eyes. Ruby didn't approve of the gesture, but she couldn't disagree with the sentiment.

"Of course, we understand," clucked Marianne as she offered Maggie a hug and scooped up her bag. "I'm Marianne, Ruby's housekeeper. I live in the guest cottage around back. Is this all you've packed?"

"No, I've got more," Maggie replied.

"She has a suitcase in the trunk of my rental," Janet interjected, "but we can get it later. I'm in no hurry."

"So we've learned," Ruby said in a dry tone.

Maggie turned to face Ruby then, eyebrows raised in delight at the sarcasm in her aunt's voice, and appeared to look at Ruby for the first time. She felt the fire in her niece's gaze, the judgment of Ruby's color-coordinated pastel sweater set and expensive but sensible jeans, and she met the girl's stare with a steely one of her own. Better for the child to know who she was dealing with from the get-go than to show up expecting to be doted upon. Ruby was not the doting type.

After a moment, Maggie's shoulders relaxed, and she turned her attention to the phone in her hand. "This house is nice," she said. Maggie held up her phone, and Ruby heard a distinct shutter sound. "My friends are gonna freak."

Ruby pressed her lips together into a ghost of a smile, but Maggie had already gone back to typing. A moment later, Marianne directed Maggie and Janet up the stairs to the guest rooms. Ruby released a puff of air from between her lips. She could hear Marianne's voice, eager to pepper Maggie with all sorts of questions about her life, but Ruby shared none of her housekeeper's interest in the girl.

At least now Ruby knew she and Maggie were on the same page. As far as she could tell, they had nothing in common except their mutual disinterest in one another, and that suited Ruby just fine.

~~~

The watery winter sunlight pierced the crack in Ruby's bedroom curtains and landed right on her face. She had dreamed of sand between her toes and tears on her cheeks, and the brightness behind her eyes made her feel like she was there on that beach. She could still hear the seagulls cry as if they knew her torment and grieved along with her.

Ruby groaned and turned away from the window. Not today.

She sat up in bed and pressed long, cool fingers to her temples. The swell of a budding headache thumped inside her skull, and Ruby knew from many similar experiences that it would be a bad morning for everyone if she didn't get up and take care of it soon.

Ruby shuffled to the bathroom that had once belonged to her parents—and her grandparents before them—and grabbed an ibuprofen. With a swish of water in her mouth and a splash of water on her face, the pressure in Ruby's head seemed to ease.

She brushed her teeth and hair and then padded back to the bedroom to change. Hers was an ancient routine, simple and unaffected. A quick rinse, a moisturizer, and some mascara. She allowed the pattern of lines on her face to shine through, having made peace with them once she realized she had no one to impress at this point anyway. Her eyes, once bright and vibrant green, had turned the color of swamp water, and her cheekbones, a point of pride for many years, now cast hard shadows on her face. Only Ruby's hair retained its youthful appearance, gray now instead of the deep auburn it had once been, but still thick, wavy, and styled down past her shoulders. Ruby would never cut it short. That was for very young women, like Maggie, or for women who'd given up. Ruby didn't care much for this life
~~~

anymore, but she retained her sense of self-preservation like any good Southern woman should.

She dressed in a long, floral skirt and white cashmere sweater and then made her way down to the kitchen, not without some effort. It was time for her to begin using the master suite downstairs— it had been for a few years now—but Ruby was nothing if not stubborn. She had already moved bedrooms once, and she had no intention of doing it again. Marianne had once suggested an elevator, more for herself than for Ruby, and she was beginning to consider it. She had more than enough money and little else to spend it on.

Seated at the breakfast table tucked in the front parlor window, Ruby turned to face the morning sun. Ruby was a nature lover, and the large Queen Anne Victorian she'd inherited from her father offered plenty of views from which to observe the acres of forest around it. As a child, Ruby would often imagine pirates skulking across their land to steal the antique treasures within her home. Although she hadn't known their monetary value then, she knew well the story of her great-grandfather, George Hurst, who had immigrated to the United States from Germany and founded the town of Hawthorn in the late 19th century. The significance of her family heritage had been a common theme throughout her childhood, but rather than give Ruby a sense of self-importance or duty, it filled her with a persistent dread that somehow, someday, it could all be taken away from her.

And it had been.

Not the house or the name, but the people she had loved most, one after the next, until no one was left but Ruby. Sometimes, it felt like her life had been one cruel joke, a poor man's version of what it could have been—what it should have been—all along. Now, all she had to show for it was a tired, old body, a tired, old house, and a niece who appeared sooner to forget Ruby existed than spend any meaningful time with her.

Ruby settled into her seat and took a sip of the coffee Marianne had placed in front of her. She liked it sweet and creamy, a cup of comfort to her soul, and Marianne made it just right every time. "That's delicious," Ruby said with a sigh of contentment.

"I know," said Marianne with a wink. "You want eggs or grits this morning?"

"Grits, please, with extra butter on top. And a few slices of bacon."

"Extra butter?" asked Marianne, her eyebrows raised. "It's about time. You need some more meat on your bones."

Ruby rolled her eyes. If she'd heard that cliche once in her life, she'd heard it a thousand times.

"I've never understood the point of that phrase," Ruby replied dryly. "I can stand, can't I? I can walk around and lift my arms and even do a little twirl if it pleases me."

"Let's see it then!" came a voice from the doorway. It was Janet, fresh-faced and wide-eyed, her hair a shaggy mess on the top of her head. Ruby said nothing. Maggie stood just behind her, looking as grumpy as Ruby felt.

"Good morning, ladies," Marianne crooned, plates of grits, bacon, and toast piled high on the plates she held. She set one down in front of Ruby, who took another sip of her coffee and nodded at her nieces as they took their seats at the breakfast table.

"Morning," Maggie replied in a scratchy voice. Her face was puffy from sleep, and a small, angry pimple had made its way to the surface of her chin. At the sight of it, Ruby felt something tight in her chest uncoil. She swallowed hard. She supposed they'd have to make the best of this if they wanted to live in peace.

"Did you both sleep well?" Ruby asked in a placid voice.

"Oh, yes," replied Janet with a sip of coffee. She sighed and curled her fingers around the mug with a soft grin. "That bed up there is dreamy, Aunt Ruby. Like sleeping on a cloud."

Maggie said nothing. She pulled her knee up to the table and leaned on it, slumped over her food like a veritable beast gnawing at a bone. Ruby held no romantic ideas about how much better life was in the past, especially for women, but she did often wish that people would still act with manners more suited for a breakfast table than a wild animal's den.

"And how about you, Maggie?" Ruby asked pointedly.

Maggie looked up at her with a bewildered expression as though she had forgotten Ruby was even present. "It was fine."

Janet glanced at Ruby and raised her brows as if to apologize. But Ruby was undeterred. "Good. I'm afraid I don't leave the house much, but there is plenty for you to do here if you use your imagination. What do you like to do for fun?"

Maggie shrugged, and Ruby set her toast down on the plate, brushing her hands free from crumbs. "I don't know what that means," she said, nodding to Maggie's shoulders.

The girl scowled at Ruby and slumped into her seat. "Talk to my friends. Watch videos of cats. I read a lot."

"Ah," Ruby replied, confused. *Cats?*

Maggie sunk deeper. "Can we go to the beach?" she mumbled.

Marianne shot Ruby a sharp glance, whose mouth turned down into a frown as she spoke. "I'd rather not. It's too cold this time of year, anyway. You won't enjoy it."

Maggie fiddled with her toast and muttered, "Yes, I would."

Janet cut in. "Maybe you can go into town sometimes and look around? We drove through the square on the way, and it looks like such a sweet place."

"Yes, we have a coffee shop and a bookstore and some great little restaurants," Marianne said as she cleared a few dirty dishes and headed back to the kitchen. "The man who owns the bookstore has a daughter about your age, too."

At that, Maggie's eyes lit up. Ruby looked to Marianne with gritted teeth, who returned her gaze with an expression of remorse. Her housekeeper knew good and well how much Ruby hated town.

"Thank you for the wonderful breakfast, Marianne," Ruby said in a sharp tone and stood from the table. "I think I'll go for a short walk."

Marianne retreated quickly, leaving Maggie and Janet to finish their meal as Ruby stepped outside. With the fresh, cold air in her lungs, Ruby felt calmer. She took slow, even strides down the dirt driveway that had never been paved in one hundred and thirty-eight years, terracotta Georgia clay still wet from rain and clinging to her shoes. The live oak trees that lined the drive on either side hung their thick limbs over her head, protective and ancient. Ruby used to climb them as a young girl, even into her teen years, and found such comfort in how the low-hanging branches stretched out to welcome her up, as though they were forever anticipating her arrival. When she reached the paved road that traveled east into town, tall iron gates flanking the entrance to the Hurst estate, Ruby turned and walked back toward the house. From a distance, the pale yellow Queen Anne Victorian looked much like Ruby herself: put together well, but old enough to be haunted and not approachable to anyone who hadn't been invited. Benjamin did his best with the grounds, but there was just too much of the estate to care for and not enough people to care about enjoying it. For years now, Ruby had only asked that he keep the house, the cemetery, and the immediate property tidy. The rest of the vast acreage she'd inherited didn't matter anymore.

As she walked, Ruby thought of her dream from the previous night, of the grief that still lived within her heart, and worried that its coinciding with Maggie's arrival was a bad sign. A sign of more loss to come.

But what else was there to lose?

If Ruby had been anxious about Maggie's visit before, she was even more anxious about her departure. She could only imagine what kind of nonsense the girl would bring into her home before it was all over.

4

Eleanor

Eleanor walked with her dad to Bluestocking Books the next morning, the sky a steel gray blanket above their heads. Eleanor longed for snow, but a wish like that was a fish in the air. It had only snowed once in Hawthorn in all of Eleanor's twelve years, and even then, it hadn't stuck. Every flake had melted as soon as it hit the too-warm ground. Eleanor could still remember the delightful sting of the flurries as they landed on her cheeks and outstretched tongue. They had tasted like the sea, like salt and brine and happy afternoons spent finding shells on the beach. For an hour, Eleanor had galloped with excitement around the backyard, the sadness of her mother's absence from yet another holiday forgotten for a moment. Poppy and Grandpa had joined her since they were old enough to know how to act like kids again and took great pleasure in doing so at every opportunity. James, however, had stood on the patio watching with a sad smile fixed on his care-worn face until Eleanor had tugged on his sleeve and demanded that he catch some snowflakes, too.

That's how it had been for as long as Eleanor could remember. She had so many memories of her mother, even though she'd disappeared when Eleanor was six, but for some reason, Eleanor couldn't remember a thing about her dad from back then. It was as if he'd come to life fully formed the moment Vera left, ready to take over as a full-time parent and fill in the gaping hole left behind by his wife. He was a good father but a sad one.

With a wave goodbye, Eleanor trotted over to Agatha's bakery and threw open the door, ready for her first day as a delivery girl. Inside, the aroma of roasted coffee beans and melted sugar filled the space. Eleanor inhaled, tasting the sweetness of Agatha's peppermint cremes and chocolate croissants. One customer sat at a table by the window, head down as he typed away on his laptop, and another sat sipping an iced coffee while she played on her phone. Agatha flagged Eleanor down from the kitchen doorway, a flour-dusted apron on top of her ugly Christmas sweater.

"Morning!" she called out. "Already got two orders for you, soon as you're ready."

Eleanor beamed. She'd dressed for the occasion in a bright green crew neck sweatshirt, red plaid scarf, and red Converse sneakers. Her long, curly hair was pulled back in a claw clip she'd painted with Christmas ornaments, and she wore earrings in the shape of tree lights. Her dad's old messenger bag was slung across her shoulders. Inside was Eleanor's favorite notebook, two spare pens, and some high-lighters for crossing off orders as she delivered them.

"Gracious, child," Agatha said with a hearty chuckle as Eleanor ap-proached and followed her into the kitchen. "It looks like a Christmas tree threw up all over you."

Eleanor clenched her teeth together. Did the woman own a mirror? "I like to be festive," she said, hurt straining her voice.

Agatha tutted and took Eleanor by the arm. "We're just two peas in a pod then, honey," she said and handed Eleanor two receipts, a to-go bag, and two to-go coffees in a tray. Eleanor struggled to keep the cups upright as she fumbled with the receipts. "The bag goes over to Mrs. McIntosh over at the antique store, and the coffees go to the front counter at Harriet's Hair. Don't forget to give them their receipts."

"Have you ever considered online ordering?" Eleanor asked, straightening her shoulders, eager to pass on her knowledge. "It's much more efficient *and* it's better for the environment."

Agatha shook her head and shooed Eleanor out of the kitchen. "Efficient isn't always better, my dear. As for the environment, you tell me how many trees those books of yours have killed, and then we'll talk."

"But, I...they're—" Eleanor sputtered, momentarily speechless. *Blasphemy*, she thought, calling to mind a word she'd read once in *The Witch of Blackbird Pond*. Eleanor liked the way the letters hissed and rolled like an angry squall out over the ocean.

"Hurry back now," Agatha continued, unbothered by Eleanor's protests. "We get real busy about ten o'clock, so I'll need you to make it quick." With an unceremonious shove, she waved Eleanor off into the frigid morning. An icy breeze had picked up, and a tornado of dried leaves swirled around her feet. Eleanor kicked them away in frustration.

With a deep breath to steady herself, she eyed the town square. Harriet's Hair was closest, just across the street from where Eleanor stood on the corner, and the antique store, Lost & Found, was clear on the opposite side of the square. Eleanor couldn't help but smile. Hawthorn residents pulled out all the stops at the holidays, with jaunty wreaths on every shop door, red and white ribbon curled around the lamp posts like peppermint candy, and menorahs peeking out from a window or two. Strings of bells danced in the breeze, and the trees blinked at her, golden sparkles of light twinkling like fairies as she passed. It was difficult to stay in a grumpy mood when Eleanor was surrounded by so much holiday spirit.

She made her deliveries without incident, except for when she slipped and almost fell on the linoleum floor at Harriet's. She would've dropped both coffees if it hadn't been for the young stylist waiting by the door for her latte. Eleanor's face had flushed crimson as she saw her principal, Mrs. Wilson, turn around in her chair to gape at

Eleanor's clumsiness. Then again, Mrs. Wilson had been wearing aluminum foil all over her head, so Eleanor recovered quickly.

Just as she returned to the bakery, Eleanor spied a curvy, middle-aged woman at the counter engaged in spirited conversation with Agatha, a young girl about Eleanor's age standing next to her. She was a bit taller than Eleanor, with a messy blond pixie cut, and she was wearing a pair of baggy, wide-leg jeans that Eleanor had seen online and begged her dad to buy. James had quipped that he had an old pair in his closet she could have for free.

Agatha's voice filled the bakery as she chatted with the woman. The girl looked bored as she peered around the store. Her blue eyes landed on Eleanor, who offered her a grin. The girl smiled back, silver braces shiny beneath the overhead lights.

Lucky! Eleanor thought. She'd always wanted braces but never needed them.

"Oh, good! You're back," Agatha hollered. Eleanor approached, eager to pick up more orders. "This is Eleanor Black. Today's her first day as my delivery girl. Her dad, James, owns Bluestocking Books next door."

"Oh, you're the girl with the bookstore?" said Braces as she scanned Eleanor's holiday attire, her eyes alight. "Marianne told me about you yesterday."

"I like your jeans," Eleanor replied by way of introduction. "My dad wouldn't buy me a pair even though I begged him to, but I probably shouldn't have asked anyway since—" Eleanor stopped short. She'd almost blurted out her secret to God and everybody. No one could know that Bluestocking Books was in trouble.

The three of them eyed Eleanor expectantly, waiting for her to continue.

"Uh, since it's so close to Christmas, you know?" she finished quickly. "Who's Marianne?"

"That's me," said the woman next to Braces. "And this is Maggie." Marianne had an interesting face, the kind that would tell a lovely story. Her hair was long and full, light brown shot through with silver, and her eyes crinkled into deep lines as she smiled at Eleanor. "I've been into your family's store a few times over the years. Such a captivating place."

"Marianne works for my great-aunt Ruby," Maggie said. "She's been her housekeeper for, like, a million years."

Marianne clicked her tongue. "Not quite that long, but Hawthorn is certainly home at this point."

"It's so nice to have you here, too, Maggie," Agatha said in a voice of pure molasses. Eleanor could already see the woman's wheels turning. No one loved to tell tales like Agatha did, and Ruby Hurst's great-niece coming to town was a story worth telling.

Ruby was the great-granddaughter of Hawthorn founder George Hurst and the daughter of publisher William Hurst and his fiancee, Alice. Everyone knew the tragic history of Ruby's mom. She'd been a recent widow who'd gotten engaged to William in the mid-1940s, and she'd died when Ruby was just a young child. As the story went, Alice had taken Ruby to Tybee Island one afternoon for a picnic at the beach and, within an hour of their arrival, had drowned. Little Ruby had been discovered by a couple walking on the beach. The search for Alice's body went on for weeks until it was finally discovered miles away in the marshes of Cockspur Island near Fort Pulaski. William later married and had more children, but Ruby always stood out, a traumatized beauty whose mother's death was the subject of many rumors, rumors that often included Ruby herself. She never married or had children, and after William died in the nineties, Ruby became a near-total recluse, hiding out in her grand Victorian mansion outside of town. Most people assumed she was off her rocker. The worst rumors, believed by few but dark enough to cling to collective memory, claimed Ruby was once possessed and had lured Alice to her death. The whole story was fascinating, but Eleanor had been preoccupied by her own tragedy for too long to give Ruby Hurst much thought.

"I'm sure Eleanor would just love to show you around town," Agatha continued. "Maybe get to know your aunt a little." She wiggled her eyebrows at Eleanor, who bit her tongue and looked back to Maggie. "Maybe you can come with Eleanor on her deliveries. I could always use another pair of hands." With those words, Agatha's husband, Richard, appeared from the kitchen, a tray of fresh-baked cinnamon scones in hand.

"You've got two hands right here," he said in a jovial tone as he placed the scones in the glass display case. "That not enough?"

Agatha swatted him with a tea towel. "You get back into the kitchen where you belong," she teased, which he did with a little bow. Eleanor and Maggie giggled.

"I was hoping to drop Maggie off at the bookstore for a bit while I ran my errands," Marianne continued as Agatha steamed milk behind the counter, her cast foot stuck out to the side.

"Oh my gosh, you'll love it," Eleanor gushed to Maggie. "You *have* to see the book tree I made for the front window. It took me hours and hours. And you'll love our couch. It's the coziest thing your butt will ever touch, I swear."

"Eleanor, honestly!" Agatha scolded. Marianne covered her smile with a gloved hand.

"Wanna go?" Eleanor asked, reaching for Maggie's arm. Agatha cut her off.

"Not yet," she said, hobbling back to the counter, face stern. "You've still got deliveries."

"Oh, right," Eleanor replied, crestfallen. She'd forgotten about work already with the promise of a new friend. "Can I just walk Maggie over? I'll come right back, I swear."

Agatha, sensing her source of intel on the infamous Ruby Hurst was about to escape, waffled for a moment. Eleanor pushed out her bottom lip and eyed Agatha with her hands clasped together, pleading. "Alright, fine," Agatha agreed with a long-suffering sigh. "Five minutes."

Eleanor squealed with delight and looped her arm through Maggie's, steering her towards the door.

"Keep your phone on you, Maggie!" Marianne called out, "And stay in the bookstore. Your aunt will have my hide if you go wandering off."

"I will!" Maggie said over her shoulder as the door closed behind the two girls.

"You have a phone?" Eleanor asked, her eyes fixed on Maggie in disbelief. "My dad would sooner become President of the United States before he let me have one. He says they're rotting our brains."

"My parents are getting divorced," Maggie said with a shrug. "Mom feels guilty about it, so she buys me stuff all the time. I didn't even ask for a phone. I think she only got it because I'm here with Aunt Ruby for the next month, and she wants to check up on me every day."

Eleanor's heart sank as she thought about her mother, wherever she was. Her eyes stung as she imagined hearing her voice again, even if just on the other end of a phone call. "That must be nice," Eleanor said softly.

Maggie grimaced. "It's annoying, honestly," she replied as they stopped by the front window of Bluestocking Books. Maggie gasped at the sight of Eleanor's book tree stacked high above their heads, glittery presents nestled around the bottom in a bed of cotton snow. "*Whoa*," she said, awe written on her pointed features. "This is so cool."

"Thanks," Eleanor replied, the warmth of Maggie's reply a cozy fire in her chest. "It took me all day to get it right. I kept knocking over books, and then I couldn't decide between multicolored lights or white ones, so my dad made me pick with my eyes closed because he was tired of hearing me waffle."

"It's nice that your parents let you help," Maggie said.

"It's just me and my dad," Eleanor replied. Better to rip the band-aid off now. "My mom's been gone for a while."

"Oh," Maggie said with a frown as they entered the soft warmth of the bookstore. "I'm sorry."

Eleanor was saved from a reply by Maggie's theatrical swoon. "Okay, I love," she sang as she turned in a circle, looking at the shop with wonder. "It's giving *You've Got Mail.*"

"Never seen it," Eleanor replied. Maggie gasped in mock horror.

"It's iconic," she said. "It has the cutest bookstore ever. My mom and I watch it together every October and dream about moving to New York City."

"I watch *Anne of Green Gables* every October," Eleanor said simply.

Maggie gave an appreciative nod. "Also iconic."

"Do you want to see the rest?" Eleanor asked.

"Um, *yes,*" Maggie answered.

Eleanor took Maggie on a quick tour and introduced her to James, who was on the phone but offered a wave and a smile. "Make yourself at home," he whispered with a hand over the receiver. Once Eleanor had Maggie settled with a collection of books on the couch, which she agreed was "definitely the coziest thing my butt has ever touched," Eleanor made a mad dash back to the bakery to continue her deliveries.

For the rest of the morning and into the early afternoon, Eleanor went back and forth across the square, delivering an assortment of drinks and pastries. Every half hour or so, she'd sneak over to the bookstore to chat with Maggie, who had stretched out on the couch watching a movie on her phone. They talked about their favorite books and where they went to school, and Eleanor learned that Maggie didn't know much about her great-aunt Ruby other than what everyone else did. She found it funny that people in Hawthorn were so fascinated with her past since Maggie considered the whole story ancient history and Ruby little more than "a rich old grump."

Eleanor herself had never bought into the rumor that Ruby was nuts just because she hid away on the massive estate she'd inherited. It sounded more like Ruby had been the victim of terrible circumstances and, perhaps, had never recovered. Eleanor knew what that felt like and how difficult it was to explain to other people. Or, more often, to have no interest in explanations at all.

What most people failed to understand, unless they had experienced a grievous loss themselves, was that pain was not a weakness. It wasn't a failure to be fixed. It simply...*was*. Six years of pain as her constant companion had taught Eleanor that. As inconvenient as she might find it, she could not be made well with good intentions or comfort food. Neither, it seemed, had Ruby ever been lured back into the community with the desire to clear up ridiculous gossip.

After the last bag of lunch bagels had been delivered and it was time to return to the bookshop, Eleanor hurried back to the bakery to collect her paycheck.

"You did good today," Agatha said as she counted through a stack of bills. Eleanor's cheeks warmed at the praise, and she held out a hand, eager to claim her reward for a job well done. When Agatha pressed a ten-dollar bill into her palm, Eleanor's face fell.

"*Ten dollars?*" she asked, incredulous. "That's all?"

Agatha scoffed. "That's *all*? Ten dollars is a lot of money for a twelve-year-old."

Eleanor crossed her arms and raised her chin. "Not when the minimum wage is seven dollars and twenty-five cents an hour."

Agatha howled and fanned herself with the bills. "Minimum wage! Oh, you're a hoot, Eleanor."

"I'm serious," Eleanor replied. Agatha stopped laughing and fixed her with a firm glare.

"Young lady, you get what you get," she replied. "What were you expecting? A full-time salary?"

Eleanor stood firm. "I expect to be paid for the five hours I just spent traipsing all over town delivering orders that you can't because you were dumb enough to fall off a step stool!" As soon as the words left her mouth, Eleanor wanted to grab them all out of the air and swallow them back again. But it was too late. Her words had tumbled out before she could even think to stop them. Customers twisted in their seats to stare.

Agatha's broad face turned as red as Eleanor's sweater as she gaped at her, a fish out of water. "Eleanor!" she exclaimed and pointed towards the entrance. "Let's go find your dad and see what he has to say about this."

Agatha's hobbled effort to lead Eleanor out of the bakery like a hardened criminal was diminished somewhat by her injury, but Eleanor hung her head just the same. How could she have been so stupid? Now, she'd never get the money they needed. With Eleanor's outburst, Bluestocking's fate had been sealed.

James was rearranging the local authors' shelf when they arrived. His smile fell into a frown as he took in Agatha's hardened expression and Eleanor's defeated shuffle.

"What's going on?" he asked, concern etched into his tired features. Agatha relayed the whole story, careful to add that they had never agreed upon a fixed amount when Eleanor agreed to work for her.

Maggie had crept up to a bookshelf on Eleanor's left as Agatha half-shouted at James to get a handle on his daughter's sass mouth. Hidden from the adults' view, Maggie stifled her giggles behind a copy of *The Secret Keeper* by Kate Morton. Then she gave Eleanor a thumbs up.

"Nice job," she whispered with a cheeky grin.

Eleanor bit her lip to keep from laughing and turned back to face her dad. He looked down at her with a stern expression, but she could see the humor in his eyes.

"Well, Agatha," he said in a serious tone, "I'm sorry about Eleanor's rudeness. She knows better than to talk to people like that."

"As well she should," Agatha added with a harrumph.

"But as far as payment goes, I tend to agree with her," James finished.

Agatha clenched her jaw. "She's twelve, Jimmy. This is ridiculous. She works with you all the time, and Eleanor said herself that you don't pay her either!"

"True," James replied, unruffled, "but I'm her dad. I feed, clothe, and care for her in about a million other ways, so I don't think it's too much to ask for her help stacking books now and then. Besides, all of this is going to be Eleanor's one day. She needs to learn how to run it."

Eleanor's heart filled with pride as she pictured herself at the helm of Bluestocking Books. Then she remembered that they were about to lose it, and her heart deflated.

"I'm really sorry, Agatha," Eleanor said, and she meant it. She needed to keep working, but she also needed Agatha to pay more than ten dollars a day if she had any hope of saving her family's bookstore. "I shouldn't have talked to you like that. It was mean and disrespectful, and even though I should have earned *at least* minimum wage for the deliveries, especially since it's so cold outside, I swear on my life it won't ever happen again." Agatha opened her mouth to protest, but Eleanor beat her to the punch. "Do you think we could compromise?"

"That sounds like a good idea," said James. "How about...five dollars an hour?"

Agatha sucked her teeth, considering. After a moment, she patted Eleanor's arm. "Oh, it's alright, sweetheart. I suppose I can give you five dollars an hour, but you'll have to wait until Fridays to get your money just like everybody else."

"'Everybody' meaning you and Richard," James joked.

Agatha sent him a piercing stare. "Exactly," she said.

"That's great," Eleanor agreed and extended a hand. "Thank you so much. Really."

Agatha cast a suspicious glare at Eleanor's hand but then laughed and shook it. "You're welcome. Now, I need to get back to the bakery before Richard sets the place on fire." She eyed Eleanor. "I'll see you again tomorrow morning, okay? Make sure you leave the attitude at home, please."

Eleanor gave a salute, and James hurried to open the shop door for her. As she limped away, Maggie emerged from her hiding place and collapsed into a fit of laughter.

"That was amazing," she said, wiping tears from her face. "I thought that woman was going to have a stroke. Did you really say all that stuff?"

"Yeah," Eleanor replied with a sheepish glance at her dad. He put his hand on Eleanor's shoulder.

"I told you Agatha was a handful, Eleanor," he said. "I need you to keep that smart mouth in check, okay? Not least of all because Agatha is our neighbor, and we have to see her every single day. I don't want to hear any more comments like that again, understood?"

Eleanor nodded, properly ashamed. "Yes, sir."

She and Maggie scurried back to the young adult section and flopped down on the couch. Eleanor was happy to have a friend to laugh with, even a new one. She'd never been skilled at making friends—books were her preferred companions—and she found most kids at her school were all too happy to ignore her. After Eleanor's mother disappeared, it was as if her classmates thought missing mothers were contagious, though these days most people had come to the conclusion that Vera was the victim of a grisly murder who'd eventually become the subject of a true crime podcast.

"Seriously, though," Maggie said, as though she'd never been interrupted. "That was hilarious."

"I bet you didn't think spending the holidays with your grumpy old aunt would be this fun," Eleanor replied with a shake of her head.

"I still can't believe she was only going to pay you ten dollars for the whole day," Maggie said. "This isn't the eighties."

"I'm just glad she didn't fire me," Eleanor said, relieved. "We need the money."

Maggie furrowed her brows. "You do?"

Eleanor cast a sideways glance at Maggie. "Promise not to tell?"

Maggie stuck out her little finger. "Pinky promise."

Eleanor twisted her pinky around Maggie's and took a deep breath. "My dad is behind on the store's monthly payments. We're going to lose it if we don't come up with the money soon. He doesn't know I know, though. I found the papers in his desk."

Concern filled Maggie's eyes. "How much money?"

Eleanor sighed and fell back against the couch cushions. "A lot. More than I can earn with Agatha, that's for sure. I know that now, but I still want to help."

"We'll think of something," Maggie said. "Do you think your dad would let you spend the night with me tomorrow? We can brainstorm ideas."

Eleanor brightened at the thought of a sleepover and seeing inside Ruby Hurst's grand old mansion. "That will be fun!" she exclaimed. "Let's ask Marianne to talk to him when she picks you up."

The plan was a success. After Marianne was done talking to James, Maggie shouted a hearty goodbye, and they headed out into the icy afternoon. "See you tomorrow!" she called.

Eleanor waved them off. Then she turned to her dad and hugged him. Tucked close against his chest like that, she could smell his Old Spice cologne and thought of her mother. Vera had loved that smell. Sometimes, she even stole James' deodorant when she ran out of her own. Suddenly, a flood of memories came rushing back to Eleanor, and she thought back to all the stories her mother had shared with her, stories of girls with big dreams and big courage. Even in elementary school, Eleanor had known that her mom was fueled by the need to instill hope in her daughter, hope Vera herself seemed to lack in moments when she thought no one was looking. Eleanor could see her mother's focus start to turn inward to a place that wasn't kind. She grew overly sensitive and anxious, afraid of something Eleanor didn't understand. But even then, Vera was always gentle with Eleanor, perhaps because she hadn't known how to be gentle to herself.

The bookstore was their whole family's happy place. Vera and James had opened Bluestocking Books back when neither of them could even imagine their daughter. Back when they had given up on parenthood after many failed attempts to get pregnant and resigned themselves to a quiet life, just the two of them. The shop had been a way to grieve the story they weren't living and a grand attempt to try and celebrate the story they were.

And then Eleanor had surprised them. Vera always said she was the best story of their lives.

Eleanor's first memory swirled around those precious words, a memory she had recalled countless times in her mother's absence. She had been lying in bed, no more than four years old, pressed close against her mother's side as they looked through a book together. The frustration that coursed through Eleanor's tiny body as her mother closed the book was potent. Eleanor couldn't remember the entire story now, but she remembered how it had ended: with the two friends separated forever, their lives destined to move in different directions.

"Why did they have to say goodbye?" Eleanor had asked in a quiet voice as her mother tucked in the blanket around her.

"Well, honey," Vera had said with a kiss to Eleanor's forehead, "there are times when people who love each other have to go different ways. It's not always a bad thing."

At those words, Eleanor had clutched her mother's hand as though holding tight to her soft, warm fingers would prevent Vera from floating away forever. It hadn't.

Eleanor's heart sank into her stomach as it had done a thousand times before, and the questions that had long plagued her days and nights dominated her thoughts once more.

What kind of mother leaves her only daughter behind without a word? What makes a woman turn away from the family she loves?

Eleanor had her suspicions, but she was no longer sure she wanted to know the answer.

5

Ruby

The first week of Maggie's visit was a turbulent one.

Ruby was so used to the perpetual quiet of her home that the increased volume caused by Maggie's lead feet on the floor above her, her enthusiastic chewing at the table, or the constant buzzing of her cell phone grated on Ruby's last nerves. The girl had no manners at all, and Ruby was not shy about sharing her opinions on the matter.

"You might want to ease up on her a bit, dear, if you plan on getting through her visit in one piece," Marianne said, her voice gentle but firm.

Ruby sighed as she shuffled to her father's old desk in the library. It helped her to feel more in control when she sat in his old leather chair, soft as butter from decades of use and as strong as he had once been.

"I'm not the one you need to worry about, Marianne," Ruby stated. "Margaret is thirteen, not three. If she cannot respect the basic rules of consideration for others in my house, then there will be consequences."

Marianne cocked her head to the side and pierced Ruby with a sharp look. Ruby began to squirm under the intensity of her glare. "Ruby Hurst. I know we've never considered ourselves to be friends, exactly, but in all my years of working for you, I've never known you to be unkind. Stern, yes. Particular? Absolutely. But mean for the sake of meanness? Never."

"Until now," Ruby finished for her.

Her housekeeper shrugged and continued dusting the bookshelves.

"Go on," Ruby insisted. "You can say it." Marianne refused to reply, but Ruby got the message clear enough.

She sat back in her father's chair and ran her fingers over the lines etched onto its surface. She could picture him there, hard at work, while she pestered him with questions about the books on the shelf. She had been forever curious about the stories they contained. At eight years old, he finally let Ruby have free rein of the library, and she had devoured the books, one after the other. For years, her favorite had been *Flower Children: The Little Cousins of the Field and Garden*, a small, charming book that contained illustrations of children dressed as flowers, each accompanied by a clever verse. They were easy to memorize. In the spring and summer, Ruby would take *Flower Children* outside and roam the estate in search of blooms she could identify by verse. She could spot the difference between pansies and peonies, sweet alyssum and apple blossom, and knew which flowers were toxic or safe to pluck from their stems.

If she closed her eyes and concentrated hard, the image of Ruby's mother seated on a blanket beneath the oak trees, her face lifted to the sun, could be conjured. It was hazy now, like looking through a foggy window, but the feeling of warmth and safety that had flowed through Ruby's tiny body on that day remained as fresh now as it was seventy-five years ago. The flower book had been a gift from her mother, and some joys just could not be forgotten. No matter how many years had passed.

The same was true of sorrows.

Marianne completed her tasks in the library and left Ruby seated like a scolded child in her father's chair. She found it hard to argue with her housekeeper's logic, and yet she returned to her time-worn reasons for strict boundaries like one would return to a familiar coat in the winter. They kept her safe from the icy bite of death. With them, she was safe to enjoy the world around her without suffering the inevitable despair that followed closeness with other people. She'd had quite enough of that in her life.

Ruby would continue with her limited time on earth the way she had since her father had died and left her with his money and secrets. It was too late now for her to be exhilarated by life anyhow. Those days had gone the way of her mother, her father, her sister, and her brother. And they would never return.

The front door slammed, and Ruby started at the sound. Maggie was back from walking Marianne's dog, Danger. He was a Dachshund puppy, no bigger than Ruby's foot.

"Marianne!" Ruby called out as she slipped off her sneakers, leash in hand. Danger pulled towards the library, but Maggie scooped him up before Ruby could protest.

Marianne poked her head out from the parlor. "I'm here," she said.

"He pooped once and peed twice," Maggie squealed with the same enthusiasm one would expect from a lottery win. "You're such a good boy, aren't you, Danger?" She pressed her face up close to the dog's, and he licked her nose. Ruby looked heavenward.

"Lord, help me," she sighed. "Margaret, please take that dog back to Marianne's cottage. I don't want it doing either of those things on my rugs."

"'*It*' is a 'he,'" said Maggie with another coo at the puppy. "And *I* am a Maggie, not a Margaret."

"Regardless," Ruby continued. "Do as I say."

Maggie gave a dramatic sigh and put Danger down. "Let's go, buddy. I'll come visit you later and bring treats."

"You're a doll," Marianne said to the girl as she led Danger out the front door again. "He's going to want to come home with you in January if you keep this up."

"Fine by me!" Maggie replied.

"Fine by me, too," Ruby grumbled. Maggie laughed—a bright, open sound that touched a tender spot in Ruby's chest—and closed the door. Ruby rubbed her breastbone as though in pain. Maggie's laugh conjured memories of Ruby's father and his big, lovely guffaw.

Another lifetime.

Her father, William, had lavished Ruby with affection. He called her his Daffodil after Ruby had declared it her favorite flower and picked every single one within a three-acre radius of the house. It was a nickname that continued until the day he died. Ruby had grown up under the bright spotlight of his adoration. He often reminded her that it was his duty to love her twice as much since he had to show her the love of two parents. It seemed a simple goal for a man with such a gregarious personality and large family inheritance, even if Ruby—in her confusion and grief—hadn't made it easy for him.

She hadn't made it easy for her stepmother or younger siblings, either. When William married Jeanice Russell, twelve years his junior, in 1952, she had been eager to start a family with him. A *new* family.

Jeanice—or Jean as Ruby had called her—had never known what to make of Ruby. She was eight years old when William married Jean, and by then Ruby was well set in her quiet bitterness. Though Ruby had desperately longed for a mother, she only longed for her own. Jean had fallen short of that expectation despite her attempts to carve out a space in Ruby's heart. It wasn't long before Jean gave William two more children to dote on— Ruby's younger sister, Caroline, and younger brother, Edward. Before they were out of elementary school, Ruby was well on her way to college.

On her visits home from Georgia Teachers College, she'd sit at the dining table and watch her family tease one another and share stories that Ruby knew little about. It seemed to her that they made a complete set, the four of them, just as they were. She loved them all with a fierceness, and yet she was not one of them. Not in the way her father had hoped, nor in the way she could see Caroline and Edward were.

Oh, but Ruby had been beautiful. When most girls were just on the cusp of breasts and hips, Ruby already had a full set of both. Her long, full locks were once the color of a setting sunset just before it disappeared over the horizon. She'd been the envy of all her peers. Her good looks made her an obvious focal point everywhere Ruby went. She became quite well known in and around Hawthorn for the bevy of pageant titles she won during her years of competition. People were eager to forget their opinions of her history once they set their sights on her beauty. Crowns and sashes and prize money became the easy boost to her confidence that Ruby could not seem to find within her family, no matter how much her father praised her or how her siblings admired her. Ruby was an outsider with a whole separate identity that didn't include them. The memory of her mother and the hole within Ruby's heart simply could not be forgotten.

She had gotten close to forgetting once. So very close. Then that hope had slipped away, too, and Ruby had given up on hope altogether.

Marianne returned to the library and knocked on the door frame. "Ruby, you got a minute?"

Pulled out of her reverie, Ruby shook off the memories and clasped her hands together on the desk. "Unfortunately, I have more minutes than I would like."

Her housekeeper huffed. "Having a pity party today, are we?" she asked, a note of humor in her charming accent.

"Not pity. Just facts," Ruby replied. "What do you need?"

Marianne brightened. "I introduced Maggie to Eleanor Black yesterday. They hit it off, and Maggie invited Eleanor to come over tonight. I've already spoken with Eleanor's dad about it, and he didn't mind. I think he wants Eleanor to get out of the bookstore more often and make some friends. Lord knows Maggie needs someone her age around."

Ruby hadn't moved a single eyelash while Marianne spoke. "And you want to know what I think?"

"I know you don't like strangers, but it seems like a good idea if you want to keep Maggie occupied and out of trouble while she's here. She can't just sit on her phone all day."

It did seem like a good idea, except for the fact that one pubescent child in the house was already one too many. Two was just asking for it.

"I wish you would have spoken with me first, Marianne," Ruby said, pinching the bridge of her nose. "It seems the decision has already been made."

Marianne had the good sense to look sheepish. "I knew you would say no," she admitted.

Ruby scoffed. "Better to ask for forgiveness than ask for permission, then, am I correct?"

"I have too much to do around here, Ruby," Marianne countered. She put her hands on her hips and glared at her employer. "I can't babysit Maggie, much as I like having her around, and you certainly aren't going to do it. She needs a *friend*. I know it's been a long time since you were thirteen, but try and remember for her sake. Maggie's been dropped here on her Christmas break while her mum moves out of the only home she's ever known and divorces her father. Think of how she must feel right now."

To tell the truth, Ruby hadn't much considered how Maggie might be feeling. She tried not to think of her at all.

Her shoulders slumped as she realized Marianne was right. How inconvenient it was to have such a compassionate housekeeper. "Fine, fine," she finally said, biting off each word. "Just...do whatever needs to be done so they don't get in my way."

Marianne smirked and shook her head. "Ruby Hurst, you are one of a kind."

Don't I know it, Ruby thought to herself as Marianne headed back to the parlor.

Her whole life had been one big sideshow. Ruby had made peace with people's whispers and stares as a child. Her mother's mysterious death had only added to the intrigue, but as she grew older and the town's expectations of what a beautiful, rich woman should do with her life failed to come to fruition, their opinion of Ruby Hurst had soured. As the years passed, Ruby hid herself away, and the people who might have once called her friend were now sleeping in their graves. She'd become an old crone with better style, a Miss Havisham in a lonely mansion, and she no longer gave anyone reasons to stare at her because she stayed as far away from her hometown as she could. Whatever Ruby needed, Marianne or Ben had always brought to her.

Ruby pulled herself up from her father's desk and ran her wrinkled hand across the wood. Too much sadness lived in her heart for Ruby to care much what people thought of her or to try and restore what had been lost. She shuffled over to the stairs and looked up, suddenly exhausted. With great effort, she pulled herself up them one by one, the weight of her memories an anvil on her thin, narrow shoulders. Then she padded down the hall to her bedroom, taking a seat in the large bay window across from her bed.

Fresh anger at everyone, from her mother and father to Maggie and even Eleanor Black, lit a fire in her gut. She stoked it with her self-pity and uncharitable thoughts as she glared out at the quiet world around her childhood home. The live oak trees looked sad to her now; their branches hung low as though they, too, were tired of holding up the weight of all the Hurst family troubles. All of *Ruby's* troubles.

Had any of it been worth what her father had given? What *she* had given?

Ruby squeezed her eyes shut and waited for the prickling in her nose to stop. She would not cry.

Even after twenty-five years, she missed her father. She longed to hear the velvet bass of his voice, his affectionate teasing. Despite her anger at all the unanswered questions he'd left behind for Ruby to solve alone, she would never regret that he had belonged to her.

Outside, holiday lights Benjamin had strung around the intricate porch railings conjured thoughts of Ruby's last Christmas with

William. Caroline had died some years before, and Edward had spent the holiday at home in Virginia, so Ruby and her father were there to celebrate together. Ruby worked all day on a delicious Christmas feast. The kitchen was a mess of flour, vegetable ends, and dirty mixing bowls, but she managed to create a more-than-palatable roast turkey. She paired it with homemade dressing and gravy, squash casserole, and pumpkin pie from Jean's old recipe book that was still stowed away in the cupboard.

William was even older than Ruby was now. A decade-old prostate cancer diagnosis, which had lain dormant, had chosen that year to finally flourish and spread to the rest of his brawny, graceful body. It was the anniversary of Ruby's mother's death, a day that never failed to haunt them both. Over dinner, they had spoken of Alice in quiet reverence, alone together in their too-brief memories of her. They spoke of so many things that night. It was in that conversation William had given Ruby his estate, in word before it was made official in deed.

Then, he confessed to a secret that changed everything.

Strangely enough, the worst part about William's confession wasn't even the truth. No, the worst part was the transformation that occurred in Ruby's soul the moment she heard his words. It was the realization that sometimes even the best people, the ones who seem to set the standard for goodness and truth, can turn out to be more flawed than anyone thought possible.

William died two short weeks later. Ruby walked around in a daze then, shell-shocked over both the loss of her father and the conversations she had still hoped to have with him. The funeral a few days after was practically a spectator sport. The entire town of Hawthorn was in attendance, alongside many of Savannah's elite who wanted to see and be seen alongside someone from the infamous Hurst family. Even a dead or crazy someone. Ruby steeled herself for the hundreds of handshakes and hushed greetings she would endure throughout the day. Then she brought William's body home to the estate and said one final goodbye as he was laid to rest in the family cemetery, right next to Alice.

It was the last time Ruby had ever been to the graveyard and one of the last times she'd ever set foot in town.

From her window seat, Ruby searched the distant horizon in the direction of the cemetery. It was tucked away in a grove of mulberry trees a few hundred yards from the house, hallowed ground for every Hurst family member who had lived and died on this property since the Gilded Age.

Ruby never wanted to see it again. Not until her own aged body was shut inside a wooden box and lowered quietly into the earth, her secrets finally at peace with her.

6

Eleanor

Unable to fall asleep the night before, Eleanor had spent hours on her laptop searching for information on how to save a business from financial ruin. There were thousands of search results, but few fit for a twelve-year-old to manage independently. She'd stuck to technology Maggie would know best and made a long list of ideas for how to promote the bookstore on social media. Bluestocking Books needed to find a place in the 21st century.

After a while, Eleanor had gotten curious about Maggie's aunt Ruby and the tragic story of her mother's death. There wasn't much to be found online. She found a few short blurbs from the early 1960s announcing Ruby as a pageant winner. She also located her father William's obituary from 1999. Eleanor searched and scoured for Alice Hurst, but the only result she'd found that wasn't behind a paywall was a Find A Grave entry that noted the location of her burial in the Hurst family cemetery.

Frustrated, Eleanor chewed on a hangnail. A thought occurred to her, but she swatted it away. She got ready for bed, washed her face, and brushed her teeth. Still, the idea hovered, a ghost over her shoulder.

Finally, Eleanor opened her laptop again. She typed *Vera Black Hawthorn, GA,* in the search bar before she could change her mind. Immediately, the page was filled with links to news articles that had covered the story. Down a little further was Bluestocking's website, where Vera Black was listed as the owner alongside James. Otherwise, it was all news about her disappearance.

Bile rose in Eleanor's throat as she peered at the headlines displayed on her screen, at her mother's beautiful face on one thumbnail after another. It seemed every outlet had printed some variation of the same story. The news hadn't made it past local and regional papers, with the *Savannah Daily News* offering the most coverage. One article, in particular, caught Eleanor's eye. The headline felt slightly less sensational than the others, so she clicked on it.

Chatham County Mother Vanishes, Local Community Left Grief-stricken

James had prevented any reporters from talking to Eleanor at the time, but they'd gotten their hands on the police reports. Eleanor felt the horrible memory of those moments prickle her skin as she read.

Wednesday, March 26, 2018

A Chatham County woman has gone missing, and police are seeking any information related to her disappearance.

Vera Elizabeth Black was last seen Monday on the property of Bluestocking Books in downtown Hawthorn, the business she and her husband, James Black, opened together in 2000. Three witnesses gave statements to police reporting that they had seen or spoken to Mrs. Black around five p.m. when she was about to close the bookstore. One such resident, Agatha Candler, owner of a bakery located next to Bluestocking Books, reported visiting with Mrs. Black at the shop before returning to her place of business. Mrs. Black was reported missing by her husband two hours after her expected return home. She has not been seen or heard from since.

"We're just heartbroken," Mrs. Candler said in an interview. "Vera is such a sweet woman, and she's been an important part of this community for a long time. We're just praying she's found safe. She has a little girl and a husband who need her home."

In the wake of Mrs. Black's disappearance, the residents of Hawthorn have organized search parties to assist local law enforcement as they comb the vast acreage of forests surrounding the town. There was no evidence of foul play in or around the property of Bluestocking Books, but it hasn't been ruled out as a possibility. Mr. Black's husband is cooperating fully with the investigation.

"All we want is for Vera to be back here with us, safe and sound," said Mr. Black through tears during Tuesday evening's press conference. "Please, please help us find her."

This is the first missing persons case reported in Hawthorn since Alice Hurst, fiancee of William Hurst, grandson of Hawthorn founder George Hurst, drowned off the coast of Tybee Island in the winter of 1949. Her body was later recovered near Fort Pulaski, and she was buried in the Hurst family cemetery. Alice Hurst's daughter, Ruby, turned eighty this year and continues to reside on the family estate in Hawthorn.

Anyone with information regarding Mrs. Black's disappearance is asked to contact the Chatham County Sheriff's Department at 912-556-7865.

Eleanor smiled through tears when she read what Agatha had said to reporters about her mother. She was just as Agatha had said: kind and beloved. To the citizens of their small town, Vera had been a respectable business owner, wife, and mother. To Eleanor and James, she had been an enigma, full of ideas and life, while also troubled by dark moods. It was a regular occurrence for Vera to shut everyone out and hide away. Her mind simply became too loud for her to engage with the world or with Eleanor. Only James had ever been able to pull Vera from those moods and settle her back into the present.

Eleanor's vision blurred as she watched a clip from the press conference for the very first time. Her dad was shaking visibly, his eyes filled with tears, as he spoke of his wife. Eleanor clutched her pillow.

She'd never realized how much her dad had aged since her mother left. His hair was still fully black back then, and the lines around his mouth were less pronounced. Eleanor's heart clenched as she thought about how much of his grief she never really saw. The entire experience was a sickening blur.

Scrolling down to the bottom of the article, Eleanor momentarily caught a glimpse of the comments. That was a big mistake. Over and over, readers made vicious accusations about her father, casting doubt on his "performance" at the press conference and calling him terrible names. Eleanor snapped her laptop shut, furious that people would accuse her dad of being anyone other than the devoted father and husband he had always been. She swiped angrily at her tears and prayed James had never read their ugly words.

After falling into a fitful sleep, Eleanor awoke the next morning to a heavy thunderstorm. Downstairs, James was sipping coffee by the kitchen sink. He turned to face Eleanor when she walked in, hair piled high in a messy bun on her head, and greeted her.

"Morning," he said, cupping his mug. "How about this storm, huh? Not going to be busy today."

Eleanor took a cereal box from the cupboard and shook some into a bowl. "Have some faith, Dad," she replied, her voice rough from tears and lack of sleep. "Rain makes for perfect reading weather."

James chuckled into his coffee. "At home, maybe. But nobody's going to leave their house to come to the bookstore in this weather."

"I would," Eleanor said. She poured milk into her bowl and took a bite. "You want to take me over to Maggie's today? Or should I call her and get Marianne to pick me up?"

James ruffled his daughter's hair. "Don't talk with your mouth full," he said. "I'll take you over. I'm curious to meet Maggie's aunt."

Eleanor raised a brow. "You've never met her before?"

"Nope," James answered, taking a seat at the breakfast table. "I don't think many people have. We just know about her because she's—"

"Richer than the pope?" interjected Eleanor. "A total mystery? Completely fascinating?"

James pointed at her. "That, yes," he replied. "We actually bought the bookstore from her. Did you know that?"

"WHAT?" Eleanor exclaimed. She plopped down into a seat across from her dad. "You bought Bluestocking Books from the woman who is basically our town mascot?"

James guffawed. Eleanor thought back to the video she'd watched last night and felt her eyes sting. It had been a long time since she'd heard her dad laugh like that.

"What a terrible thing to say," he admonished her with a grin. "The poor woman is probably just an extreme introvert who wants to be left alone. But, yes, well—*no*. It wasn't a bookstore then. It was just an old, empty space that belonged to the Hurst family. Your mother and I never even met Ruby. Everything was done through her lawyer."

Eleanor was dumbfounded. "I wonder what it was before," she said, taking another bite of cereal. "The bookstore, I mean."

James shrugged. "Her family made their money in publishing and owned large sections of the original town, so I'd hazard a guess it was an office of theirs at some point. My wingback chair and the desk in the storage room were still in the back when we bought the place."

Eleanor was thrilled at the thought of their bookstore once being the home of a publishing empire. "How serendipitous," she sighed. Another word she'd learned from a novel.

James' lips turned up at the corners. "You can say that again."

After breakfast, it was time for Eleanor's second day as Agatha's delivery girl. She had high hopes it would go more smoothly than her first.

On crutches now, Agatha made a beeline to Eleanor as soon as she arrived at the bakery. Her face was open and bright, eager in a way Eleanor knew could only mean one thing.

"Did you and Maggie have fun yesterday?" she asked, leaning toward Eleanor so much that Eleanor had to back away. "Your dad told me you're going over to her aunt's house to spend the night tonight. That'll be an adventure."

"Uh, yeah," Eleanor replied. "I guess it will." She made her way towards the kitchen, Agatha close behind now that she had crutches to lean on. "How many orders do you have for me?"

"None right now," Agatha said, a note of impatience in her voice. "Don't go changing the subject, young lady. No one ever goes over to Ruby Hurst's house. This is quite the opportunity you have here."

Eleanor raised an eyebrow at her employer. "Opportunity for what?" she asked, unable to hide her annoyance at being pried for information. "And how do you know that no one ever goes over there?"

"Didn't I tell you to leave the sass at home today?" Agatha reminded her. "And *I know* because I know everyone here. People talk."

"I'll say they do," Eleanor muttered.

Agatha continued as if Eleanor hadn't spoken. "I bet if you could get Ruby Hurst to stop haunting that old mansion of hers and come into town, Bluestocking Books might find some more customers."

Eleanor's spine stiffened as she took in the subtext of Agatha's words. She eyed the woman with apprehension. "What do you mean?"

Agatha pressed her lips together quickly. "Well...nothing, dear," she hemmed. "I just know how hard it can be for bookstores nowadays. People are always ordering books online or reading on their phones and such. A chance to see Ruby Hurst might bring people around if they heard she'd come by, you know?"

She wasn't wrong, but Eleanor felt the slice of betrayal cut deep. Her dad had told the biggest gossip in town about their troubles at the store but hadn't told his own daughter. And now Eleanor's boss wanted her to use a new friend to get more customers.

Adults were the worst sometimes.

"If you don't have any orders for me right now," Eleanor said in a quiet voice, "can I just get a hot chocolate, please? I'll read in the kitchen until you get busy."

Agatha eyed Eleanor, her brows furrowed. Then, her expression softened. "Sure, honey. That's fine."

Eleanor shuffled back to the kitchen, where Richard was cheerily mixing batter for a batch of banana bread. He greeted her with a broad smile as he sang along to the radio, dancing off-beat. Eleanor couldn't help but giggle. She sat down at the counter and pulled *Walk Two Moons* by Sharon Creech from her bag, a novel she'd found in the little free library. Her mom had had a well-loved copy of it at home in their office, but Eleanor had never read it before. She flipped to the back cover and read the blurb, then felt a hot flash of panic when she realized it was a story of a girl named Salamanca and her lost mother.

Her heart thudded in her chest as she fingered the cover. Memories of nights on the sofa, cuddled up next to her mom as she read a book aloud, prickled like ants all over Eleanor's body. She had thought those were happy times, but six years of life without her mother had convinced Eleanor even her most precious memories could not be trusted.

She opened the book with care, even though it was practically a new copy, and scanned the title page. Vera's copy at home was care-worn, pages permanently dog-eared, and the spine torn until the back cover had fallen off. The book in Eleanor's hands was used but fresh, still crisp as she turned the page and began to read. Within minutes, she was lost in the story.

"Here's your hot chocolate," Agatha said, placing a steaming mug in front of Eleanor, who started with a yelp. She'd been so engrossed in the book that she hadn't noticed Agatha's approach. Richard was still singing over by the oven, where he placed five pans of banana bread mixture on the center rack to bake.

"Goodness!" Agatha patted Eleanor on the shoulder. "I didn't mean to scare you, hon."

Eleanor's heartbeat slowed to a normal rate. "It's okay. I was just reading."

"Must be a good book. When you're finished with your hot chocolate, I have a few orders for you to deliver."

Eleanor nodded and took a sip of her drink, letting it warm her up from the inside out. "Sounds great," she replied. Sal Hiddle would have to wait.

The next few hours passed in agonizing slow motion. Agatha enlisted Eleanor to help bring out orders in the cafe when she wasn't making deliveries, but the lunch crowd was thin today. Eleanor couldn't wait to go see Maggie.

Her stomach had been a bundle of nerves that morning as she packed her overnight bag, unsure exactly about what she might need. Did Ruby Hurst have servants? A chef? Should she bring all her toiletries, or did Ruby have those little travel ones in every bathroom for guests? Did she ever *have* guests? These were the sorts of questions it would be convenient to text Maggie if Eleanor had a phone.

She had decided to stick with the basics. Best to keep it simple. She'd also packed her laptop and charger along with her notebook and extra pens for their research.

On the drive over, Eleanor asked her dad about the novel in her bag. "Dad, have you ever read *Walk Two Moons*?" she asked, holding it up for him to see. James glanced over at the cover. Recognition flashed across his face.

"Yeah, I've seen that before," he replied. "We have a copy at home, don't we?"

"Mom did," Eleanor said. "I found this one in the little free library."

"I've never read it," James answered. "I remember your mom liked it a lot. She said it was one of her favorite novels."

Eleanor wrinkled her nose. "But it's for kids."

James shot her an offended look. "You know as well as I do that good books don't have an age limit. Have I taught you nothing?"

"Do you know what it's about?" she prodded. James shook his head.

"It's about a mother who leaves her daughter behind," Eleanor said firmly, looking out her window at the passing landscape. Live oaks, their long, heavy limbs decorated with Spanish moss, flashed in Eleanor's reflection. James coughed and shifted in his seat. The silence pressed in around them.

"Why would that be one of her favorite stories?" Eleanor whispered, more to herself than her dad. He reached across the console and grabbed Eleanor's hand. Eleanor looked down at her lap.

"She didn't know she would leave us, sweetheart," James said with a squeeze of her fingers. "What happened was—"

"What *did* happen to her, Dad?" Eleanor asked, looking up at him with a hope she couldn't disguise. Maybe he knew more than he'd ever told her. Maybe she'd been wrong about her mother all this time.

"I don't know," he admitted, eyes full of unshed tears. "I wish I did."

Eleanor nodded and sank into her seat, clutching the novel to her chest like a life raft.

7

Ruby

"**I** can't wait for Eleanor to get here," Maggie groaned from the door to the parlor. Ruby was seated on a tufted Louis XV sofa that had seen better years, knitting a burnt orange scarf. The pain in her joints was growing, a sure sign that the wintry weather off the coast was about to sour, but she ignored it and continued working. "I'm so bored."

Ruby placed the scarf in her lap and looked up at Maggie. Dressed once more in a sweater that appeared to want to swallow her whole, her niece looked the part of a prepubescent boy as she slumped against the door frame and frowned. It might have endeared her to Ruby had she not also spent the majority of the afternoon scrolling ten-second videos on her phone until Ruby felt certain to form a tick from the repetitive assault on her senses.

"Boredom is good for children," Ruby replied in a dry tone. "It helps you stretch your imagination."

Maggie shot her aunt an exasperated look. Ruby set her knitting aside and rubbed her tender joints. "She'll be here soon enough, Margaret. Now wipe that expression off your face."

Her niece sighed wearily. "I already told you a thousand times, *it's Maggie,* and don't you ever get tired of being in this house, Aunt

Ruby?" she asked. "There's, like, a whole big world out there, you know."

"Yes, I'm aware."

"Did you know about the bakery's pain au chocolats?" Maggie asked, pronouncing the first word like a pain one would get in the elbow. "Because you need to get out and try those if you don't."

"I think you mean '*pahn*,'" corrected Ruby. "Yes, I do. I've had them several times. Marianne picks up pastries once in a while when she goes into town."

"I want to get them from *France*," Maggie said with a swoon, falling onto the mauve Queen Anne wingback chair. "And eat them under the Eiffel Tower."

Ruby couldn't help the corners of her mouth from turning up. "They are quite delicious."

Maggie shot up in the chair. "You've been to France?" she asked, eyes wide.

"When I was young," Ruby replied. "My father traveled here and there on business. Sometimes, I was able to go with him."

"What was it like?" Maggie asked. "Did you wear a beret and speak French and drink lots of espresso?"

Ruby picked up her knitting again and looked away from the dreamy expression on her niece's face. "On the contrary," she replied, needles working the yarn, "I only knew a few phrases in French, and I've never much cared for espresso. But I did wear a black beret once. It had a lovely red bow on the back, and I felt like a movie star when I put it on."

Maggie sighed again. "I wonder if Eleanor has ever been out of the country," she mused. Ruby looked up sharply at Maggie, who had fallen back against the chair and was tracing circles on the arm, lost in her own world. The room fell silent, except for the click of Ruby's needles. After a few minutes of quiet, she cleared her throat.

"How much do you know about Eleanor?" Ruby asked, careful to keep her voice neutral.

Maggie shrugged. "Just that she's cool, and her dad owns a bookstore."

"What else?"

"Oh, she also told me that she loves the *Harry Potter* books but has never seen the movies," Maggie amended. "Which, *how*."

Ruby swallowed hard. Eleanor Black had a story not unlike her own, and if the girl had shared it with Maggie, then surely her loquacious niece would have said so by now.

When Vera Black disappeared, Marianne had kept Ruby filled in on the latest updates for weeks, much to Ruby's chagrin. The story was in *The Savannah Daily News*, and Ruby could recall with startling clarity how it felt to read the headline one Sunday morning at breakfast. It brought her back to that day on the beach with her mother, another lifetime ago. Ruby remembered how confused and frightened she had felt as she stood there in the surf, tears falling down her cheeks. Her mother couldn't be gone. She was *just* there, holding Ruby's hand, reading a book. Telling Ruby how much she loved her. How does a person who's so adored, who takes up so much space in the world, suddenly just cease to exist?

Reading the report about Vera Black's disappearance conjured up the same questions for Ruby more than seventy years later. What would Eleanor's life be like now without a mother to love her in the way only a mother can? Ruby had felt a sudden pang of gratitude for her stepmother, who had been endlessly patient about her new daughter's repeated micro-rejections of her. At least Ruby'd had such a woman in her life, however little she'd shown her appreciation. Eleanor didn't even have that option.

Ruby decided to leave well enough alone. If Eleanor wanted to confide in Maggie, she would make that choice in her own time.

The sound of tires on gravel launched Maggie from the chair. "They're here!" she squealed and tore across the room.

Ruby's stomach did a cartwheel as she set aside her knitting and rose from the sofa to greet their guests. She had hoped to be stowed away in her bedroom for this part of the evening, but she would never make it up the stairs in time. It was just as well. Ruby would have to meet the girl at some point. Better to do it now and be done with it.

Maggie threw open the door. "Hiii!" she sang. Into the warm light of the foyer stepped a tall, gangly girl, chestnut curls long and frizzy down her back. She wore a cautious smile as she peered around and visibly started when she caught sight of Ruby in the parlor, staring at her. Just behind Eleanor, his dark hair sprinkled with gray, entered a man who could only be her father. He smiled at Maggie, who grabbed Eleanor's hands in her own and started talking a mile a minute.

Ruby's throat had gone as dry as a bone.

"We're going to have so much fun," Maggie said to Eleanor, who looked a little dumbstruck at Maggie's enthusiasm. "We can watch movies and eat all the junk food Marianne bought for me yesterday, and—"

Ruby cleared her throat. Everyone turned to stare as she took a few tentative steps towards the foyer. Her hands shook, but she clasped them together to disguise it. "Hello, Eleanor," she said with an abrupt nod. Eleanor's face broke into a wide, relieved grin, and the sight of it was as if someone had turned on the sun.

"Hi, Ms. Hurst," she said in a bubbly tone. "Thank you so much for having me over! Your house is *gorgeous*. I've always wanted to see what it looks like from the inside, and—*ohmigod!*" Eleanor broke off as she peered to the left and noticed the library for the first time. Maggie crossed her arms and put on a faux expression of hurt.

"Great," she said with a pout. "Now she's seen the library, and there'll be no getting her back after this."

Eleanor jerked back to face Ruby with her mouth hanging open so much that Ruby could see a silver filling on her molar. "That is the most amazing library I've ever seen in my whole life," she said with such wonder in her voice that Ruby smiled before she could think better of it.

"I'm glad it meets with your approval."

Eleanor's dad put both of his hands on his daughter's shoulders. "Make sure you ask permission before you touch anything," he said with a grin at Ruby. "If she goes in there at all, you're going to have a hell of a time getting her out."

Ruby offered James a curt nod. "Noted," she said, unable to offer anything more than that. Her jaw clenched with anxiety as she stood stock still, wishing Marianne would come and rescue her before she passed out cold on the floor.

"Thank you for having Eleanor over," James continued, his eyes kind. Then he pressed a kiss onto his daughter's head and turned to go. "Have fun! I'll be back sometime around lunch tomorrow to pick you up." To Ruby, he added, "Please call if you need anything. Eleanor has my cell number."

Ruby made no effort to reply. James' smile faltered for a moment, and then he tipped an imaginary hat and closed the door behind him. Maggie pulled Eleanor towards the stairs, and the two of them raced away, the sound of giggles trailing after them as they went. Ruby let go of the breath she didn't realize she'd been holding and steadied herself on the wingback chair.

Five minutes down. Less than twenty-four hours to go.

~~~

Marianne made a veggie pizza for the girls' dinner, but Ruby wasn't hungry. She retired to the library with a cup of decaf coffee and sat on the sofa adjacent to the fireplace. It crackled with warmth and soothed Ruby's raw nerves. She had long since lost her ability to interact comfortably with new people. That skill had gone the way of her pageant crowns and sashes stuffed into old trunks in the attic. Most of the time, she didn't miss it.

As she watched the flames flicker and spit, Ruby admitted to herself that the discomfort she felt was about more than having another virtual stranger in the house. It was because Eleanor Black was the
~~~

only person she'd ever met with a story like her own, and Ruby didn't like what her presence conjured in the safe, protected bubble she had lived in for so long. Ruby felt haunted. *Watched.* The hair on the back of her neck prickled.

She glanced about the room then and let out a yelp. Her coffee sloshed into her lap, scalding Ruby's thighs. Eleanor and Maggie were standing at the library's threshold, staring, their faces filled with nervous hope.

"Sorry!" Eleanor cried as Ruby wiped at her pants and ran over to take the coffee cup from the woman's hands. She placed it on a coaster and gave Ruby a once-over. "Did it burn you?"

Ruby wiped her damp palms onto her even damper trousers. "Just a bit. I'm quite alright."

Marianne heard their shrieks and came running. "Girls, you should be upstairs," she chided as she strode into the library. "Not down here bothering Ms. Ruby."

Maggie crossed her arms. "We weren't bothering her, Marianne. We just wanted to ask a question."

Eleanor nodded in agreement. "That's right, but we need a towel now, too, since we scared Ms. Ruby half to death, and she spilled her coffee all over her lap."

Ruby met Marianne's exasperated gaze with one of her own. "I'm fine. Just get me a towel and ask your question," she replied, unable to hide her irritation.

Eleanor chewed her bottom lip and looked to Maggie, who pulled back her shoulders and turned to Ruby with a determined set of her chin. Ruby's palms grew damp again, but this time, it wasn't the coffee. She glanced at Eleanor, who looked less than confident, and inwardly groaned. *Not this,* Ruby thought, beginning to stand. *Anything but this...*

"Girls, I'm not—"

"We wanted to know if we could look at your books," Eleanor blurted, clasping her hands under her chin like a prayer.

Ruby plopped back down, biting her tongue against the retort she'd been prepared to throw at them. Relieved, she answered, "You *could.*" She cocked an eyebrow in their direction, waiting.

Maggie rolled her eyes. "Oh em *gee*, Aunt Ruby. *May* we look at your books, please?"

Marianne returned with a towel and offered her arm to Ruby. "Yes, you may," Ruby replied, taking Marianne's elbow to stand. "Just be careful. Many of them are old and rare, and I would be quite upset if they were damaged."

Eleanor's eyes grew wide in earnest. "We would never do that, Ms. Ruby. Never. I'd rather *die.*"

Ruby glanced at her niece's friend and scoffed. "That won't be necessary, but I appreciate your enthusiasm."

After a quick change of clothes, Ruby returned to the library to find the girls seated on the forest green carpet. A pile of books sat nestled between them, and each girl held a thick volume in hand. It was the first time Ruby had seen them quiet. They were lost, as Ruby had been lost so many times in her life, in the pages of their books. *Her books.*

Ruby watched them for a moment, unseen, and could not account for the tears that sprang to her eyes. Surprised, she swiped at them furiously, betrayed by their presence on her cheeks. Eleanor noticed the movement and darted to her feet. Her expression was open and happy, a wildflower unfurled in the summer sun.

"Ms. Ruby, have you read all of these books?" she asked.

Ruby chuckled, a sound that made Maggie's eyes widen in surprise. "Not even close. There are thousands of volumes in this room."

Eleanor gaped. "But I read one-hundred and twenty-seven books last year, and I'm only twelve. You're way older than me!" Then, as if remembering her audience, Eleanor squeaked and clamped her lips together.

"Indeed," Ruby replied. "I've had much more time than you, but I haven't always spent it as wisely as you apparently have." Maggie elbowed Eleanor in the side as she preened under Ruby's praise.

Ruby clasped her hands together and gazed around the room. Each wall was covered by built-in bookshelves brimming with literature from the last century and a half, much of which her great-grandfather had brought with him from Germany, plus a couple thousand other books that her father had purchased over his lifetime. The luscious carpet, oak-paneled fireplace, and quaint, mullioned windows, which cast a rainbow of colors across the room when the sun shone through the glass, added to its charm. What a pleasure it was for Ruby to see the library appreciated as the small marvel it was. She had quite forgotten what it looked like through the eyes of other people.

Eleanor took quiet, careful steps around the room, head titled upwards in reverence as if she were in a church. Maggie cast a thankful smile to Ruby. Perhaps she could allow this space to be enjoyed by others, too. Just this once.

"I've always loved vintage books," Eleanor said. She stopped in front of a shelf loaded with German romantics—Goethe, Mereau, Schlegel—and gently fingered the spines. "Goethe," she said, the word awkward and halting on her lips. Ruby tilted her head, eyebrows drawn upward.

"I've never heard anyone around here pronounce 'Goethe' correctly. Except my father, of course."

Splotches of pink appeared on Eleanor's cheeks. "Jo says it to Professor Baer in *Little Women*. I tried to read one of his books in our store the day after I watched it, but Dad had to help me find it first because I didn't know the spelling."

"And what did you think of the great German poet?" Ruby inquired, genuinely curious.

Eleanor wrinkled her nose. "I didn't get past the first page."

"That's to be expected, I suppose," Ruby replied. "But I hope you've actually read *Little Women*. Please tell me you're not relying on film to tell the whole story."

Maggie stood up and crossed her arms. "Aunt Ruby, have you even seen *Little Women*?"

Ruby matched Maggie's petulant expression. "Which one?"

Maggie frowned. "Greta Gerwig's, obviously. The only one that matters."

"Oh, I love that version," Eleanor sighed. "Florence Pugh is the moment."

"I only understood half of what you just said," Ruby answered, looking back and forth between the girls. "But it doesn't matter because the novel is infinitely more stunning, I don't care what Greta's ger-wig does."

Eleanor and Ruby collapsed into a fit of giggles. Ruby stood there, nonplussed. "Aunt Ruby," Maggie wheezed, clutching Eleanor's arm. "Greta doesn't have a 'ger-wig,' whatever *that* is. Her *name* is Greta Gerwig. She's the director of the movie."

Ruby swallowed down her embarrassment. She wasn't used to getting things wrong. "Oh," she said.

With an apologetic smile, Eleanor gathered herself. "Yes, I have read the book. And you're right. Nothing compares, not even—"

"—Greta's '*ger-wig*,'" Maggie finished, choking out her words around a half-escaped howl. "Gosh, Aunt Ruby. That was good."

Ruby ignored her. "So it's a favorite of yours?" she asked Eleanor.

"*Little Women*?" Eleanor replied with an incredulous glance. "It's the best. What girl doesn't want to be Jo March?"

Maggie raised her hand. "I've never read it," she confessed with a grimace.

Eleanor gave a mock gasp and poked Maggie in the ribs. "You've never read *Little Women*? And you call yourself a bibliophile. I don't know if we can be friends now. We have three copies at our house alone!"

"Well, it's a good thing we're not in your house, then, isn't it?" Maggie poked back.

"Oh, I don't know if we can be friends now, either," Ruby added, a note of humor in her voice. Maggie and Eleanor turned to her in unison, shock written on both their faces.

"Aunt Ruby," Maggie said, "did you just make a *joke*? I had no idea that was possible."

Ruby snorted and sat back down with her book. "Your teenage years will be an absolute delight for your mother." Then she opened the cover to block the girls from view.

From behind, Maggie whispered to Eleanor, "That's more like it."

8

Eleanor

The first time Eleanor heard Ruby Hurst's name, she was five years old and sitting in Sunday school, wedged at a too-small table between Sarah McIntyre and her twin sister, Miriam. Their teacher was reading the story of Abraham, whose wife little Sarah, felt compelled to remind the class was her namesake, and it was during that moment when Eleanor caught a glimpse out the window of a tall older woman in a cobalt blue hat and suit striding outside the sanctuary. Eleanor thought she looked like the delphiniums that grew in her grandparents' garden, stretched towards the sky in one long line of color, and she pressed into Miriam's side as she watched the woman.

"Hey!" Miriam protested. "Stop leaning on me."

Eleanor shrank back into her seat, chastised, but raised her hand. Ms. Emily, her Sunday school teacher, paused in her lesson, the shock of a raised handwritten on her sweet, young face. She called on Eleanor.

"Who is that woman?" Eleanor asked with a pointed finger towards the window. Ms. Emily approached their table and peeked outside, where the woman in blue was now speaking with Pastor Arwen, her face scrunched in a way that reminded Eleanor of her mother when Eleanor refused to put her toys away.

"Erm," Ms. Emily mumbled, "That's Ruby Hurst."

"Who is she?"

"Her family founded our little town."

"Oh," Eleanor breathed, not quite sure what that meant but certain by the way Ms. Emily said it and by the fancy clothing Ruby Hurst wore, her hat bobbing in time with her finger pointed in the pastor's face, that she must be of some importance. "She looks angry."

Ms. Emily watched out the window for a moment longer and then pulled the flimsy white drapes together. She turned to face Eleanor and her friends. "Well, that's none of our never mind," she said with a thin smile, "so let's get back to Abraham."

But Eleanor had little thought to spare for the patriarch of her faith or the felt cartoon characters Ms. Emily displayed on the colorful board in the front of their classroom. Eleanor wanted to know more about the matriarch of their town, the woman in the bluest blue who possessed so much grit she'd made their pastor flinch and clutch his Bible with white knuckles.

So when Ruby Hurst welcomed Eleanor and Maggie into her sanctuary, Eleanor could scarcely believe their luck. Ruby was much older these days than when she had last seen her, but she remained as elegant as Eleanor remembered. Her thick, silver hair was pulled into a low ponytail, which revealed large diamond studs in her ears. That and a simple platinum band on her right hand were the only pieces of jewelry she wore. Ruby looked every bit the queen of her realm standing there in the center of the Hurst library. Thousands of books encircled her with their stories, just the way Bluestocking's did Eleanor. Although, Eleanor thought to herself with a frown, their collection wasn't nearly as magnificent.

Upstairs in Maggie's bedroom, Eleanor pulled out her laptop and turned to Maggie. "Okay, I've got some ideas about how to help Bluestocking. Most of them are just social media, but I think a few well-timed reels will help us."

"Totally," Maggie agreed, pulling out her phone. "But you'd have to use your dad's phone for that."

"It's fine," Eleanor replied. She clicked on a document and scanned the page. "He won't care if I use it for the business."

"We're going to need more than a few reels to raise enough money to save the store, though," Maggie said, her fair eyebrows knit together in concern. "Do you guys have author meet-and-greets? Readings? Book release parties?"

"A few," Eleanor answered, tapping the keys of her laptop. "But they cost money, too. We had a couple of mystery writers come in October for a Halloween-themed event. There are a lot of those types around here. Savannah is literally a ghost town. Every place has some story about a haunting."

"Oooh, I love that!" declared Maggie. "Do they do tours?"

Eleanor smirked at her friend. "Do they? You can ride in an *actual hearse* and eat in an *actual pirate house*. It's the best."

"We are so doing that," Maggie said. "But after we save your family's store. Any other ideas?"

Eleanor thought of Agatha's suggestion that she convince Ruby to come into the store. A bold move and a terrifying one at that. Eleanor couldn't picture grumpy, stubborn Ruby Hurst coming to town just for their shop when she actively avoided town anyway. *Unless* they told Ruby exactly why they wanted her to visit in the first place.

"There is one thing," Eleanor murmured, not convinced of the words tumbling around in her brain.

"What?"

"The bakery owner, Agatha—," Eleanor began.

"Oh, this will be good," Maggie interjected.

"—said we should ask your aunt to come."

Maggie frowned. "Why? What would Aunt Ruby be able to do?"

Eleanor looked at the floor. "Agatha thought if we could get her to show up and tell people she'd been there, then maybe more customers would start to come in."

Understanding dawned on Maggie's face. "Oh," she said. "I get it. Kind of like a celebrity sighting."

Eleanor smacked a palm to her face. "It's so dumb, I know. I'm sorry I even brought it up."

"No, no," Maggie replied, tugging Eleanor's hand away from her face. "It's actually sort of brilliant. I mean, I doubt Aunt Ruby will be up for it, but it couldn't hurt to try."

"Do you think we should just tell her why?" Eleanor asked, worry knit between her brows. "Your aunt doesn't seem like the type of person to do anything unless she has a good reason."

Maggie chewed on her thumb. "Let's do it," she answered after a beat. "I think we're on her good side now, you especially."

"Me?" Eleanor asked.

"Yeah, *you*. You with the *Little Women* obsession and the falling out over Aunt Ruby's library. She probably wishes you were her niece now."

Eleanor gave her friend a playful shove. "Whatever," she said.

Maggie shrugged. "Doesn't bother me. You can pretend to be her niece, granddaughter, or long-lost cousin four times removed, so long as it keeps her mood somewhere above Voldemort."

Eleanor cracked up. "She's not that bad."

"Again, with your *Little Women* obsession," Maggie replied, holding a hand up to her cheek and fluttering her eyelashes. "'*What little girl doesn't want to grow up to be Jo March?*'"

"It's your fault for not reading one of the most beloved classics of all time," Eleanor shot back. "You're lucky to have me as a friend. I've got all the books you could ever need."

"Except for the bajillion Aunt Ruby has downstairs."

Eleanor's face fell. "Well, yeah. If you want to get technical."

They continued plotting ideas between bites of peanut M&Ms and Twizzlers, and Eleanor was bolstered by her friend's enthusiasm. For the first time in weeks, she wasn't alone anymore. With Maggie by her side, the huge amount of money Bluestocking needed seemed to shrink, made smaller by hope Maggie projected even when Eleanor couldn't muster up any of her own.

At midnight, Eleanor finally closed her laptop. "My brain is mush," she said with a yawn.

"Same," Maggie agreed. "Let's talk to Aunt Ruby tomorrow and see what she says."

Eleanor's stomach lurched at the idea, but she nodded her head.

After they dressed for bed and settled beneath the plush down comforter, Eleanor stared up at the ceiling. She slipped out of her T-shirt and popped it open. Inside was a worn slip of paper, which Eleanor had read a thousand times. The only light came from the pale glow of the moon outside, stretching across the floor in a slant through the sheer white curtains. It was enough to make out the faded black print, not that Eleanor needed to see it. It was one of many little notes Vera would leave around the house for her daughter to find, a game they played both with each other and with James. One time, Eleanor opened the fridge to find a sticky note on an orange juice bottle with the words "I need some cuddles, it's FREEZING in here!" written in Vera's elegant script.

She unfolded the strip of notebook paper and ran her fingers over the simple message: *You're still my favorite story.* It was the last note Eleanor's mother had written to her. Sometimes, she wondered if Vera had been trying to tell her what would happen, to remind Eleanor that even though grief was on its way, she had been loved. Once.

Vera had adored this old Victorian house, with its canary yellow paint and multi-level turrets. It was storybook enchanting and not at all reflective of its owner, although Eleanor didn't think Ruby was as sour as she'd been made out to be by Maggie and so many others. Intimidating, for sure. But mean? *Crazy?*

Eleanor had read enough about villains to guess Ruby Hurst was just as misunderstood as the rest of them.

~~~
~~~

The next day, Eleanor opened her eyes to a strange cramping in her lower belly. The room was bathed in the gray light of early morning, and the house felt still, somber even. Maggie's cheek was smushed into the pillow next to hers, a tiny wet spot visible at her mouth where she had drooled. Eleanor bit back a giggle and then gasped as the ache in her belly tightened, a fist gripping her insides. She sat up and squeezed her stomach in an attempt to massage away the pain, but it wouldn't let up. After a couple of minutes, Eleanor moved quietly off the bed and padded down the hall to the bathroom, clutching her stomach the whole way. She sat down on the toilet and looked down at her underwear at a sight that made her gasp.

Blood, and lots of it.

"Oh my God, oh my God, oh my God," she whispered in a frenzied panic as she snatched tissue from the roll and wiped at her clothes. This was not happening. Not here. Not *now*.

Eleanor darted a glance around the bathroom for any item resembling a sanitary pad. But this was a house of older women, and it was doubtful she'd find a drawer full of liners or tampons in the vicinity unless Maggie had already gotten her period and had a bunch stored away in the cabinet. Eleanor leaned over and reached for the door under the sink, praying, but it contained only cleaning sprays and extra shampoo bottles. In the drawer by the toilet was a package of Q-tips, three floral hand towels, and a pair of nail clippers.

With shaky hands, Eleanor rolled up the toilet tissue around her palm and then placed it inside her underwear. Her pajama pants were stained, too, and there was no way for Eleanor to hide it until she got back to the room. She sat in disbelief, her mind a storm of swirling questions. Then she began to cry.

Eleanor was a smart girl. She had been waiting for this day to come. Unlike most girls her age, she felt excited about the prospect of getting her period for the first time. It was such a grown-up thing to say. *I've got my period.* But this? Hiding in Ruby Hurst's bathroom with no one to call to for help, no one to come and sit by her side, no one to celebrate this strange, lovely moment with her? Suddenly, Vera's absence was a gaping wound in Eleanor's chest.

Hiccups jumped up her throat, and she sobbed around them, tears streaming down her cheeks and off her chin. It felt like the grief would kill her. Eleanor was usually capable of keeping it at bay, stuffed down under a torrent of words and imaginary lives and stories of other people's hardships. Here, in Ruby Hurst's hundred-year-old bathroom, Eleanor had never felt more alone.

Why had her mother gone? Why had she left Eleanor to fend for herself, to learn all on her own what it meant to become a woman?

Why hadn't her mother thought of this moment...and *stayed*?

Eleanor's cries were interrupted by a gentle knock at the bathroom door. "Eleanor, honey?" came a tender voice on the other side. It was Marianne. "Are you okay?"

Eleanor swallowed the lump in her throat and rubbed at her eyes with her sleeve. "Yeah, I'm fine," she croaked.

"What's going on, love?" she pressed.

At those gentle, loving words, Eleanor leaned over her lap and cried some more. She wanted to make it stop—*just make it all stop*—but she couldn't. The blood. The pain. The sadness. It was all here now, flowing out of her body, a broken dam. And Eleanor was a broken girl. She didn't want Marianne. The only thing that could fix a broken girl was her mother...and Eleanor no longer had one of those.

Marianne spoke again. "Can I come in please?"

"No!" Eleanor cried. She scrambled to pull up her pants and flush, mortified now to be caught. "No, thank you," she said again, more calmly. She swiped a sleeve across her tears. "I'm okay. I just had a stomachache, that's all."

"I can get you some medicine if you need it," Marianne replied. After a silent moment, she added, "Are you sure that's all?"

Eleanor looked at her splotchy complexion in the mirror and winced. Turning on the tap, she splashed cool water on her face and let out a long, shuddering breath. "I'm sure," she said in a small voice.

Marianne was quiet, and Eleanor stared at the shadows her feet cast under the bathroom door. *Please go away, please go away*, she begged in her mind.

"Okay," Marianne finally replied. Eleanor could hear the hesitation in her voice. "But if you have any more trouble, you just let me know, alright?"

"Okay," Eleanor replied. She watched as Marianne's feet moved away, and she pressed an ear to the door, listening for the sound of her steps to recede. Then Eleanor washed her hands and tiptoed back to the bedroom where Maggie was still sound asleep. She peeked under the covers, fearful that she would find a bloom of crimson stains on the sheets, but they were clean. Maggie shifted, and Eleanor dropped the comforter, racing to her bag on quiet feet to change into a pair of jeans. Then she slipped back under the covers and squeezed her eyes shut, willing her mind to erase this moment. Was this how Ruby had felt when Alice disappeared? Had she, too, woken up one morning to find that she had grown up without her mom on accident?

Like Sal in *Walk Two Moons*, Eleanor longed to make sense of how her small, cozy world could exist if her mother wasn't in it. How *she* could exist without her mother.

After finding the book in their little free library, Eleanor had read for hours that night on the couch, lost in Sal's epic cross-country adventure with her lovable, quirky grandparents. She had cried angry tears when Sal finally found her mother. It wasn't the way Sal or Eleanor had hoped she would.

They always want to leave, Eleanor had thought. Then she'd thrown the book onto the floor, furious that even a character in a novel had to face this sad uncertainty. At least Sal had gotten some answers.

Would Ruby? Would Eleanor?

And *if* Eleanor's questions could be answered, where would she even begin to look for them?

~~~
~~~

Eleanor called her dad as soon as Maggie was up and asked him to come get her, claiming she had an upset stomach. At breakfast, Marianne cast concerned looks her way but, thankfully, kept Eleanor's breakdown in the bathroom to herself. At first, Maggie pestered Eleanor to stay longer in the hopes of talking to Ruby about the bookstore, but for once, her family's shop was the furthest thing from Eleanor's mind. All she wanted was to go home to her own bed and sleep.

"I'll see if Marianne can bring me by the bookstore when you're feeling better," Maggie told her while they waited on the porch for Eleanor's dad to pull up. "I wish you could stay longer."

Eleanor could hardly meet her friend's gaze. "Me too," she said. "I had fun, though. Thanks for inviting me."

Maggie eyed Eleanor's puffy, drawn face with curiosity etched on her own, but didn't press the issue. As soon as James' truck turned onto the long, gravel drive, Eleanor hugged Maggie and waved goodbye. "I'll text you from Dad's phone tomorrow," she called over her shoulder and made a beeline for the truck.

"Hey, kiddo," James said as she opened the door and tossed her bag on the floorboard. "You alright?"

Eleanor offered a quick smile and turned to face the window. Maggie stood watching them and waved as James began to pull away. Guilt gnawed at Eleanor. She wanted to tell Maggie about what had happened, she really did. It just felt too...big.

"Yeah, I just need to go back to bed, I think," she replied. Her fingers twisted in her lap. "Can we stop at the gas station real quick? I want to grab a ginger ale."

"Sure, honey," her dad answered. He reached over and pressed his palm gently to her forehead, a gesture that was both tender and much too touchy-feely for Eleanor right then. She pulled away. James frowned but only said, "You don't have a fever. I'll run in and grab you some crackers, too. You have to keep something on your stomach."

Panic tightened in her gut. "Uh, no," she said quickly. "That's okay. I'll go in and get it."

"You sure?"

"Totally."

When they parked in front of the convenience store, Eleanor nearly threw herself out the passenger door and raced inside. The store smelled of disinfectant, and her stomach roiled. The cashier hardly spared her a glance as she paced the aisles, searching for feminine products. The only ones available were heavy-flow tampons—*how much flow was heavy?*—and three boxes of overnight pads with wings. Eleanor grabbed one and tucked it under her coat before getting a ginger ale, then decided to go for broke and snag a bag of pickle-flavored Lay's and a bar of chocolate, too. Wasn't this the kind of food she was supposed to eat on her period? She'd have to look it up when she got home.

Eleanor's face burned when she placed her loot on the counter. The cashier, a rail-thin older man with a goatee like Captain Hook's, scanned each item and tossed them into a plastic bag without a word. The thought of his hands on the pads Eleanor would soon stuff inside her underwear made her cheeks burn. *Please hurry up*, she thought, tapping her foot. She stared at the card machine, willing it to process faster. When it beeped, Eleanor snatched both the card and bag away with a mumbled thanks.

"Got what you needed?" her dad asked when she climbed into the truck's cab. Eleanor nodded and slunk down in her seat, grateful that her first attempt to buy what appeared to be skinny diapers was over. *How do people do that all the time?* She shoved the bag behind her feet and pressed a cheek to the window's cool glass. Eleanor wanted to crawl under a rock for five to seven days.

At home, stowed away in the safety of her bathroom, she pulled the thick package out of the bag and turned it this way and that, searching for instructions. There were none, but it seemed pretty straightforward.

Taking a seat on the toilet, Eleanor withdrew the pad from the plastic wrap and unfolded it. She tossed the used tissue paper in the toilet and bunched the soiled underwear into a ball to be tucked deep in the recesses of her laundry basket. Not that her dad did her laundry anymore, but Eleanor couldn't take the risk. The thought was too humiliating to entertain.

She slipped on her clean underwear and put the pad sticky-side down, wrapping the wings around underneath to secure it in place. It was ridiculous. If Eleanor bled enough to fill a pad this size, she would die! But she pulled her underwear up anyway and shifted, uncomfortable. It felt like she was straddling a horse. How was she supposed to walk without waddling?

Eleanor peered at her reflection. Her hair was the same. Her face was the same. Her eyes were the same. Her boobs were definitely the same, which was to say *nonexistent*. How could such a monumental change be happening inside her body, and Eleanor not see it in the mirror?

Like everything else in her life, Eleanor's newest secret would stay just that.

9

Ruby

By this time of year, most people were busy with Christmas preparations, eagerly checking off their to-do lists in advance of family parties and holiday dinners.

But not Ruby.

Ruby was growing more anxious by the day as the calendar tiptoed closer to the anniversary of her mother's death, two days before Christmas. It mattered little how much time had passed since that day on the beach so many years ago. Her body remembered. It recalled with startling clarity the icy bite of the surf as it washed over her shoes and soaked into her stockings. The shiver that shook her from fingertips to toes. The fear of what had passed before her eyes. A body didn't forget. On December 23rd of each year, Ruby Hurst was very much the child she once had been.

Her mother, Alice, remained a mystery to Ruby as much as she had been a mystery to the townsfolk of Hawthorn. Her arrival in town in the spring of 1944 caused quite a stir. She'd been a widow in her late thirties who was taken in by Ruby's father, William. Her husband had died not long before she arrived, and she was a beautiful woman with wild and tangled copper curls that swept down her back like rays of sunlight. It was near the end of the Second World War, a time of great hardship and hope, and the people of Hawthorn loved William.

And, so, they grew to love Alice, as well. By the time Ruby came along, William and Alice were engaged.

But the wedding never happened.

Ruby closed her eyes and pictured her mother's tombstone, which she hadn't laid eyes on in close to thirty years. She remembered the coolness of the marble against her palm, smooth and polished. William had chosen the epitaph for Alice, and Ruby—small and afraid, deep in the recesses of her grief, unable to make sense of a world without her mother—had committed the words to memory by tracing them over and over until the stone rubbed her fingertips raw.

I must go now,
but I am only in the next room,
waiting to meet you again.

Words failed to convey Ruby's adolescent sorrow. Even an entire library of them couldn't describe the emotional devolution that occurred within her battered soul. First, the unresolved grief had injured Ruby, leaving her unable to connect with people who loved her most. Then it had stolen her hope, eaten away at it bit by bit like the most luxurious silk turned to moth-eaten rags. Until she gave up on hope entirely and decided to make do with what she had left.

Pride. Stubbornness.

And a whole lot of money.

Ruby had refused to bemoan her fate in public. She was the product of her generation, after all. Besides, she'd had no real friends to confide in any way. No family who would have ever understood.

It had been bootstraps up for her entire life, and they were expensive bootstraps.

Wrapped in a heavy woolen blanket, Ruby stepped out onto the large, covered front porch and gingerly settled into a rocker. The weight of the scratchy blanket soothed the ache in her bones and warmed her papery skin against the cold breeze. With her head tilted back, Ruby watched the Spanish moss dance lazily back and forth on the branches of the live oaks, telling stories only they could understand.

What would the story of her life be when this was all over, Ruby wondered? The house would go to her next of kin, one of Edward's children, who never bothered about this place and would sell it as sure as the nose on her face. A place was only as good as the people who inhabited it. And the wood beneath Ruby's feet, the bones of the old home her ancestor had built on faith that it would become the heartbeat of a new town, were getting weary now. Just like Ruby. Would there be anyone who cared about this house—this land—the way she had once her time had passed?

Ruby closed her eyes as the image of a man, conjured by her wandering, melancholy thoughts, rose in her mind's eye. He was not the sort of man one would have called handsome in the traditional sense. Indeed, no one ever had. He had been more Colonel Brandon than Mr. Darcy, overlooked and underrated. But Ruby had noticed him. She'd watched him pace the floors of the library from her seat in the parlor, where she could catch glimpses of his tender, serious face unnoticed. His name was Elliot, and he'd worked for her father. Once upon a time, he had sat with Ruby on this very porch, tears threatening to spill onto his ruddy cheeks, and Ruby could still hear the catch in his voice as he spoke. It was a sound that—like the scream that tore from her throat as she stood with the surf pounding her feet, terrified because she'd lost her mother—would never be forgotten. It was etched onto her brain deeper than the grooves on a vinyl record.

These were the worst moments, these late December days. Ruby had no recollection of ever truly enjoying the Christmas season. She'd *wanted* to love it. She could see why it was so wonderful, with all of its emphasis on light in the darkness, on gifts that redeemed the sorrow of broken things. As a child, Ruby would follow William around the house and help with the decorations, even when she was too small to do much in the way of actual assistance. She was his perpetual shadow. Her father's tangible presence had grounded her every December when she felt at risk of floating away into oblivion.

Then, the year Ruby turned twenty-three, Elliot Russell had come along. Sweet, kind Elliot. A good man. A man who had disappointed Ruby with such intensity that she never spoke his name aloud again after that day on the porch. It had happened right here, where she sat in her rocker, though she was a mere whisper of the woman she'd been back then. Vivacious. Headstrong. Determined.

Crazy. Hysterical. Unwell.

The memory was still sour in her stomach.

Ruby rubbed her palms together beneath the blanket and sighed a long, uneven shudder that trembled its way through her shoulders. The breeze coming off the coast bit at her nose and ears, but Ruby hardly noticed. She hadn't cried for a long, long time, but she wondered if it would help. She could feel the familiar tickle in her nose. Could she give in to it? *Should* she? She'd read an article in the newspaper once that touted the physiological benefits of crying, but maybe Ruby had read it wrong. Didn't she need the reassuring touch of another person to soothe her cries? Because when—*if*—Ruby ever cried again, she couldn't imagine it releasing much of anything within her except cortisol and ugly memories.

"Hey, it's getting dark out here," Marianne said, the front door propped open on her hip.

Ruby started. She hadn't heard her come outside. "Want me to turn on the lights?"

Ruby pulled the blanket tighter around her torso. "Alright," she said.

Marianne hesitated, her unspoken questions heavy in the air, but Ruby remained where she was, staring out at the trees. A few seconds later, the door snapped shut, and the Christmas lights blinked on. A quick flush of joy filled Ruby's chest but disappeared as soon as it arrived. Deflated, she tried to chase her dreary thoughts away. She pictured Maggie at the dining table last night, she and Eleanor scarfing down slices of pizza and chattering away like two canaries. Ruby bit back a smile. Their uneasy truce over a shared love of books had been just the ticket to settle the score between aunt and niece. They were still mostly strangers, but Ruby found she was growing fond of the girl.

Eleanor Black seemed as trustworthy a friend as Ruby could hope for Maggie to bond with during her temporary stay. In eight decades of life, Ruby had never known a person to love books the way Eleanor did and not be a sensible, if not genuinely decent, human. It was not a barometer of truth likely to garner points for scientific accuracy, but it suited Ruby just fine.

In fact, Ruby was curious about Eleanor. In more ways than just their shared understanding of loss, Eleanor mirrored Ruby as a young woman. She was bright and bookish, devoted to her family business. Officially, Ruby had never worked for William's publishing company, but she had championed it, pleased that her father had made a living as an honest, practical man intent on making books accessible to everyone.

A blush rose to Ruby's cheeks as she considered it, but she wouldn't mind a friend in someone like Eleanor. It was a silly thought; Ruby had nearly seventy years on the girl, a whole long life. But history was full of unlikely friendships, and it wasn't as though the two of them had nothing in common. In the saddest way possible, they had everything in common. If anyone could understand the grief that lived tucked away in the recesses of her heart, if anyone could empathize with years of unanswered questions and fears, it would be young Eleanor Black.

Ruby chided herself for such thoughts, the thoughts of a long-forgotten version of herself.

But a quieter voice whispered of hope.

The porch lights blinked bright as dusk grew to dark, and quick brushes of sound filled the air. Some animals scurried home to their dens, their tasks completed, while others settled into the trees for a long night of work. Ruby contemplated their fates. Each was a story of sheer survival, of predator or prey, and as far as she knew, woodland creatures did not bemoan their lot in life. They simply got on with the business of living and hunting and eating and dying. No existential crisis there. Grief, sure. Perhaps joy. Animals were sentient beings, after all. But were they moral ones? Did they understand what it meant to consider another, better way?

Did *Ruby*?

10

Eleanor

Deliveries for Agatha kept Eleanor distracted for the next few days. She felt awkward in her body now that it was busy doing all sorts of secret things Eleanor could feel but not name. The biology of menstruation was easy enough to understand; the experience of it was another story.

Maggie was scheduled for a visit to the bookshop later that day, and Eleanor couldn't wait to see her. She felt that if she had to keep her secret for one more day, she might burst. And this whole business of how long to wear a pad before Eleanor leaked all over her clothes was stressful, too. The only option more embarrassing than having her dad notice would be for a customer to see and point it out. Just the thought of it turned Eleanor's body hot and made her want to sink into the floor.

"Elle, can you grab that green cardboard box of donations from the storage room for me?" her dad asked from his office. Eleanor was manning the front counter, which amounted to loads of reading time and the occasional carol sing-a-long when no one else was in the store.

"Sure thing!" she called back.

The storage room was a long, narrow space at the back of the store. Eleanor used to sneak up the stairs to the small attic apartment when she was younger and fall asleep there, dreaming of enchanted wardrobes and far-away adventures. The storage room was filled with books and boxes of books that either needed to be sorted for donation or had already been logged for inventory. Since Bluestocking sold both new and used titles, they'd offered a buyback program for anyone who wanted to sell their gently used books for store credit. These days, they received more used copies than they sold, so James had put an end to that service last year. Every time Eleanor saw the sign upfront informing customers they no longer took donations or offered credit, she was reminded of the notice in her dad's desk. Time was running out.

Eleanor stepped to the center of the room and turned in a tight circle. Any unlogged donations were put by the door so as not to get mixed up with current inventory, but the dusty, hardwood floor was clear. In the dim light of the poky space, Eleanor crouched low to read what was written on the handful of boxes on the shelves, starting with those closest to the floor. She scanned rows, hands on her hips, until she finally saw the small green box shelved high above her head. Her dad must have already logged them all into the system.

As Eleanor pulled a small chair away from the heavy antique desk tucked in the far left corner, the room suddenly grew warmer. Eleanor glanced around, but there were no vents in the storage room. The air had grown thick like a knit blanket, cozy and comforting. Then, the scent of cinnamon and orange filled the space around her, enveloping Eleanor in its heady aroma. She felt light and happy. *Safe.* Her limbs tingled the way they did when she was about to fall into a deep sleep, and Eleanor was filled with the sensation of *home.* It was curious and strange. She stood on the chair and breathed it in, lost for a moment in the comfort of its presence.

Then, as she reached for the box above her head, Eleanor's foot slipped, and she stumbled in the chair. With a yelp, she crashed down on top of the desk and tumbled to the floor. She moaned in pain, her shin throbbing where it had slammed into the corner edge. A nasty purple bruise had already begun to form there. Eleanor winced and rubbed at the spot, blinking back hot tears that threatened to spill down her cheeks.

Just as she was about to attempt to stand and put weight on the injured leg, Eleanor glanced over at the desk and froze.

There, underneath the bottom drawer, a long, thin compartment had popped out from its hiding place. Inside, Eleanor could see a small book shoved deep into the corner.

She swallowed hard and scooted closer. Her breath came in short bursts as she reached out and retrieved the book with gentle hands.

The cover was old, cracked leather, soft as butter, and faded from black to a dull slate gray. A thrill of discovery worked its way up Eleanor's limbs, making her forget all about the bruise still throbbing on her injured shin. She opened the cover and scanned the handwritten page with hungry eyes. Scrawled in a messy, feminine hand across the top were the words *The Woman of Valbrooke Hall, Draft Chapter One.*

Eleanor spoke the words in a reverent voice, turning the page to finger through the book's contents. More than half the journal was filled with handwritten chapters, the pages wrinkled and stiff with water damage. Eleanor gasped with delight at each turn of the page. She flipped back to the inside cover, and there, in the top left corner, was a name.

Alma Gardyne.

Brow wrinkling in concentration, Eleanor searched her memories for any author of that name. Nothing came to mind. Recalling her conversation with her dad, Eleanor wondered if perhaps Alma Gardyne was one of the authors the Hurst family had published long ago. But why would one of their authors have hidden her book in a desk once owned by the Hursts in the very building where they had housed their publishing office?

Why...and when?

Eleanor's spine tingled as she considered the possibilities. She had a real-life mystery on her hands. First, the room had filled with the delicious scent of spices, and then she had fallen on the desk. No doubt, the crash had knocked loose some part of the hidden drawer, enabling it to come free for the first time in many years. Eleanor got down low on her belly and peered up at the bottom of the compartment.

There. A tiny combination wheel, no bigger than the end of her pinky finger. Whoever had last closed this compartment must have done so in a hurry if Eleanor had been able to knock it open without the combination. She slipped her hand inside once more to be sure it was empty and then tucked the drawer closed just enough to remain open without being seen should her father come looking through the storage room.

Eleanor wondered if her dad knew about the hidden compartment. With that thought, Eleanor sat up on her haunches, still clutching the small, worn book. The memory of Vera there at the desk, long hair piled in a messy knot on her head while she tallied numbers or hummed to herself, was both precious and tender, like the bruise blooming on Eleanor's leg.

She fingered the cover again, the soft leather-like velvet against her fingertips. If Alma was a writer from this area, then perhaps Bluestocking Books carried her work.

With a brush of her jeans, Eleanor stood and tucked the book under her arm. It was meant for her to find, of that fact she felt certain, and she didn't want to explain it to her dad just then. The room growing warm, the feeling of home...it sounded crazy even to Eleanor, but it was like the shop itself had wanted her to find the book.

Now, she needed to find out more about Alma.

"Dad, the box you wanted is up too high for me," she told him as she passed his office, hiding the book behind her back. "I tried to grab it, but I fell and hit my shin on the desk."

James took off his reading glasses, worry furrowing his brows. "Are you okay?"

"It's just a bruise," she replied.

"That's so strange," he muttered. "I put that box on the floor by the desk just this morning, I would swear to it."

A cold trickle went up Eleanor's spine. "Well, it's up on the shelf now, so you'll have to get it."

James sighed and shook his head. "Okay, here I come."

While he was busy in the storage room, Eleanor searched for Alma Gardyne in their inventory. Nothing. With a frown, Eleanor turned the faded journal over in her hands.

"Okay, I got the box down," James said from the end of the aisle, startling Eleanor. He eyed the book. "What's that?"

"Oh, uh," she stuttered, "it's a book."

Her dad raised a dark brow. "Yeah, I can see that. Anything I can help with?"

Eleanor's laugh was stilted. "Right. Well, it's a book by a woman named Alma Gardyne. Do you know her?"

James looked up and chewed on his lip. "Hmm, doesn't ring a bell. But I don't know every book in this store by heart, honey."

"No, I know," Eleanor replied, placing the slim volume on the shelf as if she had just found it there. "I was just curious. It looked interesting, that's all."

"Try Google," her dad said and continued back to his office, box in hand.

Eleanor had a better idea.

11

Ruby

R uby was stunned when Maggie suggested they play a game of Scrabble together with Marianne one afternoon. She was so stunned, in fact, that she agreed to a game.

After a lunch of sandwiches and pasta salad, the three of them settled down in front of the fireplace in the library. Their sweet teas, made fresh by Marianne that morning, sweated in their glasses, and Ruby wiped hers with a napkin before she took a sip.

"I must say, Margaret," she said as her niece counted out the tiles for each player. "I'm looking forward to this. I love a good game of Scrabble."

Maggie set up her tiles and frowned. "I don't know if I'm going to like this one."

"Just try to go for points," Marianne added with a pat on Maggie's hand. "Don't worry about fancy words."

Ruby thought that was a terrible idea, but she swallowed the comment and scrutinized her tiles. She schooled her expression into a neutral one and placed her first word on the board.

Maggie turned her head sideways to read. "'*Gaunt*'," she said. "Okay. With a double letter score for 'T,' that's seven points total." She scribbled Ruby's score on a lined pad of paper.

"Nice start," Marianne added. "Not many points, though."

Ruby glowered at her housekeeper. "Okay, then. Let's see what you have to offer us mere mortals."

Marianne looked back and forth between the board and her tiles. After a moment, she put down her word. "'*Torte*,'" she said, upbeat. "One of my favorite desserts."

"Not many points, though," Ruby countered, a note of sarcasm in her voice.

"That's ten for a double word score," Maggie added as she took note. "You guys are too fancy."

"Your turn," Marianne said with a flourish of her hand toward Maggie's letters.

Maggie chewed on her bottom lip, considering. The fire crackled and popped behind her, filling the room with a comfortable, lazy heat as they sat around the table, waiting. Ruby took another sip of her tea while Maggie switched tiles around, her blue eyes laser-focused. Then her face lit up, and she laid down her tiles with a triumphant smile.

Maggie's word intersected horizontally with Marianne's, using the '*e*' in '*torte*' as her second letter. It was a double-word score with a double-letter score at the end. Ruby calculated the total in her head and sucked her teeth.

"'*Feral*,'" Maggie said, victory writ large on her small face. "That's nine points plus a double word score for a total of eighteen points."

"*Maith thú!*" said Marianne with a clap of her hands. "You're going to be a formidable opponent, Maggie."

"A fitting first word for you," Ruby replied, to which Maggie scoffed. "I take it you've played this game before."

Her niece stared down her nose at Ruby, one eyebrow lifted high. "My dad and I used to play a lot," she said, biting out each word.

Ruby felt properly scorned. "Oh," she said. "Well. Looks like we'll make a game of it, after all."

Just as quickly as Maggie's mood had soured, it brightened once more as Marianne began to count out new letters for each of them. Ruby sipped her tea and peered over the glass at her niece, seeing for the first time the purple shadows under her eyes. She remembered how it felt to be let down by the people you loved, and she knew all too well what it was like to be disappointed with one's father. It couldn't be easy for the girl, being so far from home when everyone—and everything—she loved had changed. When this was all over, Maggie would go back to Virginia with a new life she'd had no say in building. Worst of all, she'd be asked to pretend it was better that way. But Ruby knew the pain of a broken family on a young girl's heart.

"So, did you enjoy your visit with Eleanor?" Ruby asked. She made her turn, and Maggie visibly brightened.

"We had so much fun," she answered with a grin. "We have a lot in common, and she asked if I could come to the bookstore later today. Would that be okay with you?"

Pleased to be asked instead of told, Ruby nodded. "Certainly. Marianne can take you."

Maggie hesitated and cast a nervous glance at Marianne before she spoke again. "Aunt Ruby, would you mind, uh—I mean, do you think you'd like to come along?"

Ruby withdrew her hands from the tiles and placed them in her lap, a sense of foreboding creeping up her spine. "Whatever for?"

Maggie looked down at the table and tapped her fingers on the wood. "I just thought it would be nice for you to see it."

"I have seen it," Ruby countered.

"When?" Maggie demanded, spearing her aunt with a critical look.

"Once or twice as we passed on our way out to Savannah."

Maggie scowled. "That's not the same, Aunt Ruby, and you know it."

"It's the same to me."

Marianne watched their exchange like a tennis match, her head snapping back and forth as they spoke.

Maggie persisted, undeterred. "Would it make a difference if I told you Eleanor's dad is about to lose the store, and she's desperate to help him save it?"

The air seemed to leave the room. The fire burned high in the hearth, casting long, dark shadows on the walls, like ghosts come close to listen. Ruby's heart thudded against her ribs.

"And what possible difference would I make in their present circumstances, hmm?" she demanded.

"If people saw you there, they might come by more often. Buy more books, you know?"

It was a different answer than the one she'd expected. Ruby pinched the bridge of her nose and took a few deep breaths. When she had considered what it might be like to befriend young Eleanor Black, it had been with the hope of connecting to the one person who seemed able to understand her, not offering herself up to the people of Hawthorn as a sideshow. Ruby'd had enough of that nonsense in her life.

"So I'm a profit generator now, am I?" she said in a sharp voice. Maggie winced.

Marianne reached a hand out to Ruby's arm. "She just wants to help her friend," she said in a steady, gentle tone.

Ruby considered her point but refused to give in. "This is utterly ridiculous. I will not be a pawn in some childish game. If James Black cannot earn enough money to keep his business afloat, then perhaps it's time to sell. That's what my father did, and look what it left me. I've never had to want for a thing."

As Ruby spoke, Maggie's face turned an angry shade of crimson. Her jaw tightened as she listened to Ruby's words, but a small tear slid down her cheek despite the fury in her eyes.

"Oh yeah?" Maggie countered. "How about friends, Aunt Ruby? How about a life where you aren't hiding in your house all the time? Did your dad leave you that, too?"

Ruby reared back as if she'd been slapped. Marianne's eyes were as wide as saucers. No one had ever dared speak to Ruby that way before, and she was stunned into silence as Maggie's words pierced their target. Before she could respond, Maggie stood up and stomped out of the room. The only sound left in her wake was the hiss and pop of the dying fire.

Marianne coughed and reached for the Scrabble board. Ruby stilled her with a touch of her fingers.

"Do you think she's right, Marianne?" Ruby asked her words only just above a whisper.

Marianne sighed and sat back in her chair. "She's a child, Ruby."

"That's not what I asked."

"Well, I don't know what to tell you," Marianne countered, defensive. "Are you asking as my employer or as a friend?"

"I thought I didn't have any of those," Ruby shot back.

Marianne pushed back from the table and stood. "Get a grip. I've always been your friend, even if you've never wanted one. So, yes, I suppose. Maybe Maggie has a point. She shouldn't have spoken to you in such a harsh way, but you said it yourself, Ruby. Look at all you have. Who is it for, huh? You don't seem to enjoy it very much, but I know plenty of people who might benefit from what you have to offer, starting with your niece."

"You think I should help the Blacks?" Ruby asked, unable to meet Marianne's glare.

"I think you *could*," Marianne answered. "And I also think you could do something to show Maggie you care about her as more than just an interruption to your life."

Ruby nodded, quiet.

"Maybe you're too close to this," Marianne said, gentler this time. "To what Eleanor has been through. Forest for the trees and all that."

Ruby looked up sharply. "I'm *in* the damn trees, Marianne," Ruby countered, defensive. "I've thought of my mother every single day of my life, and that girl only stirs up painful memories for me."

The conversation had landed in territory much too close for comfort. Ruby remembered the cold stares and vicious words from her youth that children are so skilled at directing to anyone they deem different. In any other town, Ruby's family name might have saved her from such treatment, but here in Hawthorn, where everyone knew everyone else, the tragedy that had befallen her family had made Ruby a target. Her testimony about what she saw the day her mother disappeared had filtered through official channels into the ears of family sitting rooms and kitchen tables, and it had not sat well with the children she'd wanted to call friends.

"She's only five," William had boomed at the Chatham County sheriff so long ago. The sheriff was a robust man, almost as wide as he was tall, and he had come by the house that day to inform William they were stopping the search for Alice's body. Ruby, small and frightened, had stood on the porch with her arms wrapped tight around the railing as she watched them argue on the gravel drive.

"She's traumatized!" William shouted. He glanced over at Ruby, and his gray eyes turned soft. Stepping closer to the sheriff, William lowered his voice, but Ruby heard him all the same. "Alice didn't go anywhere except into the water. She didn't leave, she *died*. And it's your job to find her, not give up looking after only a week."

The sheriff flinched at William's words but stood firm where he was. "I only have so many resources, Mr. Hurst."

"Well, I have plenty of them. Find her."

With William's money at the helm, the investigation had been expanded and extended. His access to all manner of well-connected businessmen had helped him cover the costs of additional boats, crew, and all the equipment necessary for underwater searches. Law enforcement combed the waters around Savannah and Tybee every day. And every night, William stood on the front porch, waiting for news from the sheriff.

Finally, on New Year's Day of 1950, a woman's decomposed and scavenged body had been discovered tangled in the marshland reeds off Cockspur Island. A set of rings, including Alice's emerald engagement ring from William, were found on the delicate platinum chain she always wore around her neck, which her first husband had given her many years before. Three days later, Alice's cherry wood casket, draped in handmade lace, was lowered into the red Georgia clay while Ruby stood next to her father, clutching his fingers as tightly as she could. She didn't cry, not then. Her tears had already been swallowed up by the ocean, coaxing them out of her as it had swirled around her ankles, stealing the only thing left that Ruby had to give after it had taken her mother.

William had tried to talk to Ruby about what happened. He was gentle and patient with her, even in his grief, but she closed up after she overheard his conversation on the porch. She didn't understand all that had been spoken between her father and the sheriff, but she could sense, as children often do, that what she had to say did not matter.

"I want Maggie to enjoy her time here," Ruby continued now, helping Marianne scrape letter tiles into the soft velvet pouch. "I didn't care much at first, it's true, but I do now. I just wish her only friend didn't have to be godforsaken Eleanor Black."

"Ruby," Marianne chided. "That's cruel. Eleanor can't help what happened to her mother any more than you could have stopped what happened to yours."

No, but Ruby knew she could have fought harder to tell the truth. She could have stood up for herself when children called her crazy, when her father dismissed Ruby's claim about what she'd seen as nothing more than a child's traumatized imagination. She shouldn't have spent all these years hiding as if she were ashamed.

The truth was Ruby had never felt shame.

She'd only ever been afraid.

12

Eleanor

When Eleanor spotted Maggie through the glass front door, Marianne close behind, she could immediately see that something was wrong. Maggie's face was pinched and sour, Marianne's concerned.

The blast of cold air when they entered made Eleanor shiver. "Hey!" she exclaimed with a broad smile, rushing over to greet them. "I've got something cool to show you."

Maggie lifted one corner of her mouth and met Eleanor's gaze with red-rimmed eyes. Marianne squeezed Maggie's shoulders. "Call me when you're ready to come home," she said and waved goodbye to Eleanor.

When she was gone, Maggie threw her backpack on the floor and slumped into a nearby chair. "Aunt Ruby is such a jerk," she said with such vehemence that Eleanor blinked.

"What did she do now?" Eleanor asked, taking a seat across from Maggie, who sat up and started talking a hundred miles an hour.

"She's just a grouchy old lady who never wants to do anything for anyone else even though she's got more money than God. I mean, would it kill her to come out of her monster cave and show her face here once in a while? Nobody cares about what happened when Aunt Ruby was a little girl anymore. What is she so afraid of, huh? Lots of people's mothers die. It's not like she's the only one. They just want to see that she exists. Is that really too much to ask?"

So Maggie had told Ruby about the store. Obviously, it hadn't gone well. Eleanor's heart sank to her toes, and she looked down at her hands, twisting the handmade bracelet she'd made for herself last summer.

"What?" Maggie asked, eyeing Eleanor's fidgety hands. "What's wrong?"

Eleanor released a long, shaky breath. Then she looked up at her friend, chin lifted despite the hard knot in her throat. "My mom went missing six years ago. We've never found out what happened to her."

Maggie's mouth fell open, her eyes fixed on Eleanor's face. "*What?*" she exclaimed. "Oh, Eleanor, I'm so sorry. I'm such a jerk!" Maggie pressed her face into her hands. "I shouldn't have said that about Ruby's mom. Ugh. I'm really, *really* sorry."

"It's okay," Eleanor replied. "You didn't know."

"Still," Maggie said. "Ugh, why am I like this?"

Eleanor shrugged. "Really. It's okay. I wanted to tell you. I just didn't know how."

Maggie walked over to Eleanor and pulled her up into a hug so tight she thought a rib might crack. "Okay, okay," Eleanor croaked, tapping Maggie's back. "Uncle!" Maggie laughed and let go.

"I guess I can see now why Aunt Ruby might not want to come here," she said, crossing her arms. "And I don't mean to be insensitive when I say this, but—well, it's just that it's been so *long.*"

Eleanor looked down at her feet. "Maybe it seems that way to you," she replied. "But it will never go away. It doesn't matter how much time passes. I will never stop missing my mom or wishing she would come back."

"How do you do it?" Maggie asked softly.

Eleanor had asked herself that question so many times. That was the thing about grief. She had thought it would kill her, but no. It was the slow, steady trickle of life that dripped from her heart when she realized her mother would never come home that threatened to steal her life. It was the lack of inertia. Grief didn't pull you back in time so much as it froze you, stunned, in the present. It could rot you where you stood.

When Eleanor was ten, her sadness over Vera's disappearance became accompanied by an intense need to understand her mom's motivations. The police and James had zeroed in on the belief that Vera had been kidnapped, or worse, but no clue ever actually pointed them in that direction. Eventually, the case had gone cold. That was when Eleanor had collected a pile of medical books from their shop and scoured them with her mother in mind, sure that if she could just understand the source of Vera's internal anguish, then maybe she could survive this pain. Maybe she could finally understand the grief that had made her mother leave.

One morning, a few months before Vera disappeared, Eleanor had woken in the middle of the night to the sound of her mother's sobs. Frightened, she hurried down the hall to her parents' bedroom and came up short when James opened the door. His eyes were wide with panic while he corralled Eleanor back to her bed with whispered assurances. But she had seen her mother sitting on a towel at the end of the bed, a bundle of bloody sheets on the floor by her feet. She hadn't understood then.

But she understood now.

Eleanor's dad would never agree that Vera had chosen to leave. He believed the best of his wife, and why shouldn't he? Why shouldn't *Eleanor*? There was no evidence to the contrary, nothing other than the visceral truth that tightened in her gut each time she imagined her mom trapped somewhere, captive. Or buried in the ground.

No, her body told her. *Not that.*

Perhaps Eleanor's body was simply protecting her from a horrific reality she couldn't bear to contemplate. Or maybe Eleanor's theory was correct. Which was worse? A kidnapped mother, a dead mother, or a mother who had once loved her daughter deeply, just not enough to keep showing up through her grief?

Eleanor didn't know how she survived. She just did.

"It's hard," she replied to Maggie, picking at the fuzz on her cardigan. "Especially right now."

Maggie nodded. "Because of the holidays," she said, matter-of-fact.

"Yeah, but—" Eleanor began but stopped short. A customer had just entered the shop behind them, and she didn't want another soul to hear what was about to come out of her mouth. Eleanor pulled Maggie towards the back of the store, near the storage room. "I started my period."

"For the first time?" Maggie whisper-shouted. Eleanor glanced around and then nodded.

"Yesterday, at your aunt's house."

"I knew it!" Maggie declared, and Eleanor shushed her. Maggie continued in a softer voice. "I thought I saw blood on your pants when you were packing up your stuff. Is that why you left early?"

"Yeah," Eleanor replied, her cheeks flushed "Marianne caught me crying in the bathroom when you were still sleeping. I was so embarrassed."

"Why? I got my period last year. It's no big deal."

Eleanor cocked her head to the side and pierced her friend with a moody stare. "It is when your mother isn't around to tell about it."

Maggie reached for Eleanor's hand. "You're right. I'm sorry. Do you have tampons and stuff?"

"I got some pads," Eleanor replied, shifting her feet. "They feel like diapers, though. It's honestly ridiculous. You'd think we'd have better options by now."

"You'll get used to it. I'll help you find some good brands. Or you could try a menstrual cup."

Eleanor blanched. "That sounds even worse."

Maggie giggled, then looked over her shoulder towards James' office and lowered her voice again. "Does your dad know?"

Eleanor shook her head, brown curls whipping back and forth. "No way."

"You're going to have to tell him eventually," Maggie said. "I doubt you'll be able to sneak out to the store on your own every month."

"I know," Eleanor admitted. "But I'll worry about that later."

With that, she opened the door to the storage room and beckoned for Maggie to follow. Inside, Eleanor bent down beside the antique desk while Maggie pulled the string to illuminate the space with hazy orange light.

With a flourish of her hand, Eleanor gestured to the hidden compartment and said, "There's something else I want to show you."

13

Ruby

Last night had been a certifiable disaster. Even Ruby could admit when she was in the wrong, even if she only admitted it to herself. But she didn't regret what she had done. Maggie, with her wide-eyed idealism and knowing looks, had gotten too close to Ruby's center where the truth lay dormant, quiet. Almost forgotten.

Rumors about Ruby and her family had always persisted—growing and shrinking around whatever half-lie interested people most that decade. Rumors only hovered around the story of her mother's death but never fully touched it.

Death. It was such a strange idea. Ruby wasn't afraid of dying, nor was she exceptionally interested in where she'd go after this charade of a life was all said and done, but she still thought it a curious concept. Her life had been somewhat consumed by it. Most people believed death was just the start of another, happier life, a perfect world in which the entirety of the human population—save ruthless dictators and pedophiles and war criminals and serial killers—lived in harmony with each other for all eternity. For some, death was one stop on an endless cycle of rebirth toward individual perfection. For others, death was just darkness and silence. Ruby quite liked that option. The world had always been too loud for her to feel at home here.

Until her father's death, Ruby had wondered if—for some—death was a whole other notion altogether, a paradise where the best and kindest of people would go as soon as it was their time, whatever that meant. Perhaps they didn't die. Perhaps they simply decided, or were told, they had to leave. Then they departed the moment the realization occurred, body and soul.

But William had been the kindest man Ruby had ever known. The best man. His death had shattered that silly, childish notion. Ruby had watched him waste away as the cancer stole him, piece by piece, until his body, shriveled and wasted to half the man Ruby had called father, gave up. It was a gruesome death, and Ruby hated whatever god had allowed William to suffer like that.

She walked out to the back garden, a woolen shawl wrapped tight around her frail shoulders and paced the pathway through the dormant flower beds. Come spring, the garden would be an explosion of color and scent, the south Georgia heat pulling heavy perfumes from the flowers until the air was weighed down with both. It was the perfect recipe for a nap on the hammock, lulled to sleep by the gentle sway and the coolness of the shade. Ruby took a deep breath of the cold winter air and wished for spring. The barren, silent earth, which Ruby took as much comfort from as she could each year, suddenly felt dark and depressing.

She turned to the east, where the garden wall hid behind a curtain of ivy, and pictured the crashing waves on Tybee Island, carving their memories into the sand, tempting people like Ruby to try and claim them, only to wash them all away in the next moment. The ocean was a jealous mistress, never content to share what she possessed. Ruby knew that better than anyone. How many times had she gone back to that beach, searching for answers, only to come home deeper in her grief than before? But that was years ago now. Ruby hadn't been back since the men who were supposed to love her betrayed her with their good intentions.

She was tempted to go now after Maggie had found her unguarded and vulnerable, looking for hope. The seventy-fifth anniversary of Alice's death was in a few days, and after her argument with Maggie the night before, Ruby had wrestled hard with skepticism and bitterness, her longtime companions. Whatever hope had planted itself in her heart had been torn up by the familiar thrum of disappointment. Ruby shouldn't have been surprised, but she was. And that made it all the more painful.

"Marianne," Ruby called as she walked back into the kitchen through the garden door.

Her housekeeper was wiping down the counters from breakfast. A fresh pot of coffee brewed on the counter, the aroma of Agatha's specialty blend of coffee beans leading Ruby across the room like a sailor to a siren. "I have a rather unusual request if you don't mind," she said as she poured herself a cup and stirred in sugar and cream.

"If I don't mind?" Marianne asked, a smirk playing on her thin lips. "How kind of you to consider me."

Ruby cast Marianne a glare over the rim of her cup. "I'd like to go to Tybee this afternoon."

Marianne dropped her rag on the counter and stared at Ruby. "*You* want to go to *Tybee*?"

"That's what I said."

"Yeah, I know."

"You seem to be struggling with your hearing, is all," Ruby replied dryly. Marianne paused, waiting for an explanation. "I don't know how long I'll be," is all Ruby offered.

"Okay." Marianne still gaped at her.

"Is that a problem?"

Her housekeeper pressed her lips into a firm line and shook her head. "Not at all. I can make us a packed lunch if you want."

"No picnics," Ruby answered sharply. "Just a visit."

"Of course," Marianne said, her tone softening. "I'll just bring a book and wait in the car if you'd like."

"Thank you."

They left for Tybee in Ruby's luxury sedan, which she allowed Marianne to drive once a week to run errands and keep it in good shape. The seats were a soft, buttery leather, heated against the winter chill, but Ruby sat in the front passenger seat as if she were going to open the door and leap from the car at any moment. As they crossed onto Wilmington Island and then over the Lazaretto Bridge to Tybee, Ruby forced herself to look out the window. The marshes were beautiful. The sun sparkled on the water in the high afternoon sun, but boats were generally docked this time of year. Great egrets stood in the tall grasses, the tide low and muddy, searching for food, while various waterfowl swam in deeper streams that connected the tangle of marshes to the ocean.

Ruby appreciated how life persisted in the winter. Wasn't that what she had done? Every December, she would think of her mother and, somehow, keep breathing. Despite her father's dismissal of her testimony, and regardless of her peers' crude remarks and her disbelief about what she had seen that day in 1949, Ruby hunkered down in the winter and made it through in one piece. She had even managed to love what it represented: the promise of new life on the other side of a frozen, quiet season. Each day, she nestled into a well-loved wingback chair in the library, cozy and safe within its walls of stories, and passed the darker, shorter months by living a hundred different lives in a thousand different places.

Warmth flooded through Ruby at the thought. Of all the gifts her father had given her, books had been the most precious, for they had been her refuge in every storm. If a body was too broken and tired to take one somewhere wonderful, a book would always do the job. Maggie and Eleanor were two of the few people Ruby had met in her long life who seemed to innately understand that truth.

Ruby crossed her arms and sighed. Marianne glanced over at her from the driver's seat but said nothing. The drive continued in silence, Ruby at perpetual war with herself. Soon, they parked in a lot on the north end of the island near the lighthouse, which was blessedly quiet at this time of year. Ruby tidied her scarf and coat and paused with her hand on the door handle.

She could already hear the sound of the waves pounding the sand, the way they pounded her memories, the swell and crush of them unyielding. She wanted to ask for Marianne's company. The fear of the ocean—of all it had already taken from her and could still take—was a physical presence in the car with them. But Ruby gritted her teeth and opened the door on her own, leaving Marianne behind with her book and a portable mug of tea, concern writ large on the woman's face as she watched her employer walk slowly away.

As she traversed the beach, each step in the powder-soft sand a monumental effort, Ruby was taken back to that December day when she was five years old. She'd been so happy toting their blanket across the sand, her mother a few steps behind her as they searched for a spot to lay their picnic. Ruby had called out every wren and sandpiper to her mother, delighted by their small, abrupt movements down the beach as they searched for tiny crabs hidden beneath their feet.

"Let's sit closer to the water," Alice had told her daughter, their fingers intertwined as they walked along the beach. "The sand is not so messy where the tide has been."

"But it's wet, Mama," Ruby replied, her nose scrunched.

"That's alright. Our blanket is thick enough to keep us dry."

After a picnic of tomato soup in tin cups with hot, fresh bread from the kitchen, Alice showed Ruby how to find shark teeth hidden in the detritus of shell pieces along the surf.

Hunched over, holding onto their hats, Ruby and her mother followed the trail of shells on constant alert for the tiny but conspicuous y shape of a fossilized shark tooth, black and shiny like obsidian rock.

"Ruby, look!" Alice exclaimed, her fiery curls peeking out from under the brim of her hat. Her cheeks were flushed with excitement and cold alike. "I found two teeth right next to each other!"

Ruby gasped with delight and cradled the teeth in her chubby palm, stunned at their good fortune. "Look how one is bigger than the other. Like me and you!"

Alice threw her head back and laughed. "That's right, Ruby, my girl. Like me and you."

As she stood alone on the beach now, Ruby looked out at the horizon and felt the crisp ocean breeze sting her eyes. Tears pricked, but she blinked them back. Now was not the time to break down. Now was the time to remember.

She closed her eyes and called to mind the joy of that day before it all went so very, very wrong. Ruby and Alice had sat on their blanket just south of the lighthouse. From a stack of books her mother had packed—*Girl of the Limberlost, Anne of Green Gables*, some volumes of Dickens—Ruby had plucked Alice's coveted copy of *The Secret Garden*. Ruby felt kindred to Mary Lennox, with her loneliness and independent spirit. Ruby's house was a lovely place, but it was too big. Too quiet. She sometimes wondered if the quiet was caused by her mother's sadness, which could permeate a room like a hot summer's day. Ruby understood later how her mother missed her husband, even though she rarely spoke of him. Alice having been married before was a difficult concept for a five-year-old to grasp when she also saw how much her mother and father cared for each other. But there it was. Mothers were girls once, too, and grief did not end just because new love entered the picture.

Ruby had snuggled up next to Alice for warmth, basking in the soft, soothing sound of her mother's voice as she told the story of Mary's first adventure in the garden.

"Mama?" Ruby interrupted sleepily. "Does magic exist?"

Alice peered at her daughter. "Hmm," she breathed. "That's a good question."

"Do you know the answer?"

Alice exhaled slowly. "I only know what I believe, what I've experienced for myself. I know that being a mother is a sort of magic. Carrying a child inside your body, feeling her grow and kick and change, is certainly magical. A lot of the world is, too, even if it seems ordinary at first glance."

Ruby bit the inside of her cheek and considered her mother's words. "I think books are magic," she proclaimed with a wide, bright grin.

"Oh, I believe you're right," Alice agreed. She pulled Ruby closer to her body. "More than you can imagine."

They continued to read *The Secret Garden* until Ruby fell asleep against her mother's side, warm from the heat of her body despite the weak winter sun moving lower in the sky. When she woke up, Alice was still holding her close, a sad smile playing on her lips.

"I fell asleep," Ruby mumbled with a yawn.

Alice kissed the top of Ruby's head. "Yes, you did."

"I liked the garden book. Would you read some more to me?"

"How about we look for more shark teeth before we have to head back?" Alice said, standing up and reaching for Ruby's hand.

"Oh, yes!" Ruby clamored to her feet and fixed her dress.

The two of them walked to the surf once more. The tide was coming in, and the waves had grown larger, their crashes stronger. Ruby dared the waves and put her boots in the surf. Alice followed suit. They laughed as the sand sucked their feet down with the pull of the tide and quickly moved away, only to step back into the water once it came close again.

"Our stockings are going to get wet, Ruby," Alice warned with a wink.

"We can change when we get home, Mama," Ruby replied, smiling. "I'm not worried."

Ruby snapped her eyes open as it all came tumbling back into her mind. Her knees began to shake, and she collapsed onto the sand. A sob tore up her throat, and Ruby choked on it, angry and afraid. Oh, how she hated this place. She hated how the waves kept on coming, charging at her, and how the sounds had remained the same for seventy-five years. She could be in 1949 or 2024; it didn't matter. The ocean remained. The terror remained. Her body, though changed, knew what this place had done to her, and it shouted at Ruby to flee.

But where could she go that grief would not find her? Where could Ruby run so that fear would not creep into her soul and tear into all that was once so good and true? Her mother's last moments mocked Ruby here, on this godforsaken island where she had been left all alone, the warmth of her mother's hand still alive on her skin.

Ruby sobbed on her hands and knees. The water rushed up over her fingers, biting into her flesh, but she barely noticed. God, what she wouldn't give to be free of this torment.

A sudden thought pierced her mind with fresh sharpness, horrible in its violent simplicity.

She could just go, too, couldn't she? Step into the waves, one foot after another, and keep walking until she was swallowed up and the world went dark and quiet for good. At least there would be no daughter left behind, terrorized, forever clinging to some notion of unreality that would cost her every opportunity of lasting companionship.

Maybe Ruby *was* some version of what people had always believed her to be: Wrong in the head. Mentally ill. Incapable of living a normal life. But she knew what she had witnessed that day, on that very beach, and it wasn't a drowning.

It was a *leaving*.

People could believe what they wanted to about Ruby Hurst. They could believe what they wanted about her entire family. She knew the truth, and she was so tired now. Ruby could make her own choice right here on this same beach. The folks in Hawthorn would have their rumors confirmed, and wouldn't that make everyone happy?

Ruby sat back on her knees and took a deep breath, tears dried by the wind on her cheeks. Her head was throbbing, but her mind was suddenly clear with purpose. Slowly, she made her way to her feet and brushed the wet sand from her hands. The ring Elliott had given to Ruby when he proposed, which she had worn for sixty years as a reminder of why it was better not to trust anyone, sparkled in the sun. Ruby twisted it from her finger. Before she could reconsider, she pulled back and flung it as far as her arthritic bones would allow into the crashing waves.

Her first step into the water, which rushed over her feet and into her shoes, was a shock to the system. But Ruby continued to her knees, her thighs, her waist. At that, she gasped and turned, breathing in huge gulps of air as the rush of the frigid water consumed her other senses. She shivered violently, and an unseen wave crashed over Ruby's back, knocking her forward until she was submerged in the dark, icy water. Her entire body seized in protest, the cold so intense it was as though Ruby had been pierced by searing hot knives on every inch of her flesh. She twisted and turned, unable to find purchase on the seabed, and panic lurched into her ever-tightening throat. Her lungs burned with the need for oxygen, and instinct screamed at her to push to the surface. But she didn't know where that was. Another wave crested over Ruby's head as she stuck her foot down straight, hoping to hit bottom, but she simply flailed in the water.

Finally, after seconds as long as days, Ruby's toe bumped the sand, and she pushed down. Her head broke the surface, and she gasped, choking on the salty water as she tried to capture sufficient amounts of air. Black spots appeared in Ruby's vision, and the world spun. In the distance, a woman's voice—*her mother?*—called out her name.

"I'm coming, Mama," Ruby coughed, her voice weak. "I'm coming."

With those words, the world went dark.

14

Eleanor

After she told Maggie about the strange events in the storage room and Alma Gardyne's draft novel, Eleanor was itching to investigate. Maggie, too, was delighted by the mysterious drawer, the handwritten pages, and the idea of it all having some sort of connection, however tenuous, with her stuffy, stubborn Aunt Ruby.

Eleanor also shared what her dad had said about him and Vera buying the bookstore property from Ruby all those years ago. "The hidden compartment, Alma Gardyne, the bookshop..." Eleanor mused, "it all feels connected."

She and Maggie were organizing two end caps as the afternoon turned to dusk, pink and tangerine skies peeking out from behind a cluster of fluffy clouds. The fading light slanted across the floor towards their feet as the book tree blinked happily at them from the front window.

"And that whole room-going-cozy-and-smelling-like-Christmas thing? It's giving major magical bookstore vibes," Maggie agreed.

Eleanor paused and looked around the shop. If any place in her world had remained magical after all she had lost, it was Bluestocking Books. "Is it weird that it almost makes me sadder to think that might be true?" she asked Maggie, carefully tidying copies of a bestselling fantasy novel.

"Why? Because you might lose the shop?" Maggie replied, her mouth turned down in a sympathetic frown.

"Exactly," Eleanor replied.

Suddenly, Maggie slapped her hand on the shelf and turned to Eleanor with wide, ecstatic eyes, her body practically vibrating with energy. "Holy crap, I just thought of something."

"What is it?"

"What if—and hear me out—" Maggie started, "*what if* the bookstore is haunted by the ghost of Alma Gardyne?"

Eleanor pulled back, her features twisted in disbelief. "You're kidding."

"Seriously!" Maggie exclaimed. "Think about it. You've been so worried you won't find a way to save the shop, and suddenly it goes all pumpkin spice cookie on you and reveals this book that's been hidden for only God knows how long. It could be a clue."

"A clue to help me find the book she wrote?" Eleanor laughed. "I want to read it, but I'm honestly more interested in Alma herself."

"That's what I mean." Maggie started pacing back and forth, chewing on her thumb. "Maybe Alma was rich from all the books she'd sold, and she stashed money here somewhere. Maybe *she* hid that book in the drawer! Your dad said the desk was here when your parents bought the place."

"Okay, sure. But you obviously don't know much about publishing if you think Alma Gardyne got rich off her books," Eleanor joked.

Maggie stopped pacing and shot Eleanor a look. "If my great-grandfather was her publisher, and this was his publishing headquarters, then it's theoretically possible. He was a rich man. She might have been a bestseller in her time."

"That's true. But for someone to hide her book in the desk feels more personal than that." Eleanor added.

Maggie put her hands on her hips, eyes sparkling with mischief. "She could have been William's mistress."

Eleanor blanched. "Gross."

"Where's the book? I want to see it."

Eleanor beckoned Maggie to follow as she made her way towards the front of the shop. "In my bag. I almost hate to ask, considering how she responded when we invited her here, but do you think your aunt knows anything about Alma?"

Maggie paused to straighten the "New Releases" label Eleanor had affixed to a shelf. "I don't know. She's so hard to read sometimes."

"Yeah, I gathered," Eleanor replied. "I wouldn't want to make her mad again, but I feel like she could help us."

Maggie lifted a shoulder. "If she *was* mad, it was at me. Not you. I called her a loser with no friends."

Eleanor gave Maggie a gentle shove. "Stop. You did not."

"No, for real, I did. I think you were right about what you said. Maybe being around you stirs up old memories."

Eleanor felt a stab of sympathy towards Ruby Hurst. She understood that feeling all too well.

Just then, they heard the front door burst open, followed by the quick-step shuffle of someone in a hurry. "Maggie!" shouted a panicked voice. Eleanor and Maggie snapped their heads towards the voice.

"That's Marianne," Maggie said, abandoning the label and hurrying to where her aunt's housekeeper stood, stricken and pale, at the checkout counter. Eleanor followed close behind and nearly bumped into Maggie when she came up short at the look on Marianne's face. Her eyes were as round as saucers, wild with fear, and her mascara ran in dried streaks down her cheeks.

"Oh, honey!" she cried at the sight of Maggie, who stood frozen in shock as Marianne swept her into a crushing embrace. "Maggie, sweetheart. It's your aunt."

Eleanor stepped forward. "What's the matter?"

Marianne released Maggie from her grasp and pressed a hand to her heart, breathing hard. "Ruby, she—my love, she's in the hospital. In the intensive care unit."

James had hurried up the hall from his office at the commotion, and his eyes filled with concern upon hearing the news. "What happened?"

Marianne simply shook her head and reached for Maggie. "We need to go. Ben is with the ambulance, but I drove the car here so I could pick you up."

"Wait!" Maggie exclaimed. She glanced at Eleanor and then looked at Marianne with pleading eyes. "Can Eleanor come? Please? I don't want to go by myself."

That was the last thing Eleanor wanted to do, but she felt a quiet gratitude that Maggie believed her capable of being that sort of friend, so she agreed. "Of course I will."

James, who had been watching the scene with a drawn expression, gave Eleanor's arm a gentle squeeze and said, "Marianne, is that alright?"

"Yes, of course," she nodded, looking like she was about to crawl out of her skin with worry.

James urged Eleanor to call him with updates, and then they were in Ruby's car, speeding down Abercorn Street towards the hospital. On the ride, Marianne's tears flowed with abandon, and the girls kept silent, too stunned to do anything besides clutch each other's hands until the hospital came into view.

~~~

Ben, a stocky older man with a face as drawn as their moods, met the trio in the lobby of Savannah University Medical Center and led them up to a waiting room in the intensive care unit. It was quiet, except for the low-grade hum of human activity and distant beeping, with the faint scent of lemon mixed with sweat and stale coffee.

Ben deposited them in worn plastic chairs and took Marianne aside. The girls watched them with anxious stares until Ben nodded and took off down the hall, leaving Marianne to bear the bad news.
~~~

"The doctor said she's stable now," she reassured them first, taking a seat across from Maggie. Both girls breathed a sigh of relief.

"What happened, Marianne?" Maggie asked.

Marianne shook her head. "She asked me to take her to the beach this morning," she told them in a hushed voice, as though Ruby could hear her from down the hall. "I was stunned, truth be told. She hasn't been to Tybee in decades, but I said alright. She was quiet all the way there. I could tell she was thinking about her Mam, what with the anniversary of her death coming up and all."

Oh, Eleanor thought. A cold shiver of dread danced up her spine. Maggie swallowed audibly.

"She wasn't in the right head space," Marianne continued. "So when she got out of the car, I called Ben. I wanted him to stay on the phone with me in case—" Marianne sniffled, "in case he was needed."

"You must know her better than anyone," Eleanor noted. "To able to tell what she was thinking."

Marianne sat up a little straighter in her seat. "I've worked for Ruby for a long time. She likes to pretend she's all alone in the world, but I'm here. So is Ben. We know what she needs when she needs it."

As if on cue, Ben returned to the waiting room, two Styrofoam cups of coffee in his hands. He stopped short when he caught them huddled together. "I can come back," he said in a dry, rugged voice.

"That's okay, Ben," Maggie said. "We're fine." He nodded once at her, kind eyes partially hidden beneath wiry gray eyebrows, and took a seat next to Maggie.

"So, you called Ben from the beach?" Maggie prodded.

"That's right," Marianne replied. "She was gone for quite a while, and I couldn't help but get nervous. So I got out and walked a ways down the shore." Marianne choked up and put her coffee down on a side table. "I couldn't see her anywhere and panicked, you know? I should have been able to see her, even if she had gone pretty far. There wasn't anybody else out there." The tears came in earnest now. "I started calling her name, and that's when I finally saw her out in the water. She got pushed under by a wave, and I lost it. I screamed for her over and over and ran as best I could across the sand, but I couldn't figure out where she'd gone. Then, by the grace of Almighty God, she came back up just as I was about to run past."

Eleanor and Maggie were frozen, riveted, as they listened.

"I plunged into the water, screaming Ruby's name, and dragged her out by the arms. God, but that water was cold. I thought for sure she was dead. I didn't know exactly where I'd thrown my phone in the sand, so I was trying to do what I remembered of my old CPR training while shouting for Ben to call the ambulance."

"I got there right when they did," Ben whispered into his coffee cup. "She looked so small. She's always been such a force of nature, you know? But it was like the water'd gone and shrunk her down to nothing. Like she was already gone."

"You saved her life," Eleanor said, with a swipe of her sweater across her eyes. "Both of you did."

"I'll never forget how she looked for as long as I live." Marianne sipped her coffee and blanched. "If I weren't so relieved, I'd be furious at her right now."

"There'll be time enough for that later," Ben said with a halfhearted smile. "Thanks to you."

"Will we be able to see her soon?" Maggie asked. She appears to shrink, seated cross-legged in the chair with her sweatshirt sleeves pulled over her hands.

"I hope so," Marianne replied. She wiped her face with a tissue and let out a weary sigh. "She came to when I was giving her CPR, but she was delirious and vomiting, calling me 'Mama' again and again." Eleanor's pulse quickened. Maggie shot her an incredulous look. "I stripped off her wet clothes and wrapped her in my coat until the ambulance arrived. The doctor told me she had only passed out in the water, but she swallowed a lot of it, and she was severely hypothermic by the time they got her off the beach."

"Oh my God," Maggie muttered, her skin turning ghostly.

"You can say that again," Ben said gruffly.

Eleanor didn't speak the words aloud, but she knew they were all thinking it: the fact that Ruby had survived was little short of a miracle.

"We're just waiting for the doctor to come back and let us know she's awake," Marianne finished. The wait continued for hours. Eleanor walked down to the cafeteria to get more coffee for everyone, all the while her mind a tangle of thoughts knotted up with curiosity. The secret compartment in William Hurst's old desk, Alma Gardyne's hidden draft, and now Ruby nearly drowning in the same place where her mother died. Eleanor could sense a single thread woven into the fabric of these events, but she was too close to see how it all connected. Maggie's comments about the bookstore pricked at her thoughts.

Back in the waiting room, Maggie took Eleanor aside and hugged her. "Thank you for coming with me," she said. "I know it was a lot to ask."

"It's okay," Eleanor replied with a weak smile. "I'm happy that you did."

Maggie pulled at a loose thread on her sweatshirt. "Do you need to go home? I don't know how long we're going to be here."

Eleanor shook her head, even as she thought about the secret compartment hidden in the desk and the novel draft still waiting in her backpack. "I'll stay until you guys leave. I don't mind."

Maggie pulled her phone from the back pocket of her jeans. "While we wait, do you want to take a look at what I found about Alma Gardyne?"

15

Ruby

The voices came to Ruby as if she were still underwater, elongated and muffled. She tried to open her eyes, but her lids were weighed down, heavy with exhaustion. Her limbs, too, did not want to cooperate with the signals from Ruby's brain, which shouted at her to move, to swim, to fight. But she couldn't do it. Her body had given up, just as Ruby herself had done before she entered the water.

Perhaps this was death, as dark as she had suspected but not exactly as quiet. The voices continued.

"Ruby?" one said in a warm, maternal tone. "Are you awake, honey?" She knew only one person who used that pet name.

Ruby still couldn't open her eyes, but she parted her stiff, cracked lips and moved her tongue. Her mouth felt cotton thick and dry, but she managed to speak. "I don't know, Marianne," she said in a raspy voice. "Are you dead?"

A soft giggle came from down near Ruby's feet. "There she is," said a high voice.

Maggie. It all came flooding back into Ruby's mind: the beach, her fight with Maggie, Eleanor—oh, God, *Eleanor*...Ruby felt a wave of nausea crest over her at the thought of what she'd almost done.

"No, you're not dead," said Marianne. "You're in the hospital."

With as much effort as she could force into her weak, exhausted body, Ruby flitted her eyes open and saw the hideous drop-ceiling of the hospital room above her head, smelled the antiseptic that couldn't be masked by any amount of flowers, felt the freezing cold air from the vent by her bed.

Not heaven, then.

"Can someone push me up, please?" Ruby croaked out. "I seem to be having a bit of trouble moving."

"Of course," Marianne replied in a rush. The bed whined as the top of the mattress began to elevate, lifting Ruby into a seated position where she could see the entire room. She stiffened at the sight of young Eleanor Black perched on the edge of her seat. What the hell was she doing there? Ruby grew nauseous as she realized news of her "accident" would have reached the whole town of Hawthorn by now. Already, there were vases of flowers lining the window ledge and an absurd-looking bear with a heart in his paws that read "Well Wishes!" How long had she been here?

"You've been asleep for a good long while," Marianne said as if she could read Ruby's thoughts. Her housekeeper patted her hand with a trembling one of her own, and Ruby felt her heart sink into the pit of her stomach at the sight. She looked up at Maggie, whose small, sharp features were pulled down into a frown. Ruby turned her face away in shame.

"I'm exhausted." Ruby tried to swallow, but her throat was sandpaper. Marianne reached over to hold a tumbler of water to her lips. The drink put some life back into Ruby's veins, but the icy temperature of it sent her mind back to Tybee, to the slam of the frigid waves over her head, and a sob caught in Ruby's throat. "I'm sorry," she whispered, covering her mouth with the hand that wasn't attached to an IV drip. "I'm so, so sorry."

"No, Aunt Ruby. Stop," Maggie said in a protective voice. "You haven't done anything wrong."

Ruby let out a low, bitter laugh. "If only that were true," she replied. She lowered her hand and pulled the blanket up close to her chest, still looking down and away from their compassionate gazes. "I've done so many things wrong."

Maggie and Eleanor exchanged confused looks, but no one spoke again. A nurse came in to check on Ruby's vitals and was pleased to see her awake and alert, if somber and in no mood for chit-chat. "When will I be able to go home?" Ruby demanded.

The nurse, a pregnant woman who looked to be in her late twenties, was unbothered by Ruby's sharp tone. "I'll let the doctor answer that. But we want to monitor you overnight to make sure your vitals are good. Hopefully, it'll be sooner rather than later."

"How diplomatic," Ruby muttered as the nurse left the room to fetch her a lunch tray. "That woman should be a politician."

The room settled into an uneasy silence, broken only by the sounds of various monitors at Ruby's bedside. She could sense that everyone had questions they were desperate to ask, given their frequent attempts to communicate with each other via surreptitious glances, but Ruby had her own things to share.

She took another sip of water and cleared her throat. "Eleanor," Ruby said, forcing out the name. It burned on her lips.

"Yeah?" Eleanor answered, shifting in her chair. The surprise on her face rendered Eleanor into a Margaret Keane portrait, all big eyes and wonder. Ruby schooled her expression into one of placid interest.

"I wonder if you and I might have a word alone," she said. Her words were met with stunned silence. Maggie tilted her head at Ruby, eyes alight and wheels turning. No doubt she would assume good news about a visit to the bookstore. Ruby would get to her later.

Eleanor cleared her throat. "Um, sure. Okay."

Marianne and Maggie made a swift exit, but not before Maggie made a face at Eleanor and closed the door with a soft click. Ruby took another sip of water, and the nurse returned then with a tray of chicken noodle soup, soft, warm bread, and a carton of apple juice.

Ruby took in the spread. She felt very much like a child now, sick and needy, and her stomach rumbled in response to the surprisingly delicious aroma of the hospital's version of comfort food. "Thank you," she said to the nurse, who winked at Ruby and left the room.

As she sipped the soup, Ruby thought back to the night before. The time for a confession was close at hand, a confession that Ruby had never before considered. Now that she'd nearly drowned herself because of a lifetime of secrets chained to her ankles, it appeared that she had little choice in the matter. Ruby *could* keep her mouth shut tight for a few more years. She wasn't long for this world anyhow. But what if she had been right all this time?

If she were, it changed everything.

If she were, it meant that her isolated existence could be very, very different. Even now.

Stepping into the water had earned Ruby some unexpected clarity about the trajectory of her life. She looked at the earnest girl across the room and remembered the women in her past: her mother, Alice, and her stepmother, Jean. Her little sister, Caroline. They had loved Ruby well, however imperfectly, and that mattered. It had mattered eighty years ago, and sixty years ago, and last year, and today. Until this moment, in this cold, stale hospital room, Ruby had never been able to see their love for what it was truly worth.

She could still hear her mother's steady, tender voice, the same as she had heard it from beyond the icy waves. It called to her as if Alice needed Ruby to hear her now more than ever before. Her heart ached with sadness and regret. She had believed the worst about everyone in her life, especially the women.

No. Especially *herself*.

Ruby had lived lost and scared and grieved, but she had never made space for that to be okay. She thought hiding away would make it safe, but it was the hiding away that had finally broken her.

She took tiny bites of her bread and chewed. Swallowing was a painful experience after taking in so much seawater and having tubes shoved down her throat to pump her stomach, but the rumble in her belly grew mercifully quiet. Her mind, however, was a different monster. Ruby's eyes filled as she wished, for the umpteenth time, to see her mother again. To feel her arms wrapped around her own, safe and protected. A woman is never too old to want or need her mother. She is a girl's first tie to life, her first taste of this world—in both the literal and figurative sense—and her first experience of what it means to be loved. It's an imprint that changes a woman's chemistry. It instills within her the very essence of who she is, and it never leaves. It had never left Ruby. Not when her mother's casket was lowered into the ground and not there, in a quiet bed and an old, achy body. Alice's presence had been there from the first to the last, whether Ruby was aware of it or not. Women carry each other within themselves: the daughter within the mother, then, as she grows, the mother within the daughter. A gift and a curse.

But, most of all, the truth.

Ruby decided it was time for more of that in her life.

Eleanor sat with studied patience on the fold-out couch by the window, humming to herself as she perused the cards on Ruby's flower deliveries.

"There are a lot of nice people in Hawthorn," she said, flipping a card over to read the inscription. "They're concerned about you."

Ruby snorted. "They've never seemed very concerned about my well-being before. It's the drama they love. The opportunity for gossip. I can't say I blame them."

Eleanor twisted on the couch and faced Ruby. "Once, when I was in fifth grade, a girl in my class told me you were a ghost and that your house had been empty for years. She said she saw you walking down the driveway in a long white gown one night, and it gave her nightmares for weeks."

Ruby almost laughed at the girl's unhinged confession. "That's a first. I'm surprised, though, since I am given to long walks when I need to think."

"In a white nightgown?" Eleanor pressed.

"What else?"

The girl snickered into her hand. "Doesn't it get all twisted around while you're sleeping? That would drive me crazy."

Ruby held her arms out wide and looked about the room. "Some of us are already there."

Eleanor choked on a laugh and then swallowed it with a sheepish grin. She picked at the chips in her dark purple nail polish. "I just found out that my parents bought our bookshop from you," she said, uncharacteristically timid.

Awash with fatigue all of a sudden, Ruby said, "Yes, that's true. I didn't know then who your parents were. I didn't care much, truth be told."

"'Then'?" Eleanor asked astutely.

"Well, I don't know them now, either," Ruby clarified. "Just *of* them. Marianne tells me your bookshop is quite a darling place."

Eleanor's countenance brightened. "Oh, it is," she replied in an airy voice. "It's my favorite place in the whole world."

"I remember when it was my father's office," Ruby said. In her mind's eye, she pictured the dark, heavy furniture that filled Hurst Publishing Co. back when she was a little girl when the office air was thick with cigarette smoke and the mechanical clatter of a dozen typewriters. Ruby spent hours at her father's desk, scribbling on onion skin. A real writer, just like the authors her father had published, their books lining the shelf above his desk. She loved to hold up her stories in front of the window, where the sunlight shone through the translucent paper as though they were whispers of a forgotten past. There was a time when Ruby wanted to write a book, but the years had come and gone, and her stories stayed tucked away, just like she had. "I spent a lot of time there during my formative years. It was such a busy place, so alive."

"I'm fascinated by that period," Eleanor said. "The war. The fashion. The Roosevelts. Do you remember anything about Eleanor? My mom named me after her, you know."

Ruby smiled at that. "She was First Lady when I was born. I was just an infant when FDR passed, but Eleanor Roosevelt was sometimes a topic of conversation among the more conservative gentlemen around here. There weren't many in these parts who liked her—she was too intimidating, too outspoken—but my father did. He was never afraid of women using their voices."

Eleanor nodded, still chipping away at her fingernails. "Women like Alma Gardyne?" she asked, suddenly tentative.

Ruby looked up sharply. The past and present converged in front of her eyes. "How do you know that name?"

Eleanor pressed her lips together in a line, clearly debating the wisdom of answering Ruby's question. "I found a book of hers in the shop yesterday. Have you read her work before? Do you remember Alma at all?"

Ruby's spine relaxed into the pillow. "No," she replied with a purse of her lips. "I've never read her work, and I don't remember her."

"Seems like you do," Eleanor volleyed back.

"Well, I don't," Ruby scoffed and crossed her arms. "I never even met the woman, if you must know. All I was told was that she abused the trust of my father, used him for his publishing connections, and then made off with his heart."

Eleanor frowned. "Your dad was in love with her?"

"Yes," Ruby replied. "She made him believe she loved him, too, but that was only so he would champion her work. After he made her a success, Alma left town without a word. She was a charlatan, through and through."

"But what about your mother, Alice?" Eleanor pressed.

Ruby clenched her teeth. Digging through the past was going to be harder than she thought. "What about my mother?" she asked, schooling her expression into one of polite interest.

"Well," Eleanor said, twisting the end of her shirt into knots, "didn't your father love her?"

He must have. He had given Alice his last name when the papers reported her missing, refusing to have her identity be separated from their daughter. Ruby had always appreciated that small kindness. She couldn't remember much physical affection between her parents, but she'd been so young at the time. It hadn't mattered. Before that afternoon on the beach, Ruby had simply felt safe. That was enough.

"I think he did love her, yes," Ruby replied.

"Did you spend a lot of time at your dad's office?" Eleanor asked.

"Oh yes," Ruby replied, eager for the change in topic. "It was exciting for a young girl like me. Most fathers at that time believed their children should be seen and not heard, but mine gave me freedom. He showed me how to set type and listened to my book ideas with gentle patience. He was a good man."

"My dad is like that, too," Eleanor added. Her spine lengthened as she spoke, pride pulling Eleanor almost out of her chair. "He lets me shelve books and work the register. I even decorated the store for the holidays this year. I spend most of my time there after school and on the weekends. It confuses most of the kids at my school because they'd rather be staring at their phones all day, but I don't care. My parents loved that place, and so do I. "

"Which explains why you and Margaret are trying to save it," Ruby noted, earning a stunned look from Eleanor, who merely bit her lip and nodded. "I understand the need for a haven," Ruby said. "During my formative years, many of my peers were unkind to me. After my mother..." she trailed off, "well, after that, you'd have thought they'd pity me at worst. Unfortunately, I found that neither my youth nor my father's standing in the community protected me from the taunts of my classmates. I represented a fear they didn't want to face, and it was easier to ostracize me for it instead of attempting to be my friend."

"Yeah," Eleanor agreed glumly, "kids think lost mothers are catching."

A lump formed in Ruby's throat as she peered at the girl. "Don't let it harden you, child," she croaked.

It was obvious to Ruby that Eleanor Black was made of sturdy stuff, careful to put forth a smiling countenance for the benefit of others, even parental in how she viewed her family's business, but deeply grieved underneath her bright-eyed optimism. When Ruby looked at Eleanor, she saw herself once upon a time. It made her pulse race so hard that she grew lightheaded. The monitor at Ruby's bedside began to beep at a frantic pace, surprising her young visitor, who jumped out of her chair and froze.

"Are you okay?" Eleanor cried as Ruby began to gasp, clutching at her gown. The room became a blur of colors, and the breath in her lungs seized, sending black spots into Ruby's vision. Her chest muscles contracted, squeezed through a vice until she felt sure her heart would burst. "Don't—" she choked, and the words froze in her throat. There were no more voices, only sensations, and terrible, terrible pain. An alarm shrilled, the blare of it as sharp in Ruby's ears as the tightness in her chest. Eleanor reached out for Ruby's hand just as the door to the hospital room burst open.

When the girl's soft, warm fingers enclosed her own, Ruby fell back against the pillows and into the dark once more.

16

Eleanor

The moments after Ruby's heart attack were a blur. Doctors and nurses rushed into the room, and Eleanor was swept outside, where Mariana pulled her into a hug, shushing her cries. She'd been sobbing. Eleanor didn't even remember when the tears started, but the large wet spot she'd left on Marianne's sweatshirt told her they had.

Guilt coursed through her, and Eleanor tucked her knees up against her chest. Maggie asked what happened, but all Eleanor could do was stare blindly at the floor, stunned into silence. At some point, her dad showed up and ushered Eleanor outside and into his car, but she remained silent in the face of his questions. Finally, as James closed the door behind them and turned to face his daughter, she crumpled into his arms and wailed.

"It's all right," he hummed into Eleanor's hair. She shook her head, a mess of snot and tears staining his navy polo shirt. "Yes, it is, sweetheart. Ruby is okay. She's going to be okay."

"It's my fault!" Eleanor cried against her father's chest. "She was fine until we started talking, and now she's going to die because of me!"

James guided her to the sofa and pushed Eleanor's hair, clinging in loose strands, off her wet face. "Elle, it's not your fault. The woman almost drowned this morning. She's eighty years old. Who knows what kind of damage that did to her body, not to mention the stress of it all. You don't get to carry that weight and call it yours. It's not. It just happened."

Eleanor's brain knew he was right, but her heart hadn't received the memo just yet. For the rest of the afternoon, she cuddled on the couch with her favorite fuzzy blanket and drifted in and out of sleep, warmed by the small fire. She was vaguely aware of her dad's presence in lucid moments, but not enough to come out of her cozy, safe cocoon. Eleanor dreamed in fits and spurts, dreary, hopeless dreams about books that wouldn't open and doors that stayed closed.

A gentle hand shook her awake. "Elle, wake up," came her dad's quiet voice. "It's dinnertime, and you need to eat."

She blinked up at him and scowled, hurling the blanket over her head. "I'm not hungry," she replied.

"I made chicken and dumplings," he sang. Eleanor peeked out from behind her covers as her stomach gave a low, long growl.

"Okay, maybe I'm a little hungry."

Eleanor devoured two plates full, her fears and guilt momentarily placated by the comfort of simple carbohydrates, and washed it down with a glass of sweet tea. James watched her chew on a piece of ice, a bad habit she had picked up from Vera as a kid, and smiled. "You're going to wear the enamel off your teeth, you know," he said.

"That's what dentures are for," Eleanor replied.

James shook his head. "It's easier to take care of the teeth you have."

In response, she chomped down even harder. James winced at the sound. "There goes my retirement fund," he joked.

Eleanor swallowed and sat back. Might as well go for broke. "I don't know about you, Dad, but I find it hard to focus on personal care when any day now we're going to lose the bookstore."

James choked on his tea. "What?" he asked, coughing. "What in the world gave you that idea?"

"I saw the bills on your desk."

He took another sip of tea and worked his jaw, avoiding Eleanor's piercing stare. "Why didn't you say anything before?"

Eleanor scoffed. "I could ask you the same question."

"It's not for you to worry about our finances, Eleanor. That's my job."

"Well, obviously, you need some help. It's not just your store anymore. It's mine, too, remember? Or it might be one day."

James worried his thumb with his teeth. "Eleanor, you're a child. Do you expect me to lay that burden on you? After everything else we've been through together?"

Eleanor sat up straight in her chair, chin up and out. "I'd rather know now than when we have to close our doors."

"We won't," James insisted. "I put in an Offer in Compromise to the Small Business Administration to keep them from calling in the entire loan or taking my assets as collateral."

Eleanor cocked a brow. "English, Dad."

"It gives us some time to come up with a certain percentage of the loan," he answered.

"And if we don't?"

James looked up at the ceiling and blew out a long breath. As he looked back at Eleanor, he said, "Then...we lose the store. *I* lose the store."

Eleanor put her head in her hands, half terrified and half angry at the circumstances out of her control which continued to dictate their lives. "Will the Whatever-You-Called-It let you work something out? Like a payment plan?"

James sighed. "Not this time."

Eleanor's voice went up an octave. "What do you mean? This isn't the first time?"

"Unfortunately, no." Shame fell over James' face.

Eleanor felt foolish now for her excitement about working with Agatha as if a few extra dollars a week could right this lilting ship.

"How long do we have before they take the store?" she croaked. Her throat felt like it was growing smaller by the second.

"Four months."

Eleanor calculated in her head. Springtime. *March.* The month her mother had disappeared and the absolute worst time of year. What a cosmic joke.

"I've had to live without my mother since I was six years old," she said, her voice a hard edge. "I won't live without our books, too." At James' answering hug, Eleanor felt the spiral begin, just as it always did when she made a concentrated effort to conjure sense from her grief.

Today, it was too much.

"I will handle this, honey," James said in a scratchy voice. "No matter what happens, we will be okay. This house is ours, and I can get another job. You let me worry about the shop. You just worry about being a kid."

Eleanor sat up and swiped at her runny nose. "I don't know how," she said in a small voice.

A flicker of grief shone on her dad's face before it was gone again. Eleanor didn't blame him for the mess they had become, but she would have liked to forget all that had happened between them and go back to the way things were once upon a time. Back when her grandparents were still alive, filling up the house with their laughter and joy. Back when Vera had been her mother instead of some distant, eternal heartache.

"Would you like me to call Maggie? See if she can come over for a while?" James asked in lieu of further conversation.

Eleanor simply nodded, then laid back down on the couch and covered her head with the blanket, dizzy from all she had uncovered in the last few days. Past and present sadness tore at Eleanor as she peered around the blanket at her mother's photograph on the mantle, Vera's lovely hair tangled and unruly, a perfect match for Eleanor's thoughts.

Before Ruby's heart attack, Maggie had shown Eleanor the website for a bookstore in Savannah, which carried a published copy of *The Woman of Valbrooke Hall*. "Look! It wasn't just a draft, Eleanor." Maggie pointed to the screen. "It was published by the Hursts in 1950."

Eleanor peered at the phone in shock, lightheaded from all they had discovered that day. "I have an original handwritten draft of a book written *seventy-four* years ago?"

"Wonder how much it's worth," Maggie muttered, and both girls locked eyes.

"Do you—" Eleanor began.

"Think it might be enough to save the store?" Maggie finished with a squeal. "I told you, Eleanor! *I told you.* Alma's here to save the day."

Eleanor swallowed hard as hope bubbled up her throat, addictive and sweet. But she wouldn't count her chickens before they hatched. "Give me your phone."

Maggie held it out, and Eleanor swiped through the list of search results on Alma Gardyne. Some were mismatched obituaries with people of the same name, but others were bookstore links with listings for sale. No Wikipedia entry on Alma, though, or any biography at all.

"Boo, this is not helpful," Maggie declared, swiping back her phone.

Eleanor pouted. "I wish I had the book with me. It's still in my backpack at the store."

"It's been there for decades, I bet," Maggie said pointedly. "It can sit a little longer."

"Okay," Eleanor replied with a pout. "In the meantime, let's brainstorm. Alma's draft was eventually published."

"Which means we could have a serious treasure on our hands."

"Except there's almost nothing about her online, so she couldn't have been very well known. At least not outside this area."

"I bet you someone knows about her."

Eleanor groaned. "Yeah, Maggie, and that someone is lying in a hospital bed right now."

She thought back to what Ruby had later told her about Alma, how the author had bailed on William Hurst after he'd made her a success and broken his heart. Yet another woman from Hawthorne who had left her loved ones without a second glance, forcing everyone else to pick up the pieces in her wake.

Footsteps sounded on the front walk, and then the doorbell sang through the cottage, a sweet tinkle of a sound. Maggie was here, *thank God.* "Hey," Eleanor said as she opened the front door and waved Maggie into the house. Marianne pulled away from the curb with a sad wave. "How's your aunt?"

"Stable now," Maggie replied, swinging her backpack onto the chair by the door. "Awake, but not very alert. She's going to be in the ICU for a few days at least and probably not out of the hospital until right before Christmas. Marianne is a total wreck. She called my mom and freaked her out."

"What did she say?" Eleanor asked. "You don't have to leave now, do you?"

Maggie shook her head. "No. I told her I'd made a friend here and didn't want to go, which seemed to calm her down. I'd rather have to visit Aunt Ruby in the hospital every day than go home to whatever crap she and my dad are fighting about today." At that, Maggie glanced around the living room for the first time, one corner of her mouth tilted up. "It looks like a very English Christmas in here."

Eleanor let out a soft laugh. "You can thank my grandmother for the inspiration."

"Your grandmother?"

"This was my grandparents' place before it belonged to my parents. We all lived here together until I was ten. That's when my grandparents left to live in the nursing home."

Maggie nodded. "Are they still there?"

"No," Eleanor replied. A stab of grief went through her ribs. She led Maggie into the kitchen and rooted around in the fridge for something to drink. "Both of them were diagnosed with dementia, and my grandmother died a few months after my grandfather. They were to-gether for, like, 65 years or something."

Maggie thanked Eleanor as she placed two sodas on the table. The click and hiss of their drinks were loud in the small, quiet kitchen. "I bet that was hard, especially with..." Maggie trailed off and tapped a bright pink nail on the table. Her cheeks turned pink as she met Eleanor's knowing gaze.

"It was." Eleanor had prepped herself for this conversation. She knew it was only a matter of time before the subject of her mother came up again. She hopped up onto the counter and took a long swig of soda, the sting of carbonation calming the jig in her stomach to a gentle waltz. Eleanor was just getting used to having a friend. She wanted Maggie to like her even after she knew what Vera had done.

Maggie pulled her feet up in the chair. "I wonder why Aunt Ruby didn't tell me about your mom. She doesn't get out much, but she has to know."

Eleanor had wondered that herself. "Maybe she thought it was bet-ter for me to tell you."

Maggie looked thoughtful. "I guess. Either way, I'm sorry that hap-pened to you. And your dad. Are the police still searching for her now?"

"Not actively," Eleanor replied. "The case is still open, but unless new information comes in, they won't look into it anymore."

"What do—" Maggie chewed her lip. "What do *you* think hap-pened?"

Eleanor took another sip of soda to quell the sting of her tears. She wanted to trust Maggie. No one had ever asked her outright what she believed about her mother's disappearance. Either they were too polite to broach the subject, too afraid to upset her, or they assumed Eleanor thought what so many others did: that Vera Black was dead, the victim of a heinous crime or her own broken mind. What they had never considered was how Eleanor could still *feel* her mother in the world, somewhere. It was a knowing, not a concrete fact the police could file away in a drawer, but still as true as the DNA in her blood. Vera Black had walked away from her family, from her daughter, and never looked back. Whatever darkness she carried in her heart, it had taken up too much space in this house—in this family—for Vera to stay. Maybe her mind had broken along with her heart, and Eleanor's mother didn't even remember who she was now. Either way, she was gone. And the thought of Vera Black somewhere else in the world while her daughter grew up without her was a pain so sharp it sliced into Eleanor's very bones.

"I don't know," she answered, the words catching in her throat. "But I don't think she's dead. I would know that, at least." Maggie looked dubious but didn't reply. "Anyway, I'm glad your aunt is going to be okay. I feel terrible."

"Don't," Maggie said, slurping her soda. "You didn't do anything wrong. Besides, I'm glad you were there for her. It was scary as crap, but Aunt Ruby's made of steel. Did you get to talk to her about Alma?"

Eleanor grimaced. "Kind of. We started to talk about the bookstore, and then I brought up Alma, which seemed to annoy her. She said Alma was a 'charlatan' and that her dad was in love with her, but she just used him to get published. Alma left town after a few years, and he never heard from her again."

"Boo," Maggie groaned. "My mistress theory is moot now."

"She could still be a ghost," Eleanor suggested with a halfhearted smile.

Maggie shot Eleanor a look. "Don't tease me."

"Never!" Eleanor cried with a grin.

"I can't stand the suspense," Maggie groaned. "Why was Alma's book hidden away? And who put it there? I'm *dying*."

"Maybe they weren't trying to hide it," Eleanor countered. "Maybe they just wanted to save it."

"For what?"

"Why does anyone save anything? For the memories," Eleanor said, tossing her can into the recycling bin. "It was probably William. He loved Alma, and she didn't love him back. So he kept a small piece of her in a place where it would be safe, but he'd never have to see it again." Eleanor slipped the straps of her backpack off the dining chair and retrieved the leather-bound journal from inside. Maggie's eyes grew wide with excitement.

"That's it?" she whispered. Her hands reached reflexively for the book, but Eleanor held it fast to her chest. "What's it say?"

"I haven't read it yet," Eleanor replied, though that wasn't strictly true. She had flipped through the journal, but the reality of its contents felt too weighty to consume alone. Eleanor hadn't had a real friend to share anything with in a long time, and she didn't want to waste the opportunity. "Dad brought it home while we were at the hospital, but I thought we should read it together."

Maggie's face softened, her blue eyes sparkling with warmth. "Let's do it."

Eleanor placed the journal between them on the table and opened to the first page with reverential slowness. Maggie shimmied in her seat and leaned forward to read.

The Woman of Valbrooke Hall, Draft Chapter One

Louise Murphy came from a long line of storytelling women, women who understood the deep, primal need of humans to make sense of their world with words. She also came from a long line of women whose words failed them when they fell in love.

"Uh oh," Maggie exclaimed.

"Failing the Bechdel test already," Eleanor quipped. Maggie raised a brow.

"I have no idea what that means."

"Two lines in, and we're already talking about boys," Eleanor clarified.

"Sure, okay," Maggie replied with a shrug and turned back to the page.

Louise's determination to avoid inheriting the lovesickness that plagued the women of her family came to a swift and abrupt end when she arrived on the pedimented porch of Valbrooke Hall. It was a vast estate in the low country of Georgia, measured in acres that spread across rough, sandy earth between the Savannah River and the Atlantic Ocean. The sticky, humid air, the palatial oaks, and the unseen presence of long-ago stories beckoned one to a slow, languid existence beneath the Spanish moss. Louise loved it at first sight.

"Oh, she fell in love with the house," Eleanor replied.

"The *estate*," Maggie corrected. "So no failed whatever-you-called-it."

"Maybe. But it sounds a lot like your aunt's house," Eleanor said with a glance at the page. "Like Alma's telling her own story."

"But here's a bigger question," Maggie supplied, "if Alma—Louise, *whatever*—loved this place so much, then why did she leave it all behind?"

Eleanor hugged herself against the rising chill forever creeping through the walls of their old cottage. "Because," she replied. "Isn't that what they always do?"

17

Ruby

Ruby hated hospitals, but at least she had an excuse to sleep the day away and think of nothing. The problem was she'd never been very good at either, and the intensive care unit wasn't that restful anyway. Ruby had been poked and prodded like a test subject, sent to have a CT scan, and undergone a godforsaken psych evaluation to boot. Ruby would bet her left leg that one hadn't gone very well, no matter how clear the brain scans. Her sharp tongue would be the death of her if nothing else.

In bed, with Marianne back home for a change of clothes and Maggie down in the cafeteria, long-dormant moments of Ruby's life played out in front of her, conjuring painful memories of joy and sorrow from a time when she had at least lived, however sadly, instead of hiding away. Walks with Elliott beneath the emerald canopy. Writing stories in her father's office. The gentle rhythm of her mother's voice. Ruby imagined how different her future might have been. If only.

Then there was Eleanor Black, all earnest hope and eager excitement despite the loss of her mother and the impending loss of her family's store. What had Ruby been thinking trying to talk to the girl? She was almost grateful now for the heart attack. She couldn't put her burdens on that child, no matter how much relief she would find in the confession. It simply wouldn't be right.

And Alma Gardyne. That was a name Ruby hadn't heard in decades.

She'd almost forgotten about her father's first real love. Alma was a blip on the radar of Ruby's memories, but she recalled how, days before Alice disappeared, William had found her thumbing through Alma's journal in the library and snatched it away, furious. He was so rarely angry that it had stunned both Ruby and her mother. William only spoke of Alma to Ruby once, when she was reeling from her own broken romance, to remind her that love didn't have to be a one-time thing. She hadn't believed him then. It was too late for it to matter now.

There came a gentle rap on Ruby's door. Maggie tiptoed in with a slice of chocolate cake. "Hey," she said in a tender voice that surprised her aunt. "Can I come in?"

"You may," Ruby replied, embarrassed by the state of her clothes and by all that had occurred since Maggie's arrival. Her niece found a seat by the window and blinked curiously at Ruby. For the first time, there was no fire in her gaze. Only concern. It did strange things to Ruby's heart.

"I brought you something," Maggie said, holding up a fork and wiggling her eyebrows.

"You're a regular maverick, child," Ruby answered, her stomach rumbling. She patted her tangled hair. She must look dreadful. With a glance at the door, Maggie opened the plastic container and handed it to Ruby. The cake was a little dry and overly sweet, but the kindness of Maggie's gesture made it taste as delicious as any of Marianne's home-made desserts.

"What happened, Aunt Ruby?" Maggie asked. Ruby froze, a mouth full of cake and a throat that would hardly swallow. "Why did you do it?"

Ruby had asked herself that question a hundred times since she woke up. A shiver crept up her spine as she recalled the frigid waves rushing over her head, pushing her down, down, down. There was no logical explanation for why Ruby had walked into that water. It wasn't her head she'd wanted to quiet. It was her heart.

"I'm so tired, Margaret," Ruby began.

"You've been sleeping for two days," Maggie interrupted.

"That's not what I mean."

Maggie slumped against the chair, chastised. "Oh."

"I'm tired," Ruby said again. "I've lived a lot longer than you and spent most of my life trying to hide who I am and be forgotten. I know what people think of me, what they've always thought about me, and I just wanted it to be over. All of it. There's nothing left for me here, Margaret. You said so yourself."

"That is not what I said!" Maggie protested, her cheeks flaming.

"Not in those exact words, but you implied it just the same. I'm not angry about it, either. You were right."

"Aunt Ruby, you have a lot of people who love you and want you to be happy. Marianne, Ben, me, Eleanor..."

Ruby balked. "Eleanor? The child hardly knows me."

"You could say the same about me," Maggie said, crossing her arms. "But here I am." Her niece glanced around the room, taking in the vases sent over by a dozen well-wishers, and offered her aunt a pointed look. "As much as you might not want to hear this or even believe it, I think you could say the same thing about the people of Hawthorn."

Ruby peered over at the colorful bouquets and felt a twinge of something rise in her throat. Eleanor had made the same claim. "People just want to look nice, but it's too hard for me to forget everything that's happened."

"I don't mean to be a jerk or anything, Aunt Ruby," Maggie said, a note of hesitation in her lowered voice, "but your mom died a long, long time ago."

Ruby sighed and rubbed her temples. She wanted to do this, but she was so scared. Each time she'd told the truth in the past, it had earned her nothing but confusion, scorn, and loneliness. *That's* what

Ruby couldn't forget. Alice's disappearance was still painful, but it was the emptiness she'd left behind that Ruby had struggled with most.

"You're not wrong, Margaret," she answered after a long beat. "And you're not right, either."

Maggie's brows came together as she tilted her head to look at Ruby. She was so young, so determined to believe that every problem could be solved with a bit of courage and logic. Ruby didn't want to dispel that notion for her niece. Margaret had her own heartbreak to live with back at home.

Still, as she took in the girl's curious gaze, Ruby wondered if perhaps Maggie would be the first person who would finally be able to hear the truth.

Ruby sat back against the headboard and took a long gulp of water from the tumbler on her bedside table. She could do this. No one was going to try and put her away this time. She was too old for that, anyhow. "I have something I'd like to tell you. The truth has never served me well before, but if you're willing to suspend your disbelief for a few minutes, then—" Ruby swallowed. She was actually going to tell this story. Share the truth with her thirteen-year-old niece, of all people. She had finally lost her mind. "Then I will."

Maggie sat up, prim and proper, and nodded vigorously. "I can do that."

"Very well," Ruby replied, feigning a calm she didn't feel. "It's about the day my mother left me on that beach."

Maggie shifted forward in her seat, eyes glued to Ruby's face. "The day your mom...?"

Ruby gave a single nod. "I'm sure your mother and cousins have filled you in with whatever details they've gathered over the years, but even their tales are riddled with guesswork. It's time I set the record straight."

"Alice drowned, and you sort of never got over it," Maggie replied without judgment. "But you didn't see it happen, right? That's what Mom told me."

Ruby grunted. "That's one way of putting it. I was found screaming, utterly hysterical, by a couple walking near the lighthouse. The police even had to restrain me after I bit one of them."

Maggie started to giggle but coughed when she took in Ruby's raised eyebrows. "Seems like a pretty normal response for a child who had just watched her mother drown."

It would seem so, but that hadn't been the case for Ruby. "Be that as it may," she continued softly, "I gave a statement to the police once I was able, and it made its way through this little town like wildfire. My words were nonsensical. Parents feared that I might be a danger to their children, and a child who frightens people quickly becomes an isolated child."

"'Frightens people'?" Maggie scoffed, one eyebrow cocked in disbelief. "You were, like, *five*."

Ruby clenched her jaw. "Age doesn't matter to one's peers."

"Were you bullied at school?"

"Worse," Ruby sighed. "I was rejected completely. No one would speak to me unless it was with taunts or jeers, and eventually, I just became invisible. Later, I grew into quite the beauty, and people sort of forgot to think of me as crazy once they approved of how I looked. Everyone loves a beauty queen, especially after the war when women were expected to be more ornamental than they had been before. But that only lasted so long, as you might expect." She gestured to her frail body and smirked.

"What about my grandfather and your sister? Did they have friends?"

Ruby smiled at the thought of her siblings. "Oh, they didn't share my fate. As the children of a wealthy man and his *actual* wife, they were welcomed in all the ways I hadn't been. My mother was respected in Hawthorn during the few short years she lived here, but I was the bastard child. After she was gone, I lacked her protection. Ironic, considering she was the reason I needed protection in the first place."

Maggie scooted off the chair and sat on the bed at Ruby's feet. "What about your dad? He was the richest guy in town! He should have told people to leave you alone."

"Oh, he did," Ruby said. "More than I even knew until the end of his life. But he was a busy man and a single father for some time. He didn't see much of my suffering."

"Or he didn't want to see it," Maggie added in a grim voice.

"Perhaps," Ruby admitted. "In his defense, I shut him out for a long time. It made me angry that no one seemed to believe my version of what happened. Father was safe for me in all the physical ways that mattered, but I viewed him as unsafe for me emotionally, even years after the fact. I regret that now."

Maggie chewed on her bottom lip, the question in her eyes evident. "What *did* happen on the beach that day, Aunt Ruby?"

Ruby humphed with an affectionate pat on her niece's hand. Maggie's black-painted nails were bitten down to the quick. She tried to hide them away in the sleeves of her sweatshirt, but Ruby held them fast. "I know our time together was rocky at first," Ruby answered, pivoting. "But I have to say: I'm glad you're here, child."

Maggie laughed in disbelief. "You're only saying that because you're recovering from a near-death experience. You'll go back to being annoyed at me by the end of the week."

Despite herself, Ruby chuckled. "You and I have a lot more in common than I suspected we would, Maggie."

Her niece beamed. "That's the first time you've called me that."

"People change," Ruby said. Another glance at all the flowers she'd received was a good reminder. "There are many painful reasons why I am the way I am, most of them self-inflicted. It's hard to let go when you've been carrying bitterness and regret like a shield your entire adult life."

"You can tell me, Aunt Ruby. I'm a pro at this kind of stuff."

"Oh, are you?" Ruby chuckled. "Had much experience with the secrets of the past?"

Maggie rolled her eyes. "You have no idea."

Ruby shook her head to try and clear the voice of her most critical self as it shouted about her wasted life. There was still time to figure this out, still time to make it right, once and for all. Ruby could choose to be brave, even if that was something she hadn't been in a long time.

"My mother used to read to me as a girl," she said with a small smile. "Those are my strongest memories of her. She always had a book on hand, thanks to my father's extensive library, and we often sat outside together with a novel. Mother didn't believe in limiting my access to books, even ones I couldn't yet comprehend. One of the first stories she ever told me was about the man she was married to before she came to Hawthorn, before my father was in the picture. She told me that he was a good man, smart and kind and tender, and that she missed him all the time."

"Wait—" Maggie interrupted.

Ruby shushed her with a finger. "Not right now. Be patient." After a deep breath, Ruby continued. "I remember being confused that my mother had a life before me. Father told me she was often withdrawn and sad. It was sometimes hard for her to be present with me because she was still grieving the loss of her first husband. One day, when I was five, around Christmas, Mother asked me if I wanted to go to Tybee for a picnic. I was happy to go anywhere she wanted to take me. That afternoon, we packed some clothes, a few books, and blankets and left for a day at the beach." Ruby paused, seeing that Maggie had gone rigid. She knew what came next. Everyone did.

"After we ate, she showed me how to find shark teeth among the broken shells in the surf. Then we sat down to read one of my favorite books, *The Secret Garden*. I loved the idea of a hidden place full of magic, just waiting to be discovered. But I fell asleep not long after. When I woke up, Mother asked if I wanted to look for more shark teeth. It was such fun at first. We ran around and played at the water's edge, giggling."

At this, Ruby had to stop. She closed her eyes and let out a strangled cry, her throat aching from the effort it took to hold back her tears. Maggie's face was wide open, almost afraid, as she listened to Ruby's words. "I still remember how her hand felt in mine. Warm and soft. Safe. But then it was gone. *She* was gone." Tears splashed onto Ruby's blanket, and she scrubbed at them with her finger, surprised by the intensity of her emotions. Maggie shuddered—whether from the cold, dry air in the hospital or the story, she wasn't sure—and moved up to the bed next to Ruby. The warmth of her arm on Ruby's was a small comfort.

"What happened?" she asked, her eyes bright with unshed tears of her own.

"She disappeared," Ruby replied in a whisper. This was the part she hadn't spoken aloud since she was a teenager, the words that had made her a pariah in her community until she was grown up and brokenhearted enough to make herself one. "I need you to understand me, Margaret." Gripping her niece's fingers, Ruby trembled. "She didn't just walk into the water like I did, though that would have been horrible enough on its own. She didn't drown." Here, Ruby paused and eyed Maggie carefully. "She *vanished*."

Maggie stiffened as she stared, dumbfounded, at her aunt. "Vanished? Like *a ghost*?"

"You could say that, although she was very much alive until that moment, I can assure you. At first, I thought she was playing some sort of game with me, but I realized soon enough that she wasn't. Mother was simply there one moment, holding my hand, and then she was gone."

"Oh my *God*," Maggie whispered, her hand pressed against her mouth. Her blue eyes reflected the horror Ruby still felt when she remembered that terrible moment.

"I started screaming for her over and over, running back and forth, searching, sobbing. I finally grew so exhausted at the police station that I just gave up and passed out in my father's arms."

"Then you told them what happened," Maggie confirmed. "And no one believed you."

Ruby gave a single nod. "Yes. They assumed my mother had drowned and began searching for her body. It wasn't until long after my father died that I learned the woman they discovered weeks later was some unknown person who had either drowned by accident or taken her own life."

Maggie gasped. "But...so...*she's* the one buried in your mother's grave?"

Again, Ruby nodded. Maggie shook her head in disbelief. "I was looking through some old financial documents on the estate and found a ledger that listed a large payment to Sheriff Jim Arwen, dated the same day that body was found. On the page next to it was one word: *Alice.* The police claimed the woman was my mother because she was found wearing her engagement ring on a necklace, so when I discovered the ledger, I lost it. I even went to the pastor. He's the sheriff's grandson, but he had no idea what I was talking about. I think I scared him to death, to be quite honest, but I was just so angry to find out the depth of my father's deception."

"What a crazy thing to do," Maggie said, chewing on her nail. At Ruby's narrowed eyes, she added, "Not you, *obvs.* Faking Alice's death."

"He was desperate to offer me some kind of peace," Ruby added. "I assume Father gave the sheriff my mother's necklace when they found that poor woman and then paid the man a whole lot of money to keep it all quiet."

"You must have doubted it was her all along, though, didn't you?"

Ruby pursed her lips together in a flat line. "Truth be told, I was so confused and in such horrible shock from losing my mother that I found every way possible to avoid the subject. Father tried to talk to me about it for years, but I was being mistreated so badly by my peers that I refused." Ruby looked down at the finger on her right hand where she'd worn her engagement ring. The tender, wrinkled skin there was already cracked and irritated from being exposed to the dry, wintry air. "When I finally did open up to someone, it was to a man I loved. His name was Elliot Russell, and he worked for my father. We got engaged in my twenties."

"Gasp!" Maggie said, lips curling. "Was he cute?"

Ruby laughed through sniffles. "I thought he was beautiful. After he proposed, I gathered up the courage to talk to him about my mother. He'd heard rumors by that point, of course. Everyone had. But he'd never actually heard them from me." Ruby sighed. "Elliot was a good man. He was smart, funny, and kind, even though he was older and had a tendency to treat me like a child. But when I stood firm by my claim that Mother had disappeared, he went to my father and tried to have me enrolled in an outpatient program for severe mental health disorders."

Maggie's mouth fell open, eyes flickering with righteous anger. "He did *not*."

"It's what men did in those days, my dear. It's what *husbands* did. When I confronted Elliot about it, he begged me to go and get help. I felt so betrayed that I ended our engagement right then. We were both pretty destroyed by it, but Elliot moved on eventually." Ruby's voice took on a bitter tone as she spoke these words.

"And you never did," Maggie finished for her.

"I fell out of love with him, but I've held my anger close to my chest ever since. Not just about what he did but about many other things, as well."

Maggie slumped as though she were exhausted by all she'd learned. It exhausted Ruby to tell it, but she still had more to say. "I tell you all of this to lay the foundation for what I need to say next. And, somehow, it's even more unlikely than the story I've already told you. But it's the truth, I promise you. All of it."

"I will believe anything at this point, Aunt Ruby," Maggie said. "Besides, you're not the only person in Hawthorn whose mom has vanished without a trace. The same thing happened to Eleanor."

Ruby's throat tightened. "She told you, then?"

"Why didn't *you*?" Maggie argued. "I put my big ol' foot in my mouth a few times before she told me, too, so thanks for that."

"It was her story to tell, Margaret."

"*Maggie.*"

Ruby ignored her niece's frosty tone. "Well, it's a good thing you've made the connection between Eleanor's story and my own, no matter how you got there."

"And why is that?" Maggie crossed her arms.

"Because," Ruby replied. "What I have to say next is something Eleanor needs to hear, too."

18

Eleanor

Eleanor's legs were stiff and sore after running errands all morning for Agatha, but she'd gotten paid again, and the thrill of those crisp bills in her hand made it all worth it. It wasn't enough to cover even one monthly payment towards what they owed for Bluestocking Books, but Eleanor felt proud of what she'd earned just the same.

Kicking off her sneakers, she belly-flopped onto the bed and reached into her bag for Alma's book. She and Maggie had read through a couple of chapters before bed, trying to capture what kind of woman Alma had been. She was a lovely writer, the story of her newfound sense of home both tender and deeply, achingly human. The slow romance blooming between her protagonist and Valbrooke Hall's charming owner had kept the girls up past their bedtime.

Sitting up, Eleanor flipped on her bedside lamp and leaned back to read some more.

The Woman of Valbrooke Hall, Draft Chapter Six

Upon her arrival at the house, Louise drifted towards the library with her story notes in hand, imagination aflame despite her best efforts to be rational. Working with books was satisfying work, to be sure, but over time, the story that had grown in Louise's heart was her own. One she longed to share with Silas.

Her footsteps were muffled as she padded to the library door. Inside, she could hear the gentle rumble of Silas' voice and another she recognized as that of Andrew Gelding, the Valbrooke estate manager.

"You're distracted, sir," Andrew chastised, voice stiff with formality despite the man's reproach. "She's your employee. A businesswoman." Disdain curled like smoke around his words.

"What are you inferring, Mr. Gelding?" Silas replied, his tone laced with amusement. "You may as well speak directly."

A pause, and then, "Ms. Murphy, sir."

"She's an exceptional writer," Silas said. Pleasure unfurled within Louise's chest. She pressed her ear to the door to hear every word he might speak of her. "I'm happy to have her on my staff. She's bright, hardworking, and funny to boot."

"You know as well as I do that's not the only reason that woman's here. I never took you for a butter and egg man," Andrew declared. The force of his insult knocked Louise back from the door. Shock thrummed in her veins as she swallowed down the rising defense already forming in her throat. How dare he?

"Ah, Gelding," Silas sighed. "Be reasonable. Ms. Murphy is a fine woman. She doesn't need my money or my reputation."

"That doesn't mean she doesn't want it," Andrew countered with a conviction Louise knew stemmed more from his high position on the Valbrooke staff than from any questionable behavior he'd witnessed on her part. It wasn't enough to soothe her. The nerve! Surely, Silas would never give credit to such a bold and indefensible lie.

Ice tinkled against the glass, each moment heavy with anticipation, and then Silas spoke again. "I assure you, Gelding, that Ms. Murphy will never even find herself the dame on my arm, much less the mistress of this house."

Eleanor pressed a palm to her heart as she read Silas' words. *Poor Alma.* Ruby had gotten it all wrong if this story had anything to say about it. William had loved Alma's work, admired it even, but he never fell for Alma herself. And it seemed as though the very real woman who had penned these words had lost her heart to him, along with something even greater:

Her home.

With a slap, Eleanor closed the journal, feeling like an intruder in Alma Gardyne's most intimate thoughts. But, then, why would she have written the book if she didn't want to share them? And for that matter, why would William have published a tome so clearly inspired by his unhappy relationship with the author?

Eleanor scrambled for her laptop. She scribbled the address of the bookshop carrying Alma's novel on a notepad and hurried downstairs to put on her shoes. Using the landline James had kept in service for the sake of his cell phone-less daughter, Eleanor called Maggie and explained her plan.

A short walk later, she was face-to-face with her dad at Bluestocking's register, a fresh cup of coffee in his hand.

"I know that place," James told Eleanor with a slurp. The steam rising from the mug momentarily fogged his glasses. "Great selection of rare books."

Eleanor bounced on the balls of her feet. "Perfect," she said. "Can we go there during lunch? I called Maggie to ask if we could swing by and pick her up on the way."

James laughed. "I think we can wait until the weekend, honey. You know I usually eat lunch here, and we need to finish prepping for the discounted book sale."

Eleanor blew a raspberry. She had forgotten all about that. In the meantime, she had a different bookstore on her mind. "It doesn't start until three, and I'll take over as soon as we get back. Promise. *Please,* Dad. *Pretty please?*"

James eyed the empty store. Then he sighed in resignation at the expectant look on Eleanor's face. "Alright, fine. Get your stuff, and I'll close up."

"Thank you!" Eleanor squealed.

When Maggie slid into the backseat a few minutes later, she turned to Eleanor with a solemn face. "Girl, I have so much to tell you."

Eleanor glanced at her dad, who was bobbing his head to some old song she'd never heard before. "What is it?" she said under her breath.

"I can't tell you right now," Maggie whispered back, "but oh em gee, you are going to *freak*."

Soon, James was parking on Liberty Street in the heart of Savannah's historic district. Eleanor and Maggie launched from the backseat and rushed to the covered front door of The Book Lady, James on their heels. Beneath a small green awning was an unassuming red door, behind which lay a veritable treasure trove of books. As they stepped over the threshold, Eleanor and Maggie gaped at the sight. In every nook and cranny, stacked from floor to ceiling, were books upon books upon books. They covered the entire staircase to the second floor, now inaccessible to the public due to the hundreds of printed volumes that covered every inch. It was a small shop, made even smaller by the dark green walls and the sheer quantity of books it held, but that only added to its charm. In one quiet corner sat a velvet wingback chair the color of mustard tucked beneath a half-uncovered brick archway. Eleanor wanted to cozy up there with a blanket and a latte and read until she couldn't keep her eyes open.

No, scratch that. She wanted to die there because this place was absolute *heaven*.

James bumped his daughter's shoulder. "I told you it was a great shop."

"You lied," Maggie said, swiveling on her toes. "This is the best bookstore in the world."

James snorted. "Lovely to hear, as a fellow bookseller."

Maggie blinked back to reality. "I mean, next to Bluestocking, of course." Eleanor giggled.

"I have a few Christmas gifts to pick up, and I'll grab us some lunch while I'm out," James said, eyeing both girls. "Can I trust you to stay in the store until I get back?"

Maggie saluted him, and Eleanor nodded primly. "Don't worry. We aren't going anywhere."

"Then I'm off," James said, planting a quick kiss on Eleanor's forehead. "Call me if you need me."

When he was gone, Eleanor turned to Maggie. "Okay, spill."

Maggie clutched Eleanor's hand and pulled her into a quiet corner, where she then proceeded to tell Eleanor the most insane story she had ever heard. With every word, Eleanor's nerves coiled tight. Alice Hurst had *literally* disappeared all those years ago? What was it with this town and vanishing women? The eerie similarity between Ruby's mother and her own turned Eleanor's stomach. Lunch seemed like a terrible idea now.

"This is bonkers. Why does your aunt want to talk to *me*?" she asked, pulling on the drawstring of her hoodie.

"Probably because you're the only other person she knows whose mother just up and—" Maggie snapped her fingers. "And you live in the same town! Maybe Aunt Ruby has a theory about all of this."

"Well, unless her theory includes actual information about where my mother is right now, I don't want to hear it," Eleanor replied sharply.

Maggie pulled back. "You don't?"

Eleanor had no more patience for people who wanted to dissect her mother's disappearance. She'd spent years fending off curious stares or well-meaning commentary from people like Agatha, and if Ruby Hurst thought she could simply demand an audience with Eleanor to talk about their shared losses just because she was a wealthy old woman, well, she had another thing coming.

"No, I don't," she answered, staring at her sneakers.

"But why, Eleanor? You and I both know Aunt Ruby isn't one to exaggerate or tell lies. If she says Alice vanished, then maybe that's what happened to your mother, too! Maybe she has an idea about how to bring her back."

Eleanor swiveled away from the bookcase and gritted her teeth. "If that were the case, then your aunt would have brought Alice home a long time ago. She's not coming back, Maggie," Eleanor's voice cracked, tears welling. "My mother didn't vanish. She *left* me. She's gone, and I will never, ever see her again."

Maggie stared at her for a beat, the silence reverberating with the clang of Eleanor's words, and then she yanked Eleanor in for a hug. The tears fell freely now, soaking Maggie's shoulder as Eleanor clutched her friend and cried. God, she missed her mom. It wasn't fair. None of this would ever be fair.

"I'm sorry," Maggie said into Eleanor's ponytail. "I shouldn't have brought it up."

Eleanor sucked in a lungful of air and pulled away, swiping at her cheeks. "It's okay. I mean, it's a crazy story. I would have wanted to tell you, too. But I just can't do it, Maggie. I can't go looking for hope where it doesn't exist."

Maggie peered around the shop. "But isn't that why we're here? To look for something that doesn't make sense because it might just be worth it?"

At that, Eleanor slumped into the nearest chair, defeated. Maggie was right, of course. But searching for Alma's book was a fun adventure, not a perilous journey that might break Eleanor's heart so badly it would never heal. *The Woman of Valbrooke Hall*—and the woman who inspired her—was a distraction of the best kind. She was a mystery that Eleanor didn't *have* to solve, and so the effort would never wound her. Alma was a safe bet, even if they never actually found out the truth.

Eleanor looked up at Maggie. "Let's just find the book, okay?"

Maggie huffed but didn't protest. "Okay."

The man at the counter listened to their plea and directed them to a large section of local books. "We have quite a few popular authors from this area, as you can see," he said, shuffling them forward, "as well as a whole slew of authors who love to write about Savannah. This place holds a lot of history."

Eleanor faced the bookshelf, hands on her hips, and surveyed the author names in alphabetical order. On the third shelf, near the end of the row, she spied a familiar title. "There it is!" she exclaimed, snatching the book and holding it up for Maggie, who squealed. The man closed one eye with a grimace.

"I'll just be over there if y'all need me," he said with a chuckle and wandered away.

The book was a dusty, faded red labeled with a simple black font. But it was Alma's book, no doubt about it. Her name was printed right there on the spine. The front matter confirmed *The Woman at Valbrooke Hall* was printed in 1950 by Hurst Publishing Co. Eleanor dug around in her bag for the journal and then held them up side by side. Both girls sat on the rug and leaned over to examine their finds.

It was surreal to see both the draft and the finished product together. Who knew how long it had been since that happened last? Eleanor ran her palm over the journal, then flipped to the beginning of chapter six. Maggie read the excerpt and gasped.

"Ugh, what a jerk," she declared, pouting. "Even if he is supposed to be my great-grandfather."

"I wonder if the published version is different," Eleanor replied.

The red volume was significantly longer than the journal draft, just as the girls suspected it would be. The scene in which Louise overheard Silas and Andrew was included, barely altered from its original draft, and the chapter went on to describe how Louise, dejected and embarrassed, fled the house with Silas hot on her heels, begging her to come back.

"Skip to the end," Maggie said, taking the volume from Eleanor's hand, who swatted at her playfully. "Do they end up together or what?"

They quickly scanned the last handful of chapters. Eleanor couldn't help but notice how the narrator's voice became more stilted in the latter half of the book. "This doesn't read the same as the draft," she commented, two lines appearing between her brows as she skimmed the final chapter. "It's just so...*dry*, ya know? The voice is different, like Alma had a ghostwriter for the rest of the book."

"At least they get together at the end," Maggie said with a swoon. "But what happens in the draft after Louise overhears the guys talking?"

Eleanor shook her head, flipping the journal to chapter six. "That's where I stopped."

Only two pages remained in the draft, the rest of the journal filled with empty pages, yellowed with age. The girls leaned back against the bookshelf and read quietly, the silence punctuated only by soft classical music playing overhead and Maggie's occasional "hmm"s.

Louise's heart split in two. Stunned by Silas' cold declaration, she could hardly move for the grief of it. Her thoughts raced, then slowed to a numbing halt as she tried to process what she'd just heard. Andrew Gelding was no honorable gentleman, but Silas Valbrooke had seemed to Louise the sort of fellow who might be charmed by her quirks, her restless enthusiasm for stories where others saw only an odd little bluestocking, far from home.

After reading that line, Maggie and Eleanor made eye contact. "Bluestocking," Maggie said with wonder in her voice.

Eleanor shook her head. "We didn't make it up. Lots of people used to call girls that." Still, her pulse quickened as they turned their attention back to the page.

Regret had always seemed a waste to Louise, but at that moment, she felt completely overwhelmed by it, suffocated by the breath in her lungs.

Footsteps shuffled behind the library door, and Louise snapped to attention. Head pounding, she slipped quietly out the front door and down the porch steps where she had once stood with such excitement and hope, eager to make a living as a writer and to prove herself worthy. Louise made it down the meandering tree-lined drive before her tears claimed their due.

It was a classic mistake, and Louise, who'd read enough stories to know a witless heroine when she saw one, had been blind to her own self-deception. No man could ever, or would ever, make her worthy. Not in her profession or in love. She'd been a fool to believe otherwise, just like all the women in her family before her.

With a sob in her throat, Louise recounted all the ways her grandmother had warned against a woman losing her stories for love. Then, she prayed to be anywhere else in the world.

Anywhere but here. Anywhere but now.

A nagging discomfort made Eleanor shift on the floor. Maggie dropped the journal with a thud. "Okay, that was depressing AF," she said with a purse of her lips. "Not a fan. I like the published version better."

"I'm guessing you're not the only one," Eleanor replied, pointing to the hardback in front of them. "But something else is off, too." She sat forward and scanned the last page of Alma's draft, searching. For what exactly, she wasn't sure. Then, rubbing her mother's locket between her fingertips, it hit Eleanor with the force of a careening Mack truck. Suddenly, the persistent nagging in her chest made horrible, awful sense.

"Maggie," she breathed, unable to utter another sound.

"What?" Maggie asked. Seeing the look on Eleanor's face, she sat up sharply and pressed a hand to her shoulder. "What is it? What's wrong?"

Eyes glued to the last sentence on the page, Eleanor fumbled with the brass locket and withdrew the folded paper inside with shaking hands. "Read this," she whispered and held the tiny message out to Maggie.

"*You're still my favorite story,*" Maggie read and waved her hands in front of Eleanor's face. "Okay. What am I looking at, Elle?"

Without a word, Eleanor placed her mother's note down on the draft page, just beneath the final sentence. The handwriting was a perfect match.

"My mother," Eleanor said, turning to Maggie with wide eyes. "You're looking at my mother."

19

Ruby

Ruby promised herself that as soon as she got out of this ridiculous hospital, she was going to sink deep into her father's library chair in front of a blazing fire and lose herself in a book. The doctors promised she would be released in a few days, owing as much to Ruby's clear lab results as to her direct refusal to stay any longer than necessary. *December 22nd*, she had told them in no uncertain terms. Ruby was to be in the comfort of her own home before the anniversary of Alice's death.

Marianne and Ben rotated shifts each afternoon, trading off time with Ruby and watching out for Danger and Maggie. But the girl was spending most of her free time with Eleanor Black, and Ruby had no doubt her secrets had been shared. It was just as it should be. Eleanor needed to know every detail of Ruby's story if she was going to be prepared for what came next.

Marianne was lying back on the sofa bed by the window, one hand over her mouth as she read a thriller, the cover an image of a raging sea with a small house in the distance, a single candle burning in the window.

"How do you read that nonsense, Marianne?" Ruby said, breaking the silence. Marianne started and blinked at Ruby behind her reading glasses. "You look like you're about to have a heart attack. And I would know."

Marianne lowered her chin and pierced Ruby with a maternal glare. "Not funny," she replied, removing her glasses and rubbing the bridge of her nose.

"I thought it was rather witty, myself."

"Who are you?" Marianne replied, laughter sparkling in her eyes. "I don't know how to be around you anymore, Ruby. For years, you've been this crabby, ornery old woman who doesn't dare show any vulnerability, even though she's desperate to be seen," —at this, Ruby gave an audible "harrumph"—"and now you're cracking jokes in a hospital bed after you tried to off yourself. I feel like I'm in *The Twilight Zone*."

"I don't know, Marianne. I feel..." What did Ruby feel? Was there even a word for this quieter, more weightless existence? "...free," she finished softly, surprising even herself. "Like I walked into that water and came out clean again."

Her housekeeper blanched. "Well, that was one hell of a baptism."

Ruby surveyed her with curiosity, a trickle of warmth making its way down into her belly. "Thank you," she said. Marianne looked up, suspicion writ large on her angular features. "I mean it. Thank you for saving my life. In more ways than one."

Marianne cleared her throat, eyes welling, and snatched a tissue from the box at Ruby's bedside. "Now, I don't know about all that," she said, dabbing at her cheeks.

"It's true enough, and don't you dare deny it. I was alone and sad and forgotten after Father died."

"You had Ben."

"And he's a lovely person who made sure the house didn't burn down with me inside it," Ruby said affectionately, "but you came along and treated me like a friend, Marianne. Even when I resisted you at every possible turn."

Marianne reached for Ruby's hand and squeezed. "I know what it's like to feel alone and afraid. You deserved more than that, Ruby Hurst. You always have."

~~~

Ben returned in the afternoon to trade places with Marianne, who was itching to get home to both her dog and the thriller Ruby wouldn't stop criticizing. She kissed Ruby's head as she departed—a move that the patient allowed, even if displays of affection still made her cringe. Then came the evening shift rotation and more clinical rigmarole. One nurse in particular, a young man called Trevor with tawny skin and warm, chocolate eyes, out-sassed Ruby ten to one. He was her favorite. She liked a young person who could look you in the eye and say what's what.

Speaking of, Ruby called over to Ben. "Do we know when Maggie will be back?"

The groundskeeper shook his head. "I sure don't, but I can find out. If she's with that Eleanor Black, then maybe just let her be for a while."

"She's already been there and back twice in two days," Ruby replied, fidgeting. "I don't want her to overstay her welcome. Will you ask Marianne to call and confirm plans with Mr. Black? I'd feel much more at ease if I knew for certain where she was going to be while I'm here."

As it turned out, Eleanor, James, and Maggie were back at Ruby's house with Marianne. They'd gone to a bookstore in Savannah, but Eleanor had gotten sick soon after, so she and her father were headed home. Ruby released a breath she hadn't realized she'd been holding. There wasn't much time left, but at least she'd have a small break before the two of them accosted her with more questions than she currently had the energy to answer.
~~~

Three days later, Ruby was released from the hospital with strict instructions to take it easy but stay gently active to prevent a second heart attack. Thankfully, there was no scarring from the first go-round, but she'd need regular check-ups for a few months to ensure a clean bill of health. As someone who had long prided herself on eating well—thanks to Marianne's skills in the kitchen—and maintaining her physical fitness—even if she did move much slower these days—Ruby felt certain a relapse would be avoided. She promised herself it would. She had too much left to say.

The frigid weather broke for a last-minute bout of temperate sunshine upon Ruby's arrival at the house. It seemed like a welcome home gift, the way the light filtered through the trees with golden warmth, blinking back a message of peace. It would grow cold and gray again soon, but Ruby soaked in the rays as she sat and rocked on the porch, gathering her courage for what was to come.

After a delicious dinner of local shrimp and grits, Maggie cornered Ruby in her bedroom and shut the door. Ruby eyed her niece as she plopped down gracelessly onto the bay window seat and sighed. She placed a canvas tote on the cushion next to her and asked, "Can I talk to you, Aunt Ruby?"

Ruby perched on the edge of her plush queen bed. "I'm surprised it took you this long, to be quite frank with you."

Maggie raised a brow. "I'm not even sure where to start, but a lot is going on. Like, a ton of crazy stuff, and it all comes back to you, somehow. Every time."

"Is there a question in there?" Ruby asked.

"Well, yeah," Maggie sputtered, "the question is *why?*"

"I'm not sure what 'crazy stuff' you are referring to beyond the story I told you of my mother," Ruby said, careful to keep her face neutral, "but I did tell you last time that when we spoke again, Eleanor would need to be present for the conversation."

Maggie clicked her teeth together. "I know, but we found a book. Actually, *Eleanor* found the journal draft in a secret desk compartment at the bookstore, but *we* found the published copy in a bookstore in Savannah. It was written by Alma Gardyne." At that, Ruby's eyes grew wide. "The stories are different and—as *absolutely insane* as this sounds right now—we think the original draft might be connected to Eleanor's mother's disappearance."

Everything in the room narrowed to a single point on the floor as Ruby took in her niece's words. *Alma's journal.* The one William had been so angry about Alice looking through all those years ago. He must have hidden it in the desk back when it was still his office. But *how* could a book written just after the Second World War have anything to do with Vera Black's disappearance? "That seems..."Ruby hunted for the right word, "illogical."

Maggie rolled her eyes. "Right. About as illogical as your mother poofing out of existence."

"No need to be an ass," Ruby chastised sharply. "I didn't confide in you so that you could turn around and throw those secrets in my face."

Maggie looked suitably shamed. "Sorry," she grumbled.

Ruby waved her off. "Back to the matter at hand. Why do you and Eleanor think Alma's draft has something to do with Vera Black's disappearance?"

"Because we found her handwriting on the last page. The last sentence, to be more accurate."

Ruby's head spun. *Surely not...* "What book was this?"

Maggie reached into the canvas bag and pulled out an old, dusty hardback. Ruby had never seen it before. "*The Woman of Valbrooke Hall*?" she asked aloud to no one in particular. "I don't know this one."

"It was published in 1950," Maggie said. "There are fifteen chapters in this version, but the journal only has six. We think Alma wrote it about her and your dad, but in the novel it's *Alma* who gets her heart broken. Not William."

Ruby ran a palm over the faded cover and remembered the earthy smell of freshly printed paper and the clang of machinery down the hall, signaling the creation of new and beloved books. It was the scent of her childhood, a perfume as beloved as it was tragic. "My father loved Alma. He only spoke of her that one time, but he was adamant about his feelings."

Maggie chewed her bottom lip. "Do you know when Alma left town?"

Ruby shook her head, flipping through the novel. "Not for sure. She was gone by the time my mother arrived in early '44. But wait. You said the stories were different. Different how?"

"Well, the draft is much shorter, obviously. And the end of the sixth chapter is completely opposite of the published book. Alma—or Louise, as she's called in the book—overhears Silas—"

"My father, presumably," Ruby added with pursed lips.

"Right—" Maggie replied, "—she overhears him tell this dude named Andrew Gelding that he's not in love with her, and then she runs out of the house crying before anyone can see her."

"And in this version?" Ruby asked, holding up the old hardback.

"In that one, William—*Silas*—goes running after her. Eleanor noticed the first few chapters in both the journal and the published novel are the same, but then the writing changes. She said it was like Alma used a ghostwriter to finish the book."

Ruby shook her head. "My father didn't hire ghostwriters. He always said if someone wanted to write, then they needed to have the courage to put their name on it."

Maggie lifted a shoulder. "Maybe William finished it. You told me he was in love with her."

Ruby considered what Maggie had said about Silas running after Louise in the finished version. Perhaps her niece had a point. "It's possible," she conceded. "I'd like to see the journal. Do you have it, as well?"

"No. Eleanor kept it."

"Which reminds me," Ruby sighed, "of your original statement. You found Vera Black's handwriting on the last page of the draft. What did it say?"

Maggie's eyebrows drew together as she looked up in concentration. "It said '*Anywhere but here. Anywhere but now.*'"

The hairs on Ruby's arms stood on end. "Do you recall what Alma had written last, just before that?"

Maggie shook her head. "You'd have to get Eleanor to show you. All I remember is that Louise was super upset."

Ruby struggled to put all this new information together. Who was Alma Gardyne, really? Had William hidden the journal in the desk? And if Vera Black how found the journal and wrote the final line of the draft, why had she hidden it away again?

"I think," Ruby said, "it's time to call Eleanor."

20

Eleanor

The pounding was in Eleanor's head, but it was in her house as well. Slowly, with a heaviness that felt like moving underwater, she woke to the sound. Her skull throbbed from having cried so much and slept so little, and a persistent thud came from downstairs. Someone was at the front door.

With a glance at the clock on her nightstand, Eleanor saw it was only eight in the morning. Her dad would already be gone to the bookstore, prepping for the last few days of work before they closed in time for Christmas. She had been ill for days, more heartsick than anything else, and James had been nursing her back to health with Christmas movies and soup. He had no idea that Eleanor just needed her mother.

She rose precariously to her feet, groaning with the effort, and saw the note her dad had left on the nightstand.

Didn't want to wake you. Be home for lunch. Hope you're feeling better! Dad

Tossing her long hair up in a messy bun, Eleanor made her way down the stairs. Maggie's face appeared in the small window beside the front door. Perking up, Eleanor yanked it open. "Maggie!" she exclaimed, shivering in her long t-shirt and woolly socks. "What are you doing here?"

"Hi, I'm so sorry to wake you up, but you need to come with me because this is important," Maggie rambled. "I tried to call a few times last night, but your dad said you were still sick, and I just wanted to make sure you were okay and do you need to talk?"

Eleanor blinked at her friend. "Uh, come in," she said and stepped aside. Maggie followed her to the kitchen, where Eleanor popped two pieces of sourdough bread into the toaster. She poured herself a glass of orange juice and downed it, holding out a finger for Maggie to wait. With a small belch, Eleanor rinsed the glass and joined her friend at the table.

"I'm fine," she finally said. Maggie narrowed her eyes. "Okay, I'm *not* fine, but I think I've figured out why my mom's handwriting is in that book. So that's something. Maybe."

Maggie slapped both hands down on the wooden surface. "You did?"

"She was depressed," Eleanor said, sadness creeping into her voice. "Mom always wanted another baby, and she couldn't have one. It took a long time before she got pregnant with me, and then she had two miscarriages when I was little. I guess Mom found the journal in the desk and read it. Alma wanted something she couldn't have, and that's how her story ended. Mom probably felt the same way."

"But that's not how the story ended," Maggie argued. "Not in the published version, anyway."

"Who knows if Mom even knew about the finished novel? Plus, we don't know that Alma wrote that version. It could have been anyone."

"Aunt Ruby told me her dad never used ghostwriters. It was either Alma or William who finished the book. I'm betting on William."

Eleanor stretched her extra-long pajama tee over her knees and pulled them up into the chair. "How come?"

"He was in love with Alma," Maggie said as if it were obvious. "She left town thinking he didn't love her, so he wrote the story he wished they'd had."

Silence stretched out while Eleanor thought about how the bookstore had led her to discover Alma's book. Had it only been so she could read her mom's words? It didn't tell Eleanor anything she didn't already know. She'd seen how her mother cried when she thought no one was watching. She knew how much Vera missed those two babies who had never taken a breath. Eleanor missed them, too.

Why hadn't she been enough?

"I guessed we solved it, then," Eleanor finally said, propping her chin on her knees. "The mystery."

Maggie took a deep breath. She shifted her eyes to the floor and then back to Eleanor. "Well...not exactly."

Foreboding roiled low in Eleanor's belly. "Um. Okay," she replied. "Where do we go from here?"

Maggie sat back in her seat, the corners of her lips turned up in a cheeky smile. "We go to the only other person who might have more answers. We go to Aunt Ruby."

~~~

A few hours later, Marianne dropped by to pick up the girls. Maggie promised she didn't know any more details, only insisting that Ruby wanted to speak to them together, and Eleanor's stomach flip-flopped as they pounded up the front stairs of the grand Victorian house. Ruby was waiting for them in the library, a fire lit in the grate and three mugs of hot cocoa steaming on the table. Dressed in a soft, expensive-looking lounge set the color of sand, she looked every bit the queen of her castle.

"Hello, girls," she greeted them with a smile. "Marianne made your drinks, and she's working on some cookies while we get settled."

Eleanor sat on the rug by the fire, relief coursing through her veins. "I'm so glad you're okay, Ms. Hurst," she blurted, unable to contain her guilt. "I'm sorry about what happened."
~~~

The woman flicked a genteel hand. "Don't be silly, Eleanor. All's well that end's well."

Eleanor nodded, appeased, and took a sip of her hot cocoa. The heat of it melted the tension in her body, and she felt safe and at peace for the first time in days. "Maggie said she told you about Alma's books. I brought the journal with me if you want to see it."

Ruby sat up a little straighter, if that was possible, and reached out an eager hand. "Oh, yes, I do."

Maggie and Eleanor drank their cocoa and watched intently as Ruby flipped through the pages of the journal with quiet reverence. "I remember this," she said, eyes glued to the yellowed pages. "When I was a little girl, my mother found it in this very room, and Father took it away. He was angry about it, but I didn't know why then. He must not have wanted her to see what was so obviously a story written about him." Eleanor watched as Ruby flipped to the final page of the draft and paused, running her fingers over the words written there. "I suspect your theories were right about Father penning the remainder of the novel. The published version reads like his work, though I suppose we'll never know for sure."

"He was a writer, too?" Eleanor asked.

Ruby smiled. "He was, but publishing—not writing—was the family business, so he stuck to that. Father mostly wrote for himself. I have some of his short stories in my cedar chest upstairs."

"My mom was like that, too," Eleanor mused. She tried to keep the sadness at bay, but her eyes began to water like the traitors they were. Eleanor blinked away the tears. "She read to me every night. The bookstore was like my other home. Still is. It wouldn't even exist if it weren't for Mom. Dad was convinced a bookstore would only lose money, but she wrote out her plan for it with drawings and everything, and eventually, he caved." Eleanor poked at the skin beginning to form on the top of her cocoa. "But maybe Dad was right after all."

"Yes, Maggie told me about your father's money troubles," Ruby said, not unkindly. "Small businesses can be hard to sustain, especially now when small towns are suffering the effects of big industry in bigger cities. We tend to be overlooked again and again."

Eleanor didn't know much about industry, but she could feel the truth of Ruby's words in her bones. "It must have been different when you were a kid."

"Hmm," Ruby mused. "It was already starting to change after the war. The family business soldiered on until the early seventies, but by then, even my father had to admit how drastically the publishing world had changed. He closed up shop and spent the remainder of his years serving several philanthropic interests. Sometimes, it's better to quit while you're still ahead."

Eleanor slumped. "So you think we should close the bookshop?" The very thought of it sent shock waves of pain through her skull.

Thankfully, Ruby shook her head. "No, my dear. Everyone deserves books."

Eleanor bit her lip, grinding her teeth into the skin. *Everyone deserves books.* It was exactly what her mother used to say, and the words in Ruby Hurst's mouth struck an already-exposed nerve frayed to breaking. Eleanor had a sudden urgent need to understand why she was here. "What did you want to talk to me about, Ms. Hurst?" she asked, blunt like the edge of a dull knife.

Something wounded flashed across Ruby's face before she blinked and it was gone. "Right, of course. Perhaps you should get more comfortable. I imagine we're going to be here for a while." Eleanor exchanged wary glances with Maggie but moved over to the love seat, fluffing the pillow in her lap for extra comfort. "Maggie tells me she shared my secret," Ruby said plainly. "I'm curious, as a girl who shares a similar loss, what do you think of the tale?"

Eleanor fidgeted. *This* was what she wanted to talk about? Their disappearing mothers? "I think—" Eleanor swallowed hard. "I think it's sad," she finished lamely. "Nobody should have to go through that, especially when you're a little kid. It sucks."

"That it does," Ruby agreed, folding her hands across her lap. "Losing a loved one, especially a parent, is always difficult. Even more so if the circumstances around their passing are confusing. We were just kids, weren't we? Everything was working against us. In my case, it felt like every*one* was, too. But there's more to my story that I've never shared before, and I'd like to share it with you girls now. It's...*delicate*, I warn you. It will not be easy to hear."

Maggie and Eleanor looked at each other again. The air in the room shifted, growing heavier with the heat of the fire and the weight of Ruby's statement. Eleanor suddenly wanted to run home, to be away from this woman who understood so much of what it felt like to lose a mom, but an even deeper curiosity kept her glued to the love seat. The girls nodded.

Ruby sat motionless for a moment, then took a sip of her cocoa. "Right," she said. "Well, I'll just jump right in. A few weeks before my father died, he did what dying men do: he confessed. He told me he was not my biological father and that my mother had been pregnant when she arrived in Hawthorn and began working for his company."

The only sound was the crackle and pop of the burning logs. "What?" Maggie croaked, ruffling her short blond locks. "I mean...*what?*" Eleanor couldn't have said it better.

"I shared your sentiments, dear," Ruby said. "I was devastated by the news. Father explained to me that while he loved Alice deeply, he had still been grieving Alma. My mother, too, was broken over the loss of her first husband. They never had a love affair. What they had was a deep and abiding friendship that grew out of an immediate connection. She was serious and sensitive; he was clever and kind. They both loved books as much as they loved anything else, and Father was the only person she told about the pregnancy. He knew she would struggle as a single, unwed mother, especially as a newcomer in this small, close-knit community, so he suggested that they get married. They'd only known each other for a few months, but many couples married quickly at that time. Father always said she was his best friend. My mother refused to follow through with the wedding while she was still grieving, but she agreed to the proposal, and William was recorded as the father on my birth certificate."

"Wow," Eleanor breathed. "And you never knew?"

Ruby offered her a gentle smile. "Not until he was dying."

"Holy shit, Aunt Ruby," Maggie said, braces shiny in the firelight as her mouth hung open in shock.

"My reaction was much the same," Ruby said. "After Father died, I sold off many of my family's properties to support the estate and continue his financial legacy for future generations. My lawyers took care of everything. I never paid much attention to who bought what, just that the checks were cleared and deposited into the right accounts." To Eleanor, Ruby said, "I also never met your mother or father. Ben and, later, Marianne were my only real ties to the community." Ruby took a deep, shuddering breath and closed her eyes for a brief moment. "Then, Eleanor, your mother disappeared. It was everywhere on the television, but I heard about it first from Marianne. She'd started working for me some months prior, and I was afraid the news would send her packing, but she stayed. She told me about you and your family's incredible bookshop, and I was heartbroken for you. I have never forgotten the pain of growing up without my mother. She was so dear to me."

Eleanor could feel her skin turn blotchy from the effort it took to hide her emotions. She sniffed. "So was mine."

Ruby plucked a tissue from the side table and handed it to Eleanor, who merely clutched it in her palm. "When Marianne brought me that week's *Savannah Daily News*, your mother's disappearance was the headline. I was sitting in the parlor at the breakfast table, and I saw Vera's photo on the front page. I couldn't believe what I was looking at. The story was eerily similar to what I had been through. The disappearance. The lack of evidence. The trail gone cold. But—well, it was more than that. Your mother, Eleanor, she—" Ruby looked into

Eleanor's dark green eyes, and her own filled with tears. "She looked just like mine."

It was as if all the air had gone out of the room. Eleanor gaped at Ruby, frozen, and then sucked in a sharp breath as though she were a drowning victim coming back to life. "Lots of people look alike," she said in a shaky voice. Ruby's patient gaze turned Eleanor's spine to steel. She lifted her chin defiantly. "And lots of people go missing. Or leave."

Sympathy flashed across Ruby's face. "You think your mother left on her own?"

Eleanor clenched her jaw as she looked away out the window. Night had fallen, and the Christmas lights on the front porch twinkled brightly against the dark. "Yes, I do."

Maggie pressed her hand to Eleanor's as her aunt continued to speak. It gave Eleanor a small measure of courage. "And what do you think about the similarities in our stories? I've puzzled over them many times."

Eleanor turned her gaze back to Ruby, thinking of the bookshop, the journal, and the hidden compartment. "A lot of strange things have been happening in this town lately."

"Yes," Ruby agreed. "That's true. But I would go further and say they've been happening for a long time."

"So, our mothers look alike," Eleanor stated sharply, hopping up from the love seat to pace the room. She wanted to crawl out of her skin. "Maybe they're related."

"Are your parents from Hawthorn?" Ruby asked.

"No. They moved here in the late nineties. My dad is from Atlanta, but my mom is from Savannah. Maybe our families are related somehow."

"I've considered that," Ruby replied. "It's a bit too convoluted to try and figure out, but it's a possibility."

Maggie cleared her throat. "So, what's your point, Aunt Ruby? What are you saying?"

Eleanor turned away from the bookshelf to stare at them. The tenderness in Ruby's gaze made her tears finally fall like fat raindrops on the carpet.

"My father's confession to me before he died answered a lot of my questions," Ruby said, "but it added a whole new set of them, too. I understood then why my mother had never followed through with their wedding and why Father went to such lengths to try and protect me from myself. He certainly didn't believe his five-year-old daughter had seen her mother vanish into thin air, and I'm sure he hoped my marriage to Elliot would bring an end to the dark cloud that hovered over our home—over *me*. But when I refused to change my story, and Elliot betrayed me, it only perpetuated the darkness."

"But to wait for so long to tell you he wasn't your dad," Maggie said, her eyes blazing with anger. "That was such a jerk thing to do."

Ruby fingered the edges of her blanket. "I suppose you're right. Courage is a fickle thing. It doesn't stick around forever. It shows up in a moment, available to anyone who chooses it, but if denied, it might not return for a long time. In my father's case, he got one more chance. The night he made his confession, he also told me more about my biological father, Mother's first husband. I was still so stunned by the news that I harbored little interest in the man at first, especially once my father passed and I was living in such deep grief over the loss. But I remembered his name. It was a name I never heard again until I read the news about your mother, Eleanor."

Eleanor felt all the color leech from her face. She didn't want to ask, but it was inevitable. Her voice shook as she whispered. "And what name was that?"

Ruby swallowed hard.

"James Black."

21

Ruby

Ruby stood as Eleanor swayed on her feet. Maggie helped the girl to her seat and put an arm around her shoulders. Even as her niece glared at Ruby, she felt pride that Maggie had found such a kindred spirit in Eleanor.

"This is nuts, Aunt Ruby," Maggie said. "You know that, right?"

"I'm only telling you what I know to be true," Ruby said. "That is all."

Eleanor's eyes shut as the tears streamed down and dropped onto her jeans, unhindered. The tissue in her hand was crumpled into a useless ball as she leaned over at the waist, gasping for breath. Marianne walked in with a silver tray of cookies just then and nearly dropped them at the sight of Eleanor hyperventilating.

"Oh my God!" she cried, dropping the tray with a clang on the table. "What's wrong?"

Maggie leaned over next to Eleanor and urged her to breathe. "She's having a panic attack, I think."

Ruby stood aside and let Marianne take over, feeling awkward and uncertain about how to handle Eleanor's not-so-surprising display of emotion. Guilt twinged her chest as she re-considered her straightforward approach to confession, feeling a bit villainous about the effect her words were having on young Eleanor. Ruby should have known the news wouldn't go down easily. It had taken her, a woman in her seventies at the time, weeks to recover from the shock.

It wasn't fair to her or Eleanor. Still, Ruby felt the girl had a right to know the truth whether she chose to believe it or not. Alice Hurst and Vera Black were one and the same.

Ruby and Eleanor, against all odds, were *sisters*.

Marianne continued to shush Eleanor, rubbing the girl's back and speaking in her soft, lilting voice. Eventually, Eleanor breathed normally and sat up. Her eyes went straight to Ruby, who noted with more than a little surprise they were filled with fury.

"Why would you tell me that?" Eleanor demanded, her voice raspy from tears. "Is it supposed to make me feel better? That, somehow, *my* father is *your* father, and *your* mother is *my* mother? Are you trying to make me as crazy as you are?"

Marianne gasped, glancing back and forth between them. Maggie slid from her perch on the edge of the love seat to the floor. Ruby never took her eyes off Eleanor, even though her words cut so deep she wanted to hurl everyone else from the room and hide away with her books. "I'm not sorry, Eleanor. You want me to be, but I've spent too many years living with regrets."

"My mother is not Alice. Her name is *Vera*. She's *mine*," Eleanor cried, tears trailing rivulets down her cheeks.

Ruby flinched at the anger on Eleanor's face. "What is her middle name, Eleanor?"

Eleanor blinked. "It's Elizabeth," she answered with a sniffle.

"Yes," Ruby countered, stepping towards the girl. "And Alice is a nickname for Elizabeth."

The wind outside picked up with a howl, knocking the holiday lights against the porch columns with an ominous rattle. Eleanor began to visibly shake, so Ruby put her hands on the girl's trembling shoulders.

"Something is happening here that doesn't make any sense," Ruby continued, thankful that Eleanor didn't pull away. "But it's real. I don't know why your mother's handwriting is in Alma's journal, but I do know what I saw on the beach the day my mother disappeared. And I know what I saw when yours disappeared, too."

"Wait..." said Marianne, holding out her hands as if to stave them both off. "Did you just say '*Alma's journal*'?"

Ruby cocked her head to the side. "Yes, that's right," she replied. Her housekeeper's skin had suddenly turned ashen. Ruby retrieved the leather notebook from where it lay on the chair and held it up. Marianne appeared to stop breathing.

"Where did you find that?" she whispered, reaching for the book with a shaky hand.

Ruby had never seen Marianne so out of sorts. She was the solid ground on which everything in this house stood, a pillar of determination, grace, and humor, and for the first time, she looked as though a stiff breeze might blow her away. "I didn't find it," Ruby said. "Eleanor did." When Eleanor didn't elaborate, Ruby explained. "It was in a secret drawer underneath my father's old desk in the bookshop. It appears as though it's an incomplete first draft of *The Woman of Valbrooke Hall*, a novel my father's company published in 1950. Alma Gardyne was the author, but Eleanor discovered a line written on the last page that matches her mother's hand."

Marianne flipped through the journal, one hand clasped over her mouth, and suddenly, the truth hit Ruby fast and sharp. "You've seen this before, haven't you, Marianne?"

Without looking up, Marianne nodded her head. "Oh, yes," she answered, voice trembling with every word. "I know this journal very well."

Maggie, who had been sitting quietly in a heap on the floor, shot to her feet. "Okay, PAUSE," she said, making a *T* shape with her hands. "What is happening right now? Can everybody just stop talking and take some deep breaths? I love a good mystery, but this is all too much too fast."

Ruby helped Marianne to a chair and sat down next to her. Maggie took her seat across the coffee table with Eleanor. Some of Marianne's chocolate chip cookies had fallen to the floor and been crushed, but at the moment, Ruby couldn't make herself care. The four of them faced one another in the soft, warm glow of the brass banker's lamp, firelight casting the room in dancing shadows.

"This journal," Marianne said slowly, her long, slender fingers splayed protectively over the cover, "is mine. *I'm Alma Gardyne.*"

Into the stunned silence that followed, she told them her story.

~~~

In July of 1958, Marianne was born Alma Louise Marianne Gardyne to Thomas and Mary Ellen Gardyne in Donaghadee, a coastal village in Northern Ireland. Like his father before him, Thomas left the family, and Mary Ellen became a single mother when Marianne was only three. Mary Ellen died months later in a car accident in Belfast, and subsequently, Marianne was raised by her paternal grandmother, Saoirse. A devout Catholic with a deep fondness for the mystic, Saoirse saw no reason why the holy mysteries of her faith should mean disavowing other obscure, unexplainable events. She called on Mother Mary to pray for her when Marianne tested her patience, and she dabbled in medicinal spell work when the girl became ill with the stomach flu. Marianne was more skeptical than her grandmother, but she was a dreamer nonetheless, and Saoirse encouraged her at every turn to broaden her thinking about what was possible. Saoirse penned collects, meditations, folk cures, and recipes of all kinds in leatherbound journals she kept by the stove. The journals were made from sheepskin belonging to a local healer, a mischievous and ornery old woman by the name of Biddy Clare. Hand-sewn and meticulously crafted, Saoirse gifted Marianne one of the journals as a birthday present before she immigrated to the States to find work.
~~~

"For all of your travels," she'd said to her granddaughter, a lovely velvet ribbon tied in a bow around the book. "The good, the bad, and the unexpected." Less than a year later, Saoirse passed away from a blood clot in her lungs. Marianne, destroyed by grief, saved the journal in a trunk where it would be preserved forever, out of sight and mind.

She eventually left New York and traveled around the country, writing freelance to eke out a passable existence. Melancholy, combined with a determined sense of purpose, held her fast, but Marianne longed for a more useful life. A happier, fulfilled life. One day, while unpacking her trunk in yet another cheap apartment, she stumbled across the forgotten journal. As she pressed it to her chest with eyes closed tight, she felt as though it sang to her, memories of her grandmother a dense cloud of longing in the air. Suddenly, Marianne was consumed by an almost obsessive need to write in the journal, and she poured out her emotions onto the page, speaking them aloud as she wrote in the same way her grandmother had cried out her prayers.

In a blink, she was back in Ireland, standing at the window of her childhood home at dusk. The only light from within came from the glow of a small box television set. On the couch were Saoirse and Marianne herself, no more than seven or eight years old. Marianne was fast asleep with her head in her grandmother's lap while Saoirse gently played with the little girl's hair. Adult Marianne, still clutching the journal, stared through the window for what seemed like hours, frozen by disbelief. For two days, she watched the house from the old gardening shed out back, numb with exhaustion, confusion, fear, and a greedy hunger to experience life with her grandmother again, even from a distance.

Eventually, though, Marianne broke down. She couldn't stay there. She had to go back.

Was going back even possible?

She'd puzzled over how it all happened and realized the journal—created by Biddy Clare specifically for Marianne's travels with who knew what sort of enchantments spoken over it—had taken Marianne back in time. Could she go forward, back to her real life, from here?

She'd scoured the shed for a writing utensil and eventually found a pen tucked into the pocket of her grandmother's gardening apron. With one last look at her beloved childhood home, Marianne scribbled in the journal her desire to go back and make a real life for herself in the present. Then, she read the words out loud. The next moment, she was back in her apartment. Marianne considered destroying the journal after that, terrified, but the memory of seeing her grandmother again stopped her. Instead, she shoved it down into the bottom of her trunk and buried it beneath a pile of books, blankets, and memories. In time, it seemed to Marianne as if it had all been a dream.

She began writing a novel in her few spare hours. She also continued to travel, and work took her as far as the historic city of Savannah, Georgia. One afternoon, Marianne went for a drive around the area, where she stumbled across a little town called Hawthorn and was immediately enchanted by the sight of it. It reminded Marianne of Donaghadee: colorful, quaint, and as charming as could be. She spent all afternoon walking around the square, browsing shops, and listening to locals talk to one another in their low country accents. She stood outside an empty storefront and, peeking in the windows, imagined what it would become—what, perhaps, it had already been. And for the first time since Marianne had arrived in the States more than fifteen years prior, she felt at home.

On the drive back to her rented cottage in Savannah, Marianne passed the iron gates of a large private estate. Set back from the road down a long, tree-lined drive was a buttery yellow Queen Anne Victorian house, surrounded by flowers and glowing in the golden light of dusk. It looked to Marianne like a storybook come to life, and she spent the next few weeks learning all she could about the house, its history, and the family who had built the little town of Hawthorn.

The tragedy of Alice Hurst's death and the daughter she'd left behind stayed on her mind for months.

Even though Marianne was more settled in Savannah than she'd ever been anywhere else except Donaghadee, she was lonely. Without any family to go home to at night and with no prospect of marriage or children on the horizon, she began to dream about the Hurst family and the town in which they'd lived. She visited Hawthorn often, drawn by some unseen force to imagine herself rooted there, and went home to her cottage again and again, wishing that, somehow, she could make her life become all that she had once hoped it would be.

One night, lying in the dark, Marianne remembered the journal. With barely a thought, she had it in her hands once more. Flipping to the first empty page, she began to write in feverish strokes. It was little more than the rambling wishes of an anchorless woman, but as soon as she finished reading aloud what was written there, Marianne opened her eyes to find herself standing in front of what had, at last visit, been an empty storefront on Hawthorn Square, journal in hand. But now—whenever *now* was—the words *Hurst Publishing Co., Established 1884,* were printed on the glass front door, and inside were rows of antique mahogany desks and heavy black typewriters. On the wall near the window, Marianne spied a calendar that read August 1936 in bold, elegant script, and she fell to her knees in the dark, astonished, afraid...and exhilarated.

She slept in the woods that night, still clad in her thin cotton pajamas and foraging for food among the trees, staying close to a creek that ran through the Hurst estate. She had no idea why the journal had sent her back to 1936, but Marianne's mother had been born that same year. She thought of Saoirse carrying Mary Ellen through the cottage in Donaghadee, nursing her in the gray light of dawn, and cried. She couldn't try to go back to Ireland. It wasn't her time. But maybe she could make a life here, in this town that felt so much like home. For whatever reason, it was where the journal had sent her. So, it was where she would choose to stay.

Marianne was resourceful and knew a thing or two about how to get by with next to nothing. She bathed in the cool creek water, brushing her teeth with dried grasses, and stole a plain cotton day dress and slip from a local woman's laundry line. She foraged for berries, mushrooms, and wild onions. After a few days of sleeping in the trees atop an old deer stand and walking through the woods barefoot, Marianne snuck a pair of worn Oxfords from a pile of donations set up outside the First Baptist Church when the two ladies organizing the event took a break for lunch. There was no time for guilt. Marianne had to survive.

One afternoon, after a dip in the creek, her long chestnut hair swept back in a low bun, she ventured into town, hoping to find work. That was when she saw William Hurst for the first time. He was tall and lean, bookish, but with a strong jaw and piercing gray eyes. She watched with a pounding heart as he closed the glass front door to his office and turned to walk in her direction, moving with all the smooth, easy grace of a wealthy Southern gentleman. He was beautiful, and he was alone.

Determined not to lose her focus, Marianne forced herself to walk past William Hurst with barely a glance. Until he looked up and caught her eye. She gasped, the breath leaving her body before she could catch it, and both of them stumbled at the same time. Marianne fell into the man's chest as he steadied himself by her shoulders, each mumbling swift, embarrassed apologies to the other. She introduced herself as Alma, and the name rolled off his tongue like honey. When, at last, William asked Marianne to lunch to make up for their awkward introduction, she said yes without a moment's hesitation.

Within a week, she was on the Hurst Publishing Co. payroll, working as a printing machine operative and renting out the furnished shoe box apartment above the office. It was a step down professionally, but since she was living nearly six decades in the past, Marianne was willing to work with what she had. She proved herself dedicated and driven, and even though it set tongues affectionately wagging around town, William began to invite her to his home for dinner every week. He was kind, generous, and whip-smart, and he listened to Marianne's stories and ideas. He championed her writing and, for her birthday that year, gifted Marianne a gorgeous Remington Noiseless Typewriter Model 7. When she came to him months later with the completed draft of her first novel, William agreed to publish it.

At the office, William was brimming with the confidence of a man who understood both the business and his inherited place within it. The legacy of Hurst Publishing Co. belonged to him, and he understood how its success benefited their small community. But in his relationships, William Hurst was shy and unassuming. Marianne, who was becoming more and more settled in her new life with each passing day, grew bolder in her interactions with him. Her novel became a moderate success under William's steady hand, and Marianne was thrilled to realize she was, at last, happy. Fulfilled.

For a time.

William never dated anyone during Marianne's five years in Hawthorn. He stayed busy with work, church, the estate, and several philanthropic endeavors that were still much-needed as the Second World War loomed ahead. Marianne grew frustrated and impatient. She had become William's closest friend, or so she thought, but she longed for his heart. William, in turn, respected her mind, which felt a lot like love to a woman unfamiliar with that sort of attention from her male colleagues, but his reserved demeanor masked whatever deeper emotions swam beneath the surface. Marianne decided to confess her feelings the next time she was invited to the Hurst estate, hoping that her actions would finally move him to do the same. Always hopeful and steady, love had made her stupid.

Marianne had begun work on a new novel inspired by her relationship with William and her affection for the town of Hawthorn. When he invited her for lunch one Saturday afternoon, she hurried to the house with her draft chapters—written in the pages of a journal that made words come to life—to share them with William. But when she arrived, Marianne overheard a conversation between William and his estate manager that sent poisoned barbs into her heart. She fled the house without a word.

What had she been thinking, to believe a man like William Hurst would ever love a brash village girl from Ireland? She was too driven, too abrupt, too *common* to even be seen as the "dame on his arm." And, worst of all, this place that had become home to her would never be the same now. Marianne felt more foolish than she ever had in her entire life.

She wrote it all down in the journal and prayed to be anywhere else in the world.

Biddy Clare's journal obliged.

~~~

By the end of Marianne's story, Ruby was stunned to find her cheeks wet with tears. "And then you were sent here?" she asked, reaching for Marianne's hand. Her housekeeper—her *friend*—nodded.

"Yes. I showed up in the front of the bookshop, alone at night, just as I had when it was William's office in 1936. Only this time, it was 2018, and I'd skipped forward a whole twenty years from the time I first laid eyes on this town in 1998. Instead of trying to go back to my normal life, though, I came looking for you, Ruby. I knew what you'd been through, and I knew William was gone. Even then, even after I'd run away with my heart broken, I still couldn't leave the Hurst family alone. I still couldn't leave this place I loved."

"But you were wrong, Marianne," chirped Eleanor, face bright in the firelight. "William did love you. He loved you so much that he rewrote the end of your story. I think he hoped, after everything that happened with Alice, that you would read it somehow and come back."

"You could go back now!" Maggie exclaimed loudly. "You know the truth. You could go back and do it over and live happily ever after."
~~~

Ruby shook her head grimly as Marianne's mouth turned up in a sad smile. "No, I can't," she replied with a sigh. She suddenly looked much older. "If I did that, then Ruby wouldn't be here now."

"Yes, she would!" Maggie declared, on the edge of her seat. "If everything you've both told us is true, then Ruby would be here, *with Eleanor and her parents*, as she was always supposed to be. Vera would never have gone back in time, and everything would be the way it should."

"No, Maggie," Eleanor interjected. She glanced at Ruby, forlorn, and then turned to her friend. "If Marianne went back, then William would never marry Jean. Jean would never have their children...and you—"

Maggie stared at Eleanor, uncomprehending. Ruby said nothing, waiting for the unhappy truth to dawn on her niece.

Then Maggie crumpled.

"—would never be born."

22

Eleanor

Eleanor knew it wasn't fair to call finding Alma's draft lucky; *fated* was the word she'd choose, even if fate had dealt every person in that library an inexplicably unfair hand. Had Biddy Clare performed a sort of time-traveling spell on the journal? Marianne told them Saoirse had specifically requested the book as a gift for her travels. Maybe Biddy Clare had decided that instead of mischief, she wanted chaos.

It's like the bookstore wants you to find out the truth, Maggie had said. Eleanor believed her now. Every single one of them—Ruby, Eleanor, Marianne, and Maggie—had felt drawn to the place that now housed Bluestocking Books. It was a haven for all the girls who needed a place to feel safe when nothing else in the world did. When Eleanor discovered Alma's journal in the desk, it was the comforting presence of something unseen that had directed her there. And in every moment since her mom had disappeared, the bookshop had always been her refuge.

Alice and Vera had both vanished without a trace. No physical evidence of foul play or suicide or an accident. They had both left behind daughters too young to lose their mothers, girls who were supposed to grow up under the guidance of their love and care, and now Eleanor had to contend with the reality that both she and Ruby were daughters of a James Black. That both Vera and Alice—twins in fate *and* appearance—had married a man with that name. In the light of Marianne's time-traveling tale, it seemed the most logical option was also the most unbelievable.

Vera had found the journal in the present. Eleanor guessed she had written in it on the day she disappeared, or had at least read the words aloud for the first time. And then she had gone back to 1944, to a different Hawthorn—William and Alma's Hawthorn—carrying Ruby along with her. If Ruby's hypothesis was true, Eleanor had been wrong about her mom all along. There was no way Vera could have known what writing on those pages would do to her or her family. And if the story Eleanor had just been told was not a fairy tale but real life, then Vera hadn't meant to leave her behind after all.

Once the weary foursome had trudged away to their respective beds, listless and worn out from the night's events, Eleanor lay next to Maggie, pretending to be asleep. Beneath the soft down duvet, light from the waxing moon illuminating the darkness of Maggie's bedroom, Eleanor simply stared at the ceiling. Her mother's locket was cold in her hand, and she felt numb, unable to process any of the information now swirling around in her head.

For six years, she'd been expected to rely on her memories as proof of her mom's love. But when Vera left, it didn't simply erase all the good and beautiful things that came before; it made the truth into a lie. It stole away everything Eleanor believed about herself and her mom. Because of what Alma's journal had taken, she no longer had any real concept of who she was or what belonged to her, except for the bookstore and her dad.

And, now, it seemed like Eleanor didn't even have him.

~~~

The next morning, Marianne made chocolate chip pancakes for breakfast with whipped cream and fresh strawberries. "Comfort
~~~

food," she told them, hoisting a large platter of cakes onto the breakfast table. Despite the rumble in her belly, Eleanor could hardly eat a bite. Maggie, on the other hand, devoured six pancakes in quick succession. Ruby only sipped her coffee.

Eleanor still couldn't quite grasp the enormity of her newfound relationship with Ruby Hurst. The woman was a legend in Hawthorn, her story a long series of unknowns and assumptions, each passed from one person to another over the years like a game of telephone until the truth had become so muddied there wasn't a single person who could verify what was real and what was rumor. No one except Ruby herself.

Until last night.

Now, there were four people, and Eleanor was one of them.

Borrowing Maggie's phone, she stepped onto the wrap-around porch with a blanket and sat down to call her dad.

"Hey, sweetheart," he said, answering on the first ring. "You still feeling okay?"

Eleanor snorted. Physically, she was fine. Emotionally? Spiritually? Mentally? Not passing the vibe check. Probably wouldn't ever again. "Yeah, I'm okay," she lied. "How did the book sale go?"

"Good," James replied. Eleanor could hear him shuffling around in the kitchen. "Sold about half the discounted inventory and took the rest to Goodwill this morning. You coming home today? I feel like I hardly see you now that Maggie Hurst has come to town."

"Yeah, Marianne said she'd bring me to the shop after lunch."

"Good. We can go see the Christmas lights in Savannah tomorrow after I close up for the week. How does that sound?"

Eleanor warmed at the thought of a trolley ride through the historic district, hot drink in hand, bundled up to gaze at the magical displays of holiday lights. "It sounds great, Dad," she said. "Can't wait."

Maggie joined Eleanor on the porch, still wearing pajamas, her cropped blond hair sticking up in all directions. They looked out at the long, quiet drive, a steady breeze blowing a wayward curl across Eleanor's face.

"Do you believe her?" she asked Maggie. "I mean, honestly. Do you?"

Maggie shrugged. "Why not?"

Eleanor exhaled hard, her breath visible in the cold morning air. *Why not?* It was as good an answer as any. The pages of all her favorite novels were filled with unexpected and unbelievable stories. And that was what made them so wonderful. Eleanor had never had a problem believing in their magic; she just never expected to become the protagonist of her own sort of fairy tale.

But if magic could exist within the pages of a book, then why not here?

"I've always loved winter," said a voice from behind them. Eleanor and Maggie pivoted to find Ruby standing in the open doorway, lovely in her long cotton skirt and rose-colored sweater. Her long, silver hair was pulled back from her face, which was kind as she smiled at them. "It gave me even more reason to hide away all those years. But now I think it's a reminder that even lost things can be found again."

Eleanor looked directly at Ruby and took in her elegant posture, her curious expression, and—in a flash—saw the young woman she must have been. Lithe and poised, just as she was now, but with hair the color of a setting sun. In Ruby's green eyes, as vivid as the forests of oaks in summer, she saw her mother. Eleanor sucked in a quick breath at the sight, wondering how in the world she hadn't noticed it before. "I'm sorry about yesterday," Eleanor continued, as though she hadn't just been sucker-punched by this strange new reality in which she lived.

Ruby came and sat down between the girls. Eleanor suddenly wanted to lean on the woman's shoulder and cry again, but her tears were all dried up. "I'm not worried about it, Eleanor."

Eleanor toyed with the delicate fringe on her blanket. "Is there...anything else you needed to tell me?" Eleanor asked, trying and failing to hold back the tension pulling at her vocal chords. "Please say no."

Ruby laughed, a full-body sound that took Eleanor by surprise. Maggie looked impressed. "No. I think I'm done now. But I would like to ask if you'd both take a walk with me?"

"A walk?" Maggie protested. "I was about to cuddle up by the fire and watch *The Holiday* on my laptop. It's too cold for exercise, Aunt Ruby." Eleanor glared at her friend, who rolled her eyes but grinned anyway. "Never mind, I'll wear a scarf."

Bundled against the breeze that bit into the tips of their ears and fingers, the thermometer having dropped sharply overnight into uncharacteristically cold temperatures, Eleanor and Maggie followed Ruby through the house and out to the garden. A small iron gate was built into the garden wall, half-covered by ivy vines, and Ruby brushed them aside before pulling, using all her insubstantial weight in the effort. It wouldn't budge.

"How long has it been since you've opened this gate, Aunt Ruby?" Maggie asked.

"Only Benjamin ever goes in and out of it. I usually stick to the garden."

Maggie stepped in front of her aunt and pushed the gate. Nothing. Ruby tsked. "I may not come through here often, but I've lived in this house my entire life, child. You're supposed to pull it."

Maggie gripped the thin railings and pulled as hard as she could. The gate flew open and sent her stumbling into Eleanor, who laughed.

"Well," Maggie said, adjusting her coat. "At least I got it open."

"Yes, I don't know what we would have done without you," Ruby added, her mouth twisted into a half smile. Eleanor liked this new version of Ruby Hurst. She liked her a lot.

They stepped outside the fence and made their way toward the trees behind the house, where an overgrown dirt path awaited them. "Goodness," Ruby said under her breath. "I didn't realize it was this wild out here."

"Where are we going?" Eleanor asked. She plucked a briar from where it had gotten stuck on her jeans.

Ruby appeared confident in her strides, despite the tangled limbs of nature reaching out for them along the path, and called out over her shoulder, "You'll see."

Maggie wiggled her eyebrows at Eleanor, perpetually delighted by the ongoing adventure the three of them were having. "Mysterious," she said in an ethereal voice.

"I'm learning to expect nothing less," Eleanor replied dryly.

The path widened as they walked deeper into the forest, large oaks of many varieties and towering pines surrounding them, beds of needles beneath their feet. The sun peeked through the canopy of bare branches above them, rays of sharp winter sunlight that brightened the dense forest. The three of them walked along in quiet contemplation together until they came to a grove of mulberry trees, in the center of which Eleanor could see another iron fence grown over with brambles.

"Is this what I think it is?" Eleanor asked as they neared the fence, behind which stood a few dozen headstones of various shapes, sizes, and ages. On the front gate hung a brass plaque covered in a spotty brown patina. Her pulse quickened.

Ruby rubbed a gentle hand over the plaque. "If you're wondering if this is the Hurst family cemetery," she answered, "then, yes, it's exactly what you think."

23

Ruby

Ruby's heart thudded in her chest as she removed an old skeleton key from her coat pocket and twisted it in the gate lock. With a bit of effort, it slid out of place, and Ruby pushed into the cemetery, Maggie and Eleanor on her heels.

It was still a beautiful place, even in the dead of winter. Marble reliefs of angels and brown obelisks dotted the back of the cemetery, the oldest markers there, and smaller granite headstones lined the front. In the center stood two altar tombs, gray and mossy now from a century and a half of exposure to the elements, where Ruby's great-grandfather George and his wife Charlotte had been laid to rest. Eleanor, her face fixed in an expression of wonder, approached them and traced her fingers along their names.

"There's so much history in here," she said.

"Good and bad," Maggie added, which earned her identical looks of affectionate frustration from both Eleanor and Ruby. She glanced back and forth between the two of them, head bobbing. "Okay, that's weird," she said.

"My father never knew George," Ruby continued, undeterred. "But Charlotte lived until he was a boy," Ruby said, approaching their graves. "He told me she was the most unaffected person he'd ever met, not at all like the women he knew from his own father's business dinners, who he said were, as I recall, a bunch of 'preening hens pretending to be swans.'" Eleanor chuckled. "She taught him to cook when he visited the house and read him stories in the library. My father loved books as much I do."

Eleanor faced Ruby with a softness on her face that warmed Ruby's heart. "Yes," she agreed, then paused. "He does."

By using the present tense, Eleanor declared her acceptance of all Ruby had shared with her at the hospital. It sent silent shock waves of hope returning to her heart. Ruby walked a few steps away to a marble statue of a cross tucked beneath the branches of an overhanging mulberry tree. Eleanor followed and stopped short when she saw the name inscribed on the stone.

Elizabeth "Alice" Hurst
Beloved Mother
Departed this world
December 23, 1949

And beneath those words, a curious epitaph:

I must go now,
but I am only
in the next room,
waiting to meet you again.

Ruby watched as Eleanor silently mouthed the words. Then, with a hand clasped to her mouth, she bent over and released a sob that tore through Ruby's chest until it felt like she was being ripped in half at the sound. Both she and Maggie rushed to Eleanor's side and, without words, collected her in a tangled embrace. Eleanor's cries pierced the quiet afternoon, and soon, Ruby had the young woman's face cupped between her hands, wiping away tears.

"Those are the same words my mother had engraved on her parents' headstone," the girl sobbed between shuddering breaths. "She said it was her favorite because it—" Eleanor hiccuped, "—it gave her hope that she would see them again one day."

Ruby's heart ached. "She didn't leave you, Eleanor," she finally said in a firm, tender voice. "It all makes sense now: Marianne's journal. Vera's message. My mother's disappearance on that day, so long ago." She swiped a thumb across Eleanor's cheeks. "She didn't leave us, Eleanor. She's still here, somewhere. *Sometime*."

Eleanor's face crumpled again as she nodded. Maggie moved a tendril of hair, damp from her friend's tears, off Eleanor's cheek and leaned her head on the girl's shoulder.

"Something went wrong," Ruby continued, breathless, "I don't know what...and I don't know why...but I know that our mother didn't choose to leave us behind."

"But the message she wrote," Eleanor argued, wiping away her tears. "*Anywhere but here. Anywhere but now.* That sounds a lot like she wanted to leave, just like I thought."

Maggie lifted her head. "Elle, you told me how sad she was after those miscarriages. She didn't want to leave you. She wanted more of you!"

Ruby pulled back and peered at the grave, remembering the warmth of her mother's voice. "And then she had me," she said, closing her eyes. A small hand found its way into hers.

"Sisters," Eleanor whispered, and the word filled Ruby with a joy unlike any she had ever known. Standing among the graves of her ancestors, of her gracious, beloved father and the unknown woman who had been buried in her mother's place, Ruby felt her history click into place, the last piece of the puzzle finally uncovered, back where it belonged.

"Sisters," Ruby repeated, and she pulled Eleanor into her arms. They stood there, the two of them locked in an embrace that could have lasted hours or minutes but not long enough to account for all the years they had gone without each other. There was so much time to make up for.

Maggie broke the silence. "Aunt Ruby, you've got yourself a big sister now. How crazy is that?"

Ruby gave an exasperated laugh as she released Eleanor. "And you, Margaret, have got yourself another aunt."

Eleanor and Maggie looked sharply at one another, and then both of them burst out laughing. The sound rang out like bells in the graveyard. "Oh my God!" Eleanor squealed as she pulled Maggie into another hug. "You're my niece!"

"You know, I'm all out of surprised feelings," Maggie replied with a grin. "I hope we're all on the same page about how we're never going to be able to explain any of this."

"Why should we have to explain it?" Ruby asked. "We know, and that's all that matters now."

Eleanor grimaced. "That's not exactly true."

"Why not?" Ruby asked, but then the realization hit her like a runaway train. "Oh," she sighed. "*James.*"

"Yeah."

"Dammit," Maggie said.

"Margaret," Ruby chided.

"*Maggie.*"

"Guys!" Eleanor interrupted.

"Where is James right now?" Ruby asked Eleanor.

"At the store." She stole a glance at her watch. "We don't open for another half hour..." The invitation was available to Ruby, should she want to take it.

She thought of the man she had only ever seen in news reports or stolen glances when Marianne would drive through town, hoping to catch a glimpse of him through the bookstore windows. Even as she had tried for the last six years to satisfy her curiosity about the man who possessed her biological father's name—and who had been married to a woman with her mother's face—Ruby had never been able to fully accept even her theories about Alice.

Eleanor showing up with Marianne's journal had changed it all.

Ruby thought of the line in that famous Christmas carol, the one that sang of a thrill of hope and a weary world rejoicing. This moment, here in a cold, abandoned cemetery with her newfound family, is what that felt like.

Five minutes later, the four of them were barreling out of the driveway, Marianne behind the wheel, heading east into town. Ruby's stomach twisted and flipped as they drove. She was about to see her father again, a man who, in an awful turn of events, was close to forty years her junior and never likely to look upon her as anything other than a reclusive old woman, much less a daughter. She pushed her shoulders back and set her chin. Be that as it may, Ruby would choose courage now and allow it to see her through.

As they parked in front of the store, Ruby peeked up at the sign in the front window.

Bluestocking Books, Established 2000.

Here they were, four bluestockings, who had been brought together by a book and utterly transformed by what they found there. Perhaps it had been a premonition of the future that tempted Vera Black to choose Bluestocking Books as the moniker for her family's business, knowing that it would one day represent more than just women who loved to discover new worlds in the pages of books, but women who would come to discover each other, and in each other, themselves.

Ruby got out of the passenger seat and stood on the sidewalk. She peered into the front window where a large Christmas tree was already lit and blinking to a merry tune. No one was visible from where she stood, but she could see an open door to an office down the hall, and the light was on. Her breathing sputtered. She felt like a foolish child whose emotions regularly got the best of her. But wasn't that what she was, still? Someone's child? A daughter never stops being a daughter, no matter how old she grows.

"Are you okay?" Eleanor asked as she came up beside her and looped their arms together.

Acting like a big sister already.

"Of course I'm alright," Ruby replied as she cleared her voice, reverting to her usual stoicism. "I have no expectations of your fath—of James. How could I? I just want to see him."

"Then let's do it," Eleanor replied and steered Ruby towards the entrance, Maggie and Marianne close behind. The happy jingle of tiny brass bells over the door announced their arrival.

"We're not open yet!" came a man's voice from down the hall. A moment later, that man came through the doorway of his office. Ruby scanned him up and down as she searched for any sign of herself in his appearance, taking in his comfortable jeans and sweater combo, his serious face and kind eyes, and his long, lean body. There was no doubt that he was Eleanor's father. She had his coloring and height, and Ruby could see little of herself in him except for, perhaps, her slender figure. She was surprised by the sadness that rushed through her.

James Black did a double take as he noted Eleanor's company. "Hi, sweetheart," he said, stepping closer to the group. "I didn't think you'd be back this early."

"I know, Dad," Eleanor replied. "I just wanted to bring Ruby by the store so she could see it."

James locked eyes with Ruby, and his own softened at what he saw there, the fear that this would end poorly and her blasted, persistent hope that it wouldn't. He extended his hand toward her. "It's nice to have you here, Ms. Hurst," he said. His hands were large and soft, the hands of an academic man, and they held Ruby's own like it was a small bird in need of the gentlest touch. Ruby swallowed down the lump in her throat.

"You can call me Ruby," she said. "Please."

James smiled, the thin skin around his eyes crinkling into tiny smiles of their own. "Okay. Ruby it is, then." He released her hand and stepped back like any normal human would do after seeing a virtual a stranger, but it left the air around Ruby colder than before.

"Would you like a tour of the shop?" Eleanor asked. "Then we can go next door to Agatha's and have some coffee and croissants."

"Oh, I would kill for a cheese Danish right about now," said Maggie, and everyone laughed.

Eleanor took Ruby's arm again and showed her the book tree she'd constructed in the large front window, draped with holiday lights.

"How creative," Ruby mused. "I think I might prefer this type of Christmas tree."

"You've got plenty of books to choose from."

"As do you," James said over his shoulder as he made himself a cup of coffee behind the register. "How many books are in your personal collection?"

"Seven thousand," Eleanor interjected, the awe in her voice apparent even now. "I almost fell out of my seat when Ruby told me that. Can you imagine?"

"You falling out of your seat?" James joked. "Yes, I can."

Ruby listened to Eleanor and James with a sort of wonder in her heart, and she waited for the jealousy to rise in its place at their familial teasing. But, blessedly, that old emotion never came, a quiet kind of gift on its own.

"You're welcome to come visit the library sometime if you'd like," said Ruby to James. "It's rarely had anyone but me or Marianne for company."

"That would be wonderful," James replied. His smart watch buzzed, and he shuffled over to flip the *Open* sign on the front door. Then he offered Ruby an apologetic smile. "Thank you for coming by. I have to get back to work, but please stop and say hello any time you'd like."

Ruby looked into the eyes of her father and reveled in the kindness she saw reflected there. It would have to be enough for now. "I will."

As James retreated to his office, Ruby turned back to Eleanor. "The desk," she said in a low voice. "Would you mind showing it to me?"

Eleanor peeked around the bookshelf closest to the register to be sure that James was gone. Before leading them to the stock room. "Yeah, it's back here."

Inside, there was little space for Maggie, Marianne, and Ruby to do anything other than stand and watch as Eleanor approached the heavy oak desk. Immediately, the room grew warm, the delicious scent of cinnamon and sugar filling the air. The four of them gasped in unison, and Ruby was overwhelmed by the feeling of home. "You said that the bookstore wanted us to find the truth, Maggie," Eleanor said, cheeks flushed. "I think you were right."

"I have a question, though," said Maggie. "How did the journal end up in the desk to begin with, and why did Vera not use it to come back to the present immediately once she got to 1944? She sounds like a smart woman. She must have known it was the journal that sent her to the past."

Eleanor furrowed her brows. "You're right. It doesn't make sense."

Marianne stepped forward. "When I left William's house that day, I came back here to my apartment upstairs. On the way back down, I dropped the journal on his desk so he would find it. I wanted him to know I'd heard what he thought of me." She paused. "Or what I *assumed* he thought of me."

"And then Mother found it in the library a few days before she disappeared," Ruby added. Her thoughts raced as she tried to piece it all together. "But Father got angry when he saw her reading it and took it away. She must have already tried to look in the desk, but it wasn't there yet."

"And the journal didn't travel with her, or you wouldn't have found it here, Eleanor," said Maggie.

"True," Eleanor agreed. "If it had, there would have been two copies in the past and Mom would have had no problem coming back."

"You have to be holding the journal for it to travel with you," Marianne added. "It's how I brought it to 1936 in the first place."

"Okay, so after Marianne left it on William's desk, he put it in his library," Eleanor said. "Then Mom found it, William took it away again, and sometime after Mom left Ruby on the beach he hid it inside the desk."

Ruby nodded. "I assume so. Once he had completed *The Woman of Valbrooke Hall*."

Eleanor shook her head. "Okay, but from everything Marianne said last night, it sounds like you have to be reading the words you've written aloud in order to time travel."

"Like a spell!" Maggie interjected and crossed her arms, frowning. "That Biddy Clare was a menace."

Eleanor scoffed. "Right, and that means Mom would have been looking right at the journal when she disappeared, even though she wasn't holding it. So, who put it in the hidden compartment after she was gone?"

A familiar voice rang out from behind them. "I did."

The group whirled to find Agatha standing there at the entrance to the stockroom, her hands pressed against her ample chest as she stared in horror at the four of them.

"Agatha!" Eleanor exclaimed. "What are you doing here?"

The woman glanced at Ruby, terrified curiosity written all over her normally cheerful face, and made a sound somewhere between a whimper and a cry. "I saw you pull up outside. I nearly spilled my coffee at the sight of Ruby Hurst walking into your store, so I came over to say hello." Maggie made a face at her aunt that said *Or find some good gossip.* "But—but then I heard y'all talking about time travel and a hidden journal." She lowered her voice. "And I got curious."

"So you took it upon yourself to just stand outside the door and listen?" Ruby demanded.

Agatha winced. "When you hear someone mention time travel like they're being serious, tell me you don't stop to eavesdrop just a little."

"Forget the eavesdropping, Agatha," said Eleanor. She stepped closer to her neighbor with fire in her eyes. "What do you mean *you* put the journal in the desk?"

Agatha began to visibly shake. "I saw Vera with it," she said, pointing a finger at the desk. "She was sitting on the floor there holding a leather journal the day she went missing."

Eleanor stilled, her eyes fixed on Agatha. "That's right," she breathed.

"What?" Maggie asked.

"You told police you saw her here that day," Eleanor replied, still staring at her neighbor.

"I brought her some coffee. We'd usually visit with each other in the afternoons when work slowed down. Vera was sitting right here in this room, right next to her desk, when I came in. She was scribbling in that book, but that wasn't anything new, so I just waved hello and went over to the counter to put our drinks down."

All time and sound had slowed to this moment, to the nervous timbre of Agatha's voice as she spoke. No one moved.

"I was chatting away from behind the register, thinking Vera was listening quietly, as was her habit, until I finally realized it had been more than five minutes of total silence on her end." Maggie coughed to cover up a snort, but no one seemed to notice. "And then—" Agatha said, looking around as if for someone to save her from what she was about to reveal, "I walked over to the stock room, and...she was gone. Just...*gone*. I knew she hadn't left because I was talking to her the whole time. I would have seen her. She would've had to walk right past me to go out the front or back doors."

"But you didn't tell the police any of this," Eleanor said, accusatory.

"Well, what was I supposed to say?" Agatha protested, her cheeks aflame. "That my friend just magically disappeared into thin air? They'd have thought I was lying! That I had something to do with it!"

Ruby could do without the woman's dramatics, but she felt empathy for poor Agatha. She understood her fears more than anyone else in that room ever could.

"What about the journal?" Maggie interjected. "You said you saw it, too?"

"I did," Agatha replied with another frightened glance at the desk. "After I came in here, I called out Vera's name a bunch of times and walked around the store, but she was nowhere to be seen. I came back, scared out of my wits, and saw the book on the floor. I picked it up and saw her handwriting, and it just felt...*wrong*. You know? It felt like I was holding something haunted. *Possessed*."

"So you hid it again and ran," Ruby said. It wasn't a question.

"How did you even know to put it in the secret compartment?" Eleanor asked.

Agatha glanced down at it and back to Eleanor. "I saw it there where Vera'd been sitting, wide open, and shoved it in. I wasn't thinking except to wonder if I'd lost my mind." Her chin wobbled, and her voice shook. "I didn't know what to do or feel or say, so I just told the police I'd seen Vera at the store, and everything was fine. I knew they wouldn't find her because...well...I knew she wasn't *here* anymore. But how do you tell someone that?"

No one had the answer, so no one spoke.

"And how do you keep a secret like that?" Eleanor mused sadly. "It must have been eating you alive."

Agatha stepped forward, a desperate request for forgiveness engraved on her features. "I'm so sorry, Eleanor. Please know I would never want to cause pain for you or James. Forgive me. For keeping it all a secret. For not at least telling the police about the journal so you could have tried to figure this out sooner."

Ruby placed her hand on Agatha's arm, and the woman looked at it as if it were a snake poised to sink its fangs into her flesh at any moment. Ruby wanted to laugh but held her composure. "We've all kept our secrets, Agatha. Some for far less justifiable reasons than you kept yours."

"But what does it all mean?" Agatha demanded, suddenly suspicious. "You think Vera went back in time that day?"

Ruby, Maggie, Eleanor, and Marianne all eyed one another. Then Ruby clasped Agatha's hand between hers, resigned. She was done hiding now.

"How about you make us some coffee, and we tell you all about it?"

24

Eleanor

Eleanor had never felt so exhilarated. Or so drained. As happy as she was about finding out she had a long-lost sister—and a niece!—the emotional toll of the previous week had left her poured out. It wasn't the same kind of emptiness Eleanor had experienced after her Mom disappeared—that had been the hollow, lifeless sort—but rather a simultaneously sad and relieved kind of emptiness. For the first time in six years, Eleanor felt truly capable of joy, but it would have to come in time. New family or not, the fact remained that her mom was gone, and no amount of mysterious messages, secret journals, or surprise confessions would change that reality.

Eleanor would always grieve.

But she was beginning to be okay with that now.

The bookstore was quiet just two days before Christmas. Curled up in her dad's office, Eleanor nibbled on a handful of Agatha's ginger snaps and zoned out to the latest and greatest Hallmark movie. They were so predictable and earnest, but Eleanor needed that right now. It was the first Christmas that she actually *wanted* to watch a sappy holiday rom-com instead of using it as a distraction from her anger and sorrow. It was nice. Her mind was at rest, at least for the moment.

James padded into the office and rolled his eyes when he saw what was on the computer. "Do we have to?" he asked.

"Hey, nobody's making you watch, old man. You're still on the clock," Eleanor said as she pointed to the shop.

"Old?" James replied, feigning hurt. "And only for another thirty minutes. Then I get to spend the next week celebrating the best holiday ever with my only daughter." For the hundredth time, Eleanor thought of Ruby. *Her sister.* Her father's other daughter, even though he would never know. It didn't change the fact that she wished Ruby could have more time with James, even if that looked as simple as joining the two of them for a cheesy Christmas movie.

"What would you prefer I watch?" Eleanor asked. "*National Lampoon?* Please kill me now."

"You know me well." James leaned on the desk and ruffled Eleanor's hair. "What's new with you, kiddo?"

If only I could tell you, she thought. Instead of answering, Eleanor stood up and threw herself in her dad's arms, squeezing hard. James pulled Eleanor in a little tighter. She hadn't been hugged by him like this, just for the sake of being close, in longer than she could remember. For six years, her dad's hugs had been attempts to either console or congratulate her for some reason, and Eleanor hadn't known how much she missed them. James had been the safe parent, the stable and reliable one, and Eleanor had taken for granted his transparent efforts to spend time with her. She had never truly considered his terrible grief over the loss of his wife and how it might be soothed with the knowledge that he could still find joy in the presence of his daughter.

"Dad," Eleanor said as she released him. James looked at her with an expectant smile. "I'm sorry I've never asked how *you're* doing."

He blinked, and his smile faltered until it fell into a frown. "Eleanor," he began, his voice a gentle warning against her guilt.

"I'm serious," Eleanor continued. She collapsed back into his swivel chair, spinning slightly, and pulled her knees up to her chest. "I know you were hurting when Mom disappeared, and I was too young to understand how much. But now?"

"I didn't expect you to ask," James replied as he leaned over to meet her eyes. "I'm the parent here, Eleanor, not you. It was—*is*—my job to protect and support you."

"So? I should have shown up for you, too."

"You did, honey. You were here with me, Elle, and that was enough. Needing to be your dad even when I didn't want to get out of bed some days kept me alive. It kept me eating and working and breathing until, eventually, I was able to forget my grief, even if just for one minute of the day."

"Did that feel like a betrayal to Mom?" Eleanor asked.

"Sometimes, yeah," her dad admitted. "But it was also a reminder that you can suffer the unimaginable and, as much as you hate that the world keeps turning and people move on, one day you find yourself in a place with a bit of light. And the closer you move towards it, the brighter it gets. That's what I tried to do. For both of us."

"That's what I'm trying to do now."

"And how's that been going so far?"

Eleanor scoffed. "Not too great. Not until recently, anyway."

"It helps to have friends," James replied with a knowing smile. "Anti-depressants help, too."

Eleanor started. "You're on meds?" She was impressed. "Since when?"

"A few years ago," James answered. "And I went to counseling for about a year."

Eleanor felt betrayed by the news. She had seen a child psychologist who specialized in grief trauma for a while when she was in first grade, but she never felt as peaceful in that office as she had in Bluestocking Books. James had never mentioned his own treatment before.

"I'm glad," she said. "But why didn't you tell me?"

"I didn't want to put that pressure on you to go back or have you feeling like it was your responsibility to fix me," he replied. "I guess I thought that if I got better, then you would get better by proxy."

"I didn't know you had a savior complex, Dad," Eleanor teased.

"It comes with the territory," he replied with a shrug. "Sometimes we do stupid things in the name of protecting our kids without realizing we're actually hiding behind them."

"Wow," Eleanor said with a nod."Insightful."

"It's all the therapy."

"I guess your savior complex worked a little," Eleanor told him as she scooted back and stretched out her legs. "Letting me help so much in the shop was a big deal for me. It still is."

"I worried about that at first. You just threw yourself in, begging to work at the tender age of seven. It was a little unhealthy, now that I think about it."

Eleanor laughed. "There is no such thing as an unhealthy affection for books."

"It was more than that, and you know it," James said, parental concern knit between his brows. "I've always worried about you, Elle. You never seemed interested in the kids at school or being in clubs. All you wanted to do was be here at Bluestocking."

The image of the secret desk compartment popped into Eleanor's mind. "It's a good place to hide," she noted.

"There are worse places," James conceded. "That's true. But I don't want you to hide, sweetheart. Not out of fear and especially not for my sake. There's still a whole lot of life we have to live." He reached over and grabbed the last ginger snap from Eleanor's plate. "At first, I wanted to stay away from here, maybe close up shop and move. But eventually, I realized I didn't want to go anywhere Vera hadn't been. This is her home, her life. *Our* life."

Eleanor watched her dad chew, his gaze off somewhere inside his thoughts, and gathered her courage. "Dad?" she asked.

"Hmm?"

"Do you really believe Mom is dead?"

James dropped the cookie. "I—" he began. His shoulders sank along with his face. "I pray every single day that she's not." Eleanor waited, silent, for him to continue. "I get why you would rather believe that she's here in the world, happier somewhere—" he choked up "—than not here at all."

Eleanor swallowed back her response.

She is here, Dad. She never left, not in the way we think. We'll never be able to get her back, but she didn't walk away from us, and she wasn't hurt by anyone. Oh, and guess what? You have another daughter because you never knew that Mom was pregnant when she disappeared. How's that for a surprise?

"But if I had to choose an answer, sweetheart," James said forlornly, "I would have to say yes. I do think your Mom is gone. Nothing else makes sense."

Eleanor couldn't bear the sorrowful look on her father's face. She thought of Ruby and of William. How he had tried to protect Ruby but never dared to be truthful until the very end. Would James have enough courage to believe his daughter—*his daughters*—if she told him the truth about what they'd discovered together? Eleanor nearly reached out to him as he looked down at his hands, lost in thought. But she stopped herself.

No. She couldn't. It wasn't her story to tell. Ruby had told one father the truth and been dismissed for too long. She deserved another chance to try again.

Eleanor prayed that this time would be different than the last.

~~~

Eleanor helped her dad close up the shop at noon and they walked back home together in the chill. She wondered if they should stay open another day in case of last-minute shoppers, anything to give their dismal finances a boost before the end of the year. But one day of little better than average sales wouldn't accomplish the rescue they so desperately needed. Besides, the day after Christmas was a better bet anyway, when people exchanged books they'd received or spent their stocking stuffer gift cards.
~~~

She pushed for James to share a little bit of information about their struggles and ask for community support, but he shot down the mention of Bluestocking's financial woes in a hot second. He reasoned that Vera's disappearance had brought them enough sympathy money, and he didn't want to ask for anymore. Eleanor told him pride goeth before the fall, to which he replied, "'*Goeth*,' really? Have we been transported back to Middle England?"

"We could be," she mumbled under her breath and then patted herself on the back for making a time travel joke. Progress.

"Aunt Ruby wants to go into Savannah to see the Christmas lights tomorrow," Maggie said to Eleanor later on the phone. Eleanor paused in her tidying of the living room.

"That's a sentence I never thought I would hear," she replied and went back to karate-chopping the pillows. "You guys should just come with us this afternoon. We're doing a trolley tour."

Maggie made a shivering sound. "Open air? It's *freezing*."

Eleanor laughed. "It gets so much colder where you live! I don't understand why you're always such a baby about this."

"Because I stay inside like a sane person," Maggie retorted. "I thought winters in Georgia were mild, but the past two days have had me feeling like I never left Virginia."

"Good. Maybe it will snow here like it does there."

"Be careful what you wish for, dude," Maggie said. "We don't play around. You'll be buried in your house for days."

Eleanor rolled her eyes. "Christmas is in two days. It's not like we're going anywhere."

"Then let's hope for snow," Maggie exclaimed. "But don't say I didn't warn you."

Eleanor tossed a blanket onto the couch. "Ask Ruby and Marianne. Ben, too." Christmas lights in Savannah with her newfound family—*her family!*—sounded exactly like what Eleanor needed.

"Okay, fine," Maggie replied. "How can I deny my newest aunt the pleasure of my company?"

"That's so freaking weird," Eleanor said with a chuckle. "Do you think Ruby will want to come since Dad will be there?"

She could almost hear Maggie lift an eyebrow. "Honestly? I think she's hoping he will." Eleanor's stomach fluttered at the thought of them all together, bundled up against the cold, marveling at the absurd and wonderful displays of Christmas lights. It was more than she could have ever hoped to ask for or even thought to ask for, but her nerves went a bit haywire on behalf of Ruby and James. They deserved to get to know each other, even as neighbors, since they would never have the opportunity to know each other as they really were: father and daughter.

With the plan in place, Eleanor trudged up the stairs to her bedroom, thoroughly overwhelmed by the events of the past few weeks and longing for the comfort of her soft, sensuous bed, even for just a few minutes. Down now from the high of all she had learned about her mother, her body was screaming at her to take a little cat nap.

Scrambling beneath the heavy, down comforter, her face pressed deep into the pillows, Eleanor happily obliged.

~~~

Vera moved down the main street, wild and tangled copper curls swirling around her head as though they were living creatures, and a pulse of fear shot through Eleanor's chest.

Wait? Hadn't she just gone upstairs to take a nap?

This was a dream. Somehow, as she struggled to keep up with her mom, calling out her name again and again, Eleanor was aware that this wasn't reality. Indeed, the town square, normally a bright and busy place at this time of day, was empty.

Not just empty. Silent and gray. Dead.

But Eleanor's mom was very much alive.

"Mom, wait!" Eleanor cried once more, willing the dream to go on. If she could just hear Vera's voice again, just feel her touch. "Please!"
~~~

Her mother stopped in front of the bookstore, a place filled with so much warmth and light, and peered, cautious and searching, through the window. Eleanor stopped running, her breath caught in her throat.

"Mom?" she whispered. Her mother's eyes were fixed on a point inside the shop, and she pressed her hands to her mouth as a sound, almost feral with emotion, escaped from between her fingers. Slowly, Vera stepped towards the door. And then, with the quickness of a child scrambling for her long-lost toy, she disappeared inside.

"Mom!" Eleanor shouted as she ran, her vision blurred by tears. She jerked at the door handle, but it was locked.

"No," she gasped, pulling harder. "Mom, *please*. Come back."

Inside, the bookstore was aglow with soft, yellow light, the shelves full and inviting. Eleanor longed to walk between them and run her fingers across the spines of every book as she lingered, safe and home. But still, the door wouldn't budge.

Eleanor pressed her face to the glass, desperate for her mom to return and let her into the shop. She banged on the door.

No one answered. Again and again, Eleanor called for her mother, but the bookstore was empty.

Her mom was gone. Inside, the lights went out.

25

Ruby

December 23rd had become frigid, with a gray overcast sky and freeze warnings on the news. The clouds hung low over the estate, heavy and full of what would likely turn into ice showers, which would transform every blacktop in town into a slippery, invisible path toward certain death.

In other words, December 23rd was turning out to be exactly what Ruby expected.

But today was better than all the previous anniversaries because today, Ruby was not alone anymore. Today, Ruby had a *family*. It was enough to make her kiss Marianne on the cheek that afternoon as she prepped cinnamon rolls for the oven, nearly causing her housekeeper to burn her hand on the stove in shock.

Ruby made herself a cup of Earl gray tea and leaned against the counter top where Marianne stood, cutting the rolled-up dough into thick, beautiful coins. "I'm so glad you're here," Ruby said, steeling herself against the emotion that made her throat feel as though it were stuffed with cotton.

Marianne put her knife down and reached a flour-covered hand out to Ruby, who returned the gesture. "You're welcome, honey," she said simply. "There's no other place I'd rather be."

For one, the pet name didn't bother Ruby at all.

A companionable silence settled between the two women, no longer just employer and employee but actual friends. Ruby turned the phrase over in her mind, examining the definition against what she had known of friendship in the past, which was very little. The flavor of it was no longer a sour taste but an intriguing and delicate sweetness that had Ruby reaching for more. She gave Marianne's hand a tender squeeze and left the kitchen for the library.

In her favorite chair, Ruby pictured Alice as she had been back then, a beautiful woman with long, red curls. Statuesque and, yet, never threatening. Just proud. Marianne could never have known what she set in motion when she first wrote in that journal, even if Biddy Clare did when she hand-stitched each page and spoke words of mischief over it. Ruby knew her friend was in mourning for William all over again. But, like Ruby herself, she also knew Marianne wouldn't choose to change it now. Against all odds, Ruby finally believed her life had not been a waste. It had simply been a long, slow walk in the trees toward this moment on the horizon.

The magic of the bookstore had done its good work. Eleanor—lovely, brave Eleanor— had been the conduit for it all, and without her, Ruby would have remained the broken woman she had become. Angry. Bitter. Terribly, awfully sad. Perhaps another woman would look at her now and think it was too little, too late. But not Ruby. The secret hope she had harbored deep within her spirit was as stubborn as she was. It had never given up on her, even when she had given up on it.

A knock at the front door broke through Ruby's reverie, and she started, rising to answer the door. "I've got it, Marianne," she said to her friend, who had emerged from the kitchen with flour on her cheek. "Go wipe your face."

Ruby pulled open the door as another knock sounded and found Eleanor—her hair nearly blown out of its bun and her clothes a rumpled mess, gasping as though she had just run a marathon—behind it.

"Eleanor!" she cried, pulling the girl into the foyer. She scanned her for bodily injury. "How did you get here? Are you hurt? What's wrong?"

"She's coming back," Eleanor said in a rush of words, clasping Ruby's warm hands inside her own, chilled by the cold. "My mom. *Our mom.* She's coming back."

~~~

"This just keeps getting better and better," Maggie said, a feral grin on her face as she opened up the refrigerator and swiped a soda. Then she grabbed a bottle of Chardonnay from the wine rack and held it up to her aunt.

"What are you doing?" Ruby demanded, swiping the bottle from her niece's grip.

"I'm getting you a drink, Aunt Ruby," Maggie said, grinning. "I figured you might need one."

"Pour me one, too," Marianne said. Ruby glanced back and forth between the two of them and then, after a visible war with herself, nodded at Maggie.

"Yes!" her niece replied with a triumphant raise of the bottle. "Three cheers all around for the lost bluestockings of Hawthorn." She poured Marianne and Ruby a glass of wine and handed them out.

Ruby started to sip hers but decided to screw decorum and gulped nearly half of the glass instead. Maggie whooped and hopped up onto the counter, looking ready to watch her aunt toss back the entire bottle.

"Get down from there," Ruby said as she pressed the back of her hand to her lips, lightheaded. Good Lord, this child. "That counter wasn't made to host your bottom."

Maggie rolled her eyes but dropped back to her feet. "Anyway," she said in a sing-song voice. "Why aren't you guys more excited?"
~~~

"Because we only have a theory," Eleanor answered, taking a long swig from her drink.

"A theory that sent you racing over here like your hair was on fire," Maggie pointed out with a tip of her can.

Ruby bit her lip as Eleanor glanced her way. "She has a point."

"Yes, but now that I've said it aloud..." she trailed off.

"You don't want to get your hopes up?" Ruby finished for her.

Eleanor nodded. Ruby watched her sister stare off into space and put her glass down on the counter. "Eleanor, look at what we've already done," she said, raising her arms out to the side. "We found one another. And now we know each other. Best of all, we still have time to know each other *more*. If our mother—" Here, Ruby paused with a smile. *Our mother.* "If she doesn't ever come home to us, won't that still be enough? How much more extraordinary magic does a person need in her life to celebrate it?"

Eleanor's chin trembled as she listened. After a deep, shuddering breath, she said, "Ruby Hurst, that salt water really did a number on you."

Ruby burst out laughing, a sound that stunned even her, and it was such a lovely moment that time seemed to pause around them, offering itself as a gift. Both eyebrows raised, Maggie watched the scene unfold with her habitual delight, and Eleanor began to laugh, as well.

"This wine is amazing," Marianne said, holding her glass up in the air as if to toast the others.

Maggie clinked her can with Eleanor's.

"Trust Aunt Ruby to have the good stuff."

"I aim to please," Ruby replied flatly.

"Okay, let's get back to business," Maggie continued, her face flushed from wine and excitement. She cleared her throat and began to count her fingers. "One, Eleanor had a dream about her mother going into the bookshop. Two, Alice vanished today, seventy-five years ago, when Aunt Ruby was five. Three, Vera disappeared almost six years ago *from the bookshop.* So, now that we know Alice and Vera are more than likely the same person, and assuming Vera was pregnant when she went back to 1944 and time moves at the same pace in both the past and present, then that means when Alice vanished on that beach, it was because she actually came back to the present, which, calculating her total time in Hawthorn with the years since Vera disappeared, would be...*today*." Maggie, out of breath, leaned back against the counter and took another sip of her wine.

"That about sums it up," Eleanor said.

"We can talk about this all day," Ruby interjected, "but we haven't solved the biggest problem. How does she come back without the journal?"

"Oh, I figured that out," Eleanor replied. At their confused stares, she crossed her arms. "*C'mon*, guys. There's no rule that the person who time travels has to be the same person who writes in the journal. Like Maggie said, it's a spell. You just have to want it really badly, the way Marianne did. The way my Mom did when she was so sad about her losing her babies. The bookstore wanted *me* to find Marianne's draft and fix everything Biddy Clare screwed up. So I'm going to be the one who brings Mom back."

Maggie blew out a star breath. "Well, okay then."

"Oh, and we have to go back to the bookstore, too," Eleanor added.

"Are we still going to see the Christmas lights?" Maggie asked, childish hope written on her elfin features.

Eleanor giggled, but Ruby frowned. "We can't," she said. "We need to be at the shop."

"Right now?" Eleanor asked. "We have time, I think."

"And how can you be certain of that?" Ruby asked. Her brows inched closer together.

Eleanor finished off her soda and tossed it into the trash. "Well, what time did Mom take you to the beach that day?"

Ruby blinked. "Oh."

Maggie breathed, "*Oh.*"

"Right," Eleanor said as the realization dawned on them. "Whatever time Alice disappeared is the time—"

"That Vera shows up at the bookshop," Ruby finished. "It was almost evening when I was found. The sun was setting, and it was starting to get dark."

"So it was, what, four o'clock when you got to the beach?" Marianne guessed. "That's in two hours."

"Close to it," Ruby replied.

Eleanor asked for Maggie's cell phone. She typed for a few seconds and then looked up at them all with triumph in her eyes. "According to Google, the sun set on Tybee Island at 5:24 p.m. on December 23rd, 1949."

Impressed, Ruby said, "Then, yes, I'd say we arrived about four o'clock. Perhaps I should give one of those phones a try."

"Okay, okay, don't get ahead of yourself," Maggie quipped.

"Do you have a copy of the police report?" Eleanor asked, moving towards the library. Everyone followed. "It would have the time you were found, wouldn't it, Ruby?"

"That's genius," Maggie said.

Ruby walked around behind her father's desk and pulled a tiny key out from a marble stone jar that looked like a paperweight. Then she unlocked a bottom drawer and pulled out a thick file folder. It was old and faded, as though it had been sifted through many, many times over many, many years. Ruby pulled out a typed sheet of paper and put her glasses on. "Here it is." She scanned the page. "I was found at approximately 5:13 p.m. The police arrived at 5:20 p.m., so she must have disappeared right around five," Ruby said, her face softening at the memory.

"Which gives us plenty of time to go see the Christmas lights," Maggie said.

Marianne jumped in. "Maggie, collect yourself, child."

"Look outside, Marianne," Maggie replied. "It's pretty dark already, and it's not even two. Besides, the shop is closed, and it will give us something better to do than sit here and get anxious."

"Or drunk," Eleanor added, looking at both Marianne and Ruby. "Besides, Dad already bought all of our tickets, and I, for one, am tired of sitting around feeling sad. Even if this doesn't work, Ruby's right. We should do something fun to celebrate."

Ruby's heart skipped. "I agree."

"Is that okay?" Marianne asked, taking in Ruby's pale face. "Spending a whole afternoon with James after all of this?"

It was more than okay. Ruby would take all the time she could get, even though she had decided never to tell James who she was. *Not unless...*

"Yes," she said quietly. Eleanor reached over and pulled Ruby into a sharp hug. She smelled like molasses and cinnamon. Ruby inhaled a deep breath and relaxed into her sister, held close by someone she loved.

The stubborn hope within her cheered.

<div style="text-align:center">~~~</div>

The trolley was packed to gills, tourists and locals alike bundled up against the ever-decreasing temperatures and a sky that threatened to burst open with icy rain at any moment. Eleanor and James sat on the bench seat in front of Maggie, Marianne, and Ruby, who stared at the back of her father's head, fascinated by the simplest things. Like the freckle just above his jacket collar and the silvery threads that peeked out of his otherwise jet black hair. This was the man who had helped create her, the man who had never known, as Vera had never known, that his daughter had been living right next to him for almost twenty-five years.

Life was strange.

Reds, greens, blues, whites, and golds shimmered and blinked all around them as the trolley car moved slowly through the Plant Riverside District, historic homes of Georgia's first city lit up with holiday spirit. Ruby gazed at them in wonder, the festive air and hot chocolate in her hands warming her up from the inside out. She decided right then and there that, from now on, she'd do more than just have Benjamin string a few twinkly lights on the front porch. Next year, the Hurst Estate would host a grand holiday lights tour of its own. It was time for Ruby to create a legacy for herself, and she wanted to do it with the people of Hawthorn, starting with the two seated right in front of her.

Ruby smiled into her cup as she sipped the rich, frothy drink. She was already making progress in that direction.

In between detailed descriptions of the homes they passed, the driver cranked up Christmas carols, and it didn't take long before the entire trolley was filled with the sounds of holiday revelers singing at the top of their lungs.

"You know," Maggie said as she leaned up to shout in Eleanor's ear. "This tourist thing is pretty excellent."

James laughed. "Isn't it?" he shouted back. "We haven't done this since Eleanor was a little girl." He swiped up on his phone for the camera and flipped it around to face the four of them. "Everyone lean in and smile!"

Ruby scooted close to Maggie and Marianne and beamed at the camera. Just as James took the photo, a call notification popped up on the screen. *Coastal Town Lender.* With a groan, James put the phone to one ear and covered the other with his hand. Ruby watched Eleanor bite her lip, her eyes fixed on the phone like it was a dangerous animal that might go on the attack.

"Hello?" James answered in a near-shout. "Yeah, I'm sorry. I'm on a tour of Christmas lights right now, and I can barely hear you. Is this an emergency?"

The four women were still as statues as James listened to the voice on the other end of the line. Maggie glanced at Ruby with a wink and waited, a small smile beginning to form on her lips. Ruby's chest constricted as she saw James' expression shift from frightened to utterly disbelieving.

"Say that again?" he said, turning to look at Eleanor, who appeared ready to jump out of her seat. James shook his head. "Is this a joke?"

Eleanor mouthed to her father. "What's wrong?" James shook his head again as he slapped a hand over his mouth.

"My God," he said, muffled. "*All* of it?" Ruby looked down at her hands, unable to bear the beauty of his surprise and delight. The sound of it was enough. "Thank you," he said. "Thank you so much. Oh my God. Yes, Merry Christmas to you, too." Ruby looked up, cautious, as James ended the call and then pressed his fists against his forehead, staring at his daughter with wide, wild eyes.

"You're scaring me, Dad," Eleanor said. "Was that about the shop? What did they say?"

James swiveled and looked at each of the women as though searching for the answer to the myriad of questions that were surely forming in his mind right now. When his eyes fell on Ruby, who met his stare with a smile that shook, the shock in his once-tired face transformed into glorious understanding.

"They said—" he began in a breathless voice, still looking at Ruby. "They said our loan has been paid in full. The bookshop is ours. *Forever.*"

Eleanor gasped and swiveled in her seat, piercing Ruby with a look that asked a thousand questions at once, happy tears in her eyes. Just then, the driver turned the volume up on the chorus of "Joy to the World." The trolley car shook with the sounds of fifty different voices shouting the lyrics as they rumbled down the cobblestone street, the glow of holiday lights enveloping them in their warm embrace. Maggie leaned her head on her aunt's shoulder, and a lump formed in Ruby's throat so that she could barely form the words, but she placed a gloved hand on Eleanor's face and whispered what she could anyway.

"'*Repeat the sounding joy,*'" she sang as the tears spilled over and Eleanor closed her eyes. "*Repeat the sounding joy, repeat, repeat the sounding joy.*'"

26

Eleanor

They finished the trolley tour in a delighted daze, voices hoarse from singing, hearts and bellies full. Ruby never confirmed nor denied that she had been their generous benefactor, but when the four of them split off to their respective vehicles afterward, Ruby and James moved towards his car while Eleanor followed Maggie and Marianne. The three of them watched in silent awe as her dad and Ruby engaged in a hushed conversation that ended with James breaking down in front of the woman who had saved their family, his shoulders quaking with sobs. Eleanor grasped Maggie's arm as Ruby pulled their dad into a quiet embrace, her beautifully lined face crumpled into his chest.

"Turns out," Maggie said as she grinned at her aunt, "that woman's not as cold as I thought she was."

Eleanor scanned Maggie's coy expression with a raised brow. "You did this, didn't you?"

Maggie offered a characteristic shrug. "I don't know what you're talking about."

"You're the worst liar," Eleanor scoffed. But then she threw her arms around Maggie and squeezed as hard as she could. "And the very best niece."

Maggie choked out a laugh. "I'll be a dead one soon if you don't let me breathe."

"Just one more second," Eleanor said, tightening her grip and then falling back to look at her dad again. She still couldn't comprehend what had gone down on that trolley. It was simply too wonderful to be true.

But that was the beauty of this new, hard life. The pain had made way for unexpected joy, joy that might not have been possible without the suffering that preceded it. And, now, she stood here on a half-empty street, awash with the magic of Christmas and so much more.

A whole family.

Well, *almost.*

"I love you, Maggie," Eleanor said to her friend, unashamed.

"As well you should," Maggie replied cheekily. "Now, c'mon." She waved to Ruby, who gave her stunned dad a quick peck on the cheek and opened the car door. "It's time to go see your mom."

~~~

At 4:30 on the dot, Eleanor, Maggie, Marianne, and Ruby left the Black cottage and walked down the street to Bluestocking Books, the sun hidden by nimbostratus clouds that pressed down lower and lower in the sky. The street lamps had already come on, bathing the town square in a soft, golden light that appeared to hush the world around them, making way for the magic they all hoped would come.

As they approached the shop and stood there gazing at the darkened book tree in the window, Eleanor saw it as her mother might see it. Altered in the six years she had been gone, but not diminished. Because of the people of Hawthorn, frustrating as they might be, Vera's legacy in this town had been honored and cherished. Eleanor had never given them the credit they deserved. She hadn't been able to see past her own suffering. She tried to give herself grace as she peered into the shop where she had offered so much of herself in return for
~~~

a haven into which she could disappear from life. Much like Vera had, but in one very different way.

Vera had never meant to disappear. Eleanor might never understand the power that had taken her mother away or why it had stolen Alice from Ruby at such a precious age, but she trusted in the power of the words that would bring her back.

Because they weren't the words of a spell or an enchantment. They were the words of love.

Maybe that was the legacy that would sustain them, even beyond the bookshop. Maybe that was the truth that would be passed down from generation to generation long after Eleanor, Ruby, Marianne, and Maggie were gone.

When all seems lost—when the world seems to offer nothing more than hopelessness and grief—all it takes is a little bit of courage to write it down and trust that, in the end, there will always be another story to tell.

Eleanor was proof of that. So were the women standing next to her.

She unlocked the front door and stepped into the solid warmth of the shop, the others quiet on her heels. The dusky orange light of the late afternoon filtered through the stacks of books as they each moved into the center of the room. They said nothing, for nothing needed to be said, and the quiet that filled the space seemed to breathe with a holy wonder while they waited for the clock to strike 4:45.

Nine minutes.

Eight.

Seven.

Eleanor closed her eyes and pictured the shop as it had appeared in her dream. It was empty of people but full of life, the bookshelves standing like a beloved family to welcome Vera back to the place she called home. Only this time, she was here with Ruby, Marianne, and Maggie.

An actual family.

Without a word, Eleanor opened her eyes and moved like air through the store, switching on lamps that glowed with soft, orange light as the afternoon inched closer and closer to evening, until the room was cast in the same cozy warmth that she had seen through the window in her dream.

And, still, they waited.

"I've always loved this building," Ruby said in a whisper so as not to disturb the anticipation. "It looked much different inside when I was a child, but a lot of it remains the same." She pointed to the window ledge in front where the book tree stood sentry. "Like that bench. I used to sit there and play with my dolls while Mother worked at her desk."

"When did William stop using this location?" Eleanor asked, her voice gentle.

"A few months after her funeral," Ruby replied, fingering the spine of a book on the shelf next to her. "Or that poor unknown woman's funeral, I should say. They had a warehouse near the port, so they converted a section of it into office space and moved there. I think he did it as much for me as for himself. He didn't want me to have to come back to the place where she'd worked or see people I didn't want to see."

"My dad—" Eleanor stopped short.

Ruby pressed her lips into a smile and said, "He *is* your dad, Eleanor. You can say it."

"Yeah. Okay," Eleanor replied. Her pale face flushed. "My dad was the same way. This was the last place Mom was seen, and he didn't want me here as much as I was. He wanted me to make friends and play a sport or something, but I was only interested in the bookshop."

Maggie snorted. "He should have called me."

Eleanor winked at her. "I honestly wasn't interested. No one was unkind to me, but I was just like you, Ruby. I didn't want to be around people. I wanted to read books and work in the bookshop and let that be my life."

"It's not a bad one," Ruby replied.

"No. But it's lonely sometimes."

"Well, you're not lonely anymore," said Maggie, ever the optimist. "You guys are lucky. You've got me now."

"Jesus, be a fence," Ruby muttered.

Eleanor giggled as she glanced at the clock. Her nerves were shot, and her stomach was performing a special sort of gymnastics routine.

Four minutes.

"What if she doesn't show up?" she said in a small voice, staring at the window and the sidewalk beyond.

Ruby put her arm around Eleanor's waist and pulled her close. "Then nothing has changed. We still have each other."

With a hard swallow, Eleanor dipped her chin once. Ruby was right. Their grief would stay with them for the rest of their lives, but it would no longer define them. Instead of loneliness, the future now held a promise. No matter who did or didn't walk into Bluestocking Books that night, Eleanor would choose to hold onto what was with her here and now. Her sister. Her niece. Her family's bookshop.

It was enough.

Two minutes. She reached into her bag and pulled out the journal. Scribbling onto the page beneath her mom's words, she was suddenly overcome by what could only be described as the most powerful, loving embrace Eleanor had ever experienced. Peace—all-surpassing peace—filled her from the inside out.

One minute.

The four of them stilled just before the antique clock on the wall behind them struck a quarter to five. The chime made them all jump as it sounded, piercing the hushed bookshop with its metallic clang. They watched the door, expectant. Hopeful. Eleanor opened her mouth to read what she'd written just as the front door opened.

A familiar head of silver and black, perched atop a heavy winter coat, came bobbing into the room. James huffed as he took in Eleanor, Ruby, Marianne, and Maggie standing in the center of the shop like they had been caught casing the joint. The doorbell jingled as it shut behind him.

"What are y'all doing in here?" he asked, somewhat breathless, as he unzipped his coat. "I was putting our recycling out by the curb and saw the lights on. I thought you guys were headed back to Ruby's place."

Eleanor wriggled free of Ruby's grasp and stepped forward, eyes still on the window behind him, ears attuned to the tick of the clock. "Dad—"

"This was always a hard day for me," Ruby interrupted with a glance at Eleanor. "Now that we've become friends, and there are no customers around, I asked if I could come back and meander a bit."

James' shoulders dropped as he took in Ruby's earnest expression. "Of course," he nodded. "As I said before, you're always welcome."

"I'll promise to ask you next time," Eleanor added with an apologetic smile.

She watched James turn a little circle and look around the shop. "I can't believe it's ours." He looked aside at Ruby, who pressed her hands to her heart as she gazed back at her father. "We have so much to look forward to."

"Yes, we do," Ruby replied.

Maggie clutched Ruby's arm. "Um, guys..." she muttered under her breath, tipping her head towards the journal still open in Eleanor's hands.

"Oh, right," she stammered with an uneasy glance at James. "Dad, gimme a second, okay? I promise—well, I *hope*—this will all make sense in just a minute." Reaching out for Ruby's hand, Eleanor took a deep breath and began to read.

"Mom, you're still my favorite story, too. Come home to us now."

In one fluid motion, Eleanor, Ruby, Marianne, and Maggie pivoted together towards the front of the shop. Then, a strangled cry escaped from Eleanor's throat. It was like she was in the dream again. Her heart thundered a gallop against her rib cage, and her breathing hitched as she tried to grapple with the reality of what she was seeing through the glass.

She was as beautiful as Eleanor remembered. Her long, red hair swirled like a halo around her head, curls dancing in the wintry breeze as evening settled over the town square. Her eyes met James' first, who reached out mindlessly, blindly, for the back of the nearest chair, steadying himself against the vision in front of them. All color leached from his skin. He looked ready to faint.

Then she turned her gaze to Eleanor, and though she couldn't hear the gasping cry that sounded from her mother's lips, Eleanor knew from her dream that it was a wondrous sound.

It was the cry of a woman for her lost love, the cry of a mother for her beloved girls.

Alice.

Vera.

Home at last.

The previous six years hurtled through Eleanor's mind, racing through time and space in the second it took for their mother to make a decision. The memory of that horrible moment when Eleanor was informed her mom was missing shifted into a memory of Eleanor lying, motionless and hollow with grief, on her bed. It then sped through the years until that day when she fell onto a desk that would finally reveal its secrets and discovered what she would soon learn were her own mother's words. Intent on being seen, somehow. Some-way.

And then she saw herself standing at Alice's grave, embraced in a circle of loving arms, safe to release her pent-up, pushed-down pain where it was held, understood, in the arms of the three other women in the room. Finally, her mind settled here. Right now. Where nothing made any sense at all, and yet, she was looking at the face of her mother.

Whole and alive and *home.*

The front door burst open, banging against the wall behind it. The jingle bells rang echoes through the store as Eleanor, Ruby, Marianne, Maggie, and James held their breath. Ruby took one uneasy step forward, eyes wide and transfixed. Eleanor could feel the tension in her sister's body as she stood there, longing rolling like waves off her skin, and Eleanor reached out for her slender, shaking fingers. It was as much a comfort as it was a talisman, a final act of hope for this precious, fragile moment.

Vera stared at her daughters, her green eyes lit from within and without, and then she fell upon Ruby and Eleanor weeping, clutching them to her body as though to keep them close forever.

"My girls," she whispered over and over into Eleanor's hair and Ruby's cheek. James and Marianne watched them, dazed, and Maggie wiped tears away with a grin that almost touched her ears. "My beautiful, darling girls."

Eleanor was dizzy with the absolute wonder of her mother's touch. She leaned into it to remind herself that it was real. She didn't have to be afraid or sad ever again.

Their mother was home.

Ruby suddenly let out a cry of such harrowing relief that it broke Eleanor's newly healed heart right in two. The old woman clung to her much younger mother, looking for all the world like just the opposite, and cried stricken, heaving sobs. Then, Eleanor felt the press of her father's arms around them all, heard his whispered cry of "Vera," and they stood there, all tangled up together, until Ruby pulled away, taking Eleanor with her.

James took Vera's face in his hands and kissed her, their tears mingling with their mouths, as he asked, "Why?" and "What?" and "How?" between each furious press of their lips.

Eleanor thought of the epitaph on Alice's grave just then and realized it had been William's answer to their questions all along.

I must go now,

but I am only
in the next room,
waiting to meet you again.

Vera, gone too soon through time and space. Vera, back again where—and with whom—she belonged. She had done what they'd all done, but with purpose and strength and a deeper faith than any Eleanor had ever witnessed. Vera had survived.

Overwhelmed, Eleanor watched her mom and dad and knew the time would come when explanations would fall short. When she would have to face more uninvited stares and inquiries into the deepest, most personal pieces of her story. When she would have to share her mom with people who might not see her return as the miracle that it was. But she knew now that none of that mattered and that this bookshop—this magical, wonderful bookshop— held everything she needed within its sturdy, secretive walls. That was all she cared about.

"Thank you," she whispered, gratitude overflowing as she touched her hand to the wall. As if in reply, the holiday lights that James had strung around the shop, as well as those draped with care around the book tree in the window, sprang to life. The whole shop filled with the fragrant scent of cinnamon and cloves, warming each of them from the inside out. Eleanor felt as if she'd just settled into a bubble bath.

All six of them turned to one another, faces lit with color and joy.

"I told you this just keeps getting better and better," Maggie said, swinging her arms from front to back, delighted by the turn of events.

"And you were right," Ruby said.

Maggie stopped short. "I'm sorry, could you repeat that?" she asked, teasing, a hand to her ear. "I was *what?*"

Ruby touched a finger to Maggie's nose and repeated, "You were right, Margaret. Now pull the string on your inflated head before you float away."

"Never," Maggie replied. "In fact, I think I've decided to come back more often."

Eleanor's mouth fell open. "For real?"

"I like Hawthorn," Maggie said simply and looked over at Vera. "It's got good people. And I need some more time to get to know my aunts and their mother. After all, we've got a lot to catch up on."

James' brows shot up, and he glanced back and forth between Maggie and his wife, who patted his shoulder. "What did she say?" he asked. "What was that?"

Eleanor laughed in reply and cocked her head at Maggie. "You think Ruby will let you stay at her house, or should you just come to hang out with your other—favorite—aunt?"

Maggie smirked. "Like I said. Better and better."

Ruby pulled on Eleanor's sleeve, turning her to face the window once more. "Truer words have never been spoken," she said as she pointed outside where fat, white flakes sparkled in the fading sunlight, painting the world in white.

It was snowing.

27

Epilogue

A canopy as colorful as a sunset over Tybee stretched across and down the length of the long, circular drive, which had finally been paved last year to accommodate the thousands of visitors who stopped by each year to see the fabled Blackhurst Victorian mansion. They came to walk the expansive grounds—a hundred acres of horticultural paradise—attend a wedding or enjoy the annual Hawthorn Holiday Lights Parade, a driving tour across the estate now hosted every Christmas.

But, mostly, they came to see the house and town that Vera Black had made famous.

Five years ago, a woman who had mysteriously disappeared for more than half a decade showed up, unharmed, at her family's bookshop. Where she had gone and how she had returned was kept a mystery that had the—confused, delighted, and, on the rare occasion, hostile— residents of Hawthorn, Georgia, wagging their tongues.

Until one year after her return, Vera Black penned a bestselling novel called *The Bluestockings* that told the entire mysterious, magical story of how she had traveled decades back in time, changing the course of her own life alongside that of her family, her daughters, and her hometown.

No one believed it, of course. Not really.

But it made for one hell of a story. And as all good Southerners know, a good story trumps the truth almost every time.

Ruby Hurst—now Blackhurst—Hawthorn's founding daughter, had been the book's loudest and most ardent supporter, hosting book clubs and advanced readings in her stunning library, which was now so beloved by visitors that it had its own Instagram account. Gone were the days when reclusive Ruby never left her house. Now, she spent her afternoons at Bluestocking Books, the last place Vera Black had been seen before she disappeared and the place that, according to her novel, had helped her home. These days, Ruby was as permanent a fixture in the bookshop as the mural the Blacks had commissioned for the large interior wall: a floor-to-ceiling rendering of passages from Vera's book. A few boring people thought it was a little too on-the-nose.

Of course, they had to paint that nonsense on the wall. At least they're committed to their lies.

But most of Hawthorn's residents had welcomed the spotlight, happy to celebrate the good news of Vera's return rather than the sadness of her disappearance. The influx of business into town certainly hadn't harmed anyone, either, and it did their hearts good to see the Black family happy and whole again. The ugly comments remained mostly online, where Eleanor could swipe left and erase them without another thought to the Internet trolls who would always find some reason to doubt. She didn't blame them, but life was too short to give up even an inch of valuable real estate in her mind.

She was too busy for that. She had a bookshop to help run.

"Okay, guys," Eleanor said with a clap of her hands. The room, full of staff, caterers, and decorators, turned to face the seventeen-year-old party planner. "We need to make sure everything is in place by five o'clock so that there's a bit of lag time between the shop closing and when guests start to arrive here at the house."

Today was a very special day. Today was Ruby Blackhurst's 85th birthday, and a massive celebration had been planned, public to both the town of Hawthorn and anyone else who found themselves swept up in the revelry, which wouldn't be difficult.

The party stretched across Hawthorn from the bookshop to Ruby's home on the other side of town. First, James and Vera were hosting a smaller do at Bluestocking for local business owners as Ruby's thank-you for their ongoing collaboration with the shop, and each other, over the past few years. Now that Hawthorn was on the map, so to speak, they'd come together to form an association of sorts to help ensure that every place of business in the city limits would benefit as much as the other. The result had been an ever-growing list of successes and, most importantly, friendships. Ruby considered her birthday as much their celebration as it was hers since it was their love and support that had kept Bluestocking afloat when it was floundering. And without Bluestocking Books—without Eleanor, Maggie, and their persistent curiosity—none of this would have been possible to begin with.

Oh, how life had changed. Once, Ruby had told herself it was too late, too pointless, to hope for joy. She had never been happier to be proved wrong.

And if Ruby had anything to say about it—which she usually did—there were many more years left of it to come.

Later in the day, the plan was to open up both the Blackhurst home and the grounds for partygoers to enjoy. Each room in the lower level of the house had been utterly transformed into a different theme, thanks to Maggie's genius, all of them an ode to Ruby herself and the things that made her happy. A ridiculously expansive coffee bar in the formal dining room. A veritable greenhouse in the parlor for guests to create their own floral arrangements. And, of course, the library, which needed no addition other than a stunning display of portraits that showed Ruby throughout her life: as a young girl seated at her father's desk, as a teenager on stage in a form-fitting gown, with her siblings as a grown woman, embracing Maggie and Marianne on her front porch, and with the Black family at Bluestocking Books.

There was also a single shot of a toddler Ruby in the arms of a tall, elegant woman with a book in her hands, masses of long curls down both their backs. It had been discovered in the pages of one of William Hurst's favorite novels, tucked away on a shelf in the library untouched for many years. Vera found the photo. Or, rather, it found her, falling into her lap one afternoon while she, Maggie, Ruby, and Marianne combed through the library to catalog every single book for the estate.

One could always count on a book to reveal the truth.

"Everything's ready on our end," Maggie said to Eleanor with a clipboard in her hand. She'd taken to her role as the Blackhurst Foundation intern with aplomb. After deciding to move to Hawthorn after high school, she'd marched straight to Ruby with a proposal for how the estate could get listed on the National Register of Historic Places, one day open to the public, and then provide a pathway for anyone in their community to get a college degree, no matter who their families were or where they came from. In the past year and a half, enough scholarship money had been raised to send five students from the surrounding counties to the state university of their choice, completely free of charge.

Eleanor nodded. "Great," she exclaimed. "Ruby will be home in about half an hour, and then guests arrive at six."

"We've got it covered," Maggie said and turned to the group. "You guys can take a break, but please make sure you're all back to your stations by 5:45 in case people show up early."

Everyone murmured in agreement and then spilled out of the crowded foyer, most of them headed to the kitchen for refreshments.

"I hope Ruby likes it," Eleanor said, releasing a heavy sigh once it was just the two of them left. "I'm exhausted."

Maggie laughed and placed her hand on Eleanor's shoulder. "She's going to love it, of course. It was her idea."

At five-thirty, Vera, James, and Ruby came laughing into the kitchen, just back from the bookshop.

"Was it a good party?" Marianne asked, handing them each a headband with sparkly gold leaves bouncing from springs. She was already wearing one on her head.

Ruby eyed hers with a suspicion that bordered on distaste. "You do not expect me to wear that."

"Oh, come on," James said, shoving his on with a silly grin. "It's not every day you turn eighty-five years old."

"Yeah, you're only young once," Vera added with a wink, pulling Ruby close.

Ruby scoffed. "Speak for yourself." But she put the headband on anyway, laughing despite herself as the leaves bounced wildly in front of her eyes. "I look ridiculous."

"You look like you're having fun," Marianne corrected. "And it's a good look on you."

As magical as Vera's homecoming had been that December night in the bookshop, the healing journey had been more precarious. Marianne had destroyed the journal, burning it in the library fireplace as the rest of them looked on, knowing what it took for her to fully let go of the life she'd lived before. Ruby'd had so many years to catch up on with her mother, and so many memories, and the heartbreak of a life without her mother didn't go away without lots of work on both their parts. James had been overjoyed at Vera's return but confused almost to the point of anger when the five women tried to explain the answers to his "Why?" and "What?" and "How?"

Eleanor explained about the bookshop and finding the journal. Marianne told him her whole life story. Ruby shared all that had happened to her as a child and what she'd learned from William just before his death. And Vera spent many evenings at the shop with James, offering details about her experience that even Eleanor wasn't privy to. He tried to understand, but doubts persisted, as they often do.

It wasn't until the photograph of Alice and Ruby had fallen out of William's book that James had finally chosen to believe, even if it meant he would never fully understand.

It was the beginning of a whole new faith for all of them.

As guests began to arrive at the house and the party hit its stride, the women mingled around the grounds, welcoming locals and strangers alike. The Blackhurst Estate, once a quiet, lonely shell of a place, was now a lively, welcoming home, resurrected by a power none of them would ever be able to explain but which looked and sounded and felt a whole lot like love.

Outside, behind the house, partygoers danced on a rented floor in the center of the sunken rose garden. The crisp air smelled of salt and peaches, the tea olive trees encircling the iron fence with their fragrant, heady blooms. Eleanor and her father danced a clumsy waltz, and then she stood back to watch him take Ruby for a spin, albeit a gentle one. She moved like water, smooth and graceful, even at eighty-five. When James dipped her lightly to the side, Ruby giggled like a girl in her father's arms.

Eleanor was so glad to know her.

Classical music played a soundtrack over the party, pumped from inside the house to the outdoor speakers in the garden and on the front lawn. Laughter clinked like champagne glasses, and the steady hum of jovial conversation filled Ruby with peaceful contentment. This was her party, but what it felt like was the culmination of a dream, a lifelong desire to be seen and known and loved for exactly who she was. Ruby felt younger now than she had in years.

At eight o'clock, Maggie approached the podium set up by the towering birthday cake in the garden and greeted their guests. "I just want to thank you all for being here and for celebrating this wonderful woman we have the privilege of calling aunt, sister, daughter, and friend," she said to the hushed crowd.

Eleanor caught a few side glances between guests at the word "daughter," but that was par for the course. They didn't have to believe everything Ruby claimed to love her, and so long as her sister was loved well, Eleanor didn't mind a few disbelieving looks now and again. She'd made her peace with them.

Maggie continued. "Speaking for the Blackhurst Foundation, I also want to thank you for your generous donations this evening, which will go directly to supporting the educational needs of people in our community." Applause sounded as Maggie beamed and handed the microphone to Eleanor.

She was going to try her best not to cry, but her chin began to tremble as soon as she took the microphone. "Many of you know Ruby as a philanthropist or as a descendant of Hawthorn's founding father. She's been a fixture in this town for eight-and-a-half decades, and in recent years, her presence has guided us through an era of flourishing unlike any we've ever seen before." Cheers resounded. Eleanor took a deep breath to steady herself as many in the crowd smiled encouragingly at her. "But we—" she raised her arm towards Maggie, Marianne, Vera, and James, who were standing around a seated Ruby, still wearing the sparkling headband, a broad smile on her face, "—we know Ruby as family.

"Not all of us knew her that way at first. It took some time. But now that we do, we can't imagine what our world would be like without Ruby in it. She is a firecracker and a force to be reckoned with. She is also tender, just, and kind. Her life tells a story of hope, and it's because of that hope that we all have the privilege of standing here today to celebrate who she is and what she has given us. Not just her time and her generosity. But herself." At this, Eleanor turned to face her sister, who was dabbing at her eyes with a tissue. "And she is the greatest gift of all. Happy birthday, Ruby. We love you."

The crowd raised their glasses in unison and began to sing, their voices rolling across the grounds like rivers to the sea.

"That was beautiful, sweetheart," Vera said to Eleanor as she moved their way.

"I meant every word."

Ruby reached out for her hand and kissed it. "Thank you," she said in a voice tight with emotion. Eleanor leaned down to hug her. "Thank you for all of it."

As the cake was cut and slices were handed out to eager guests, the sudden, deafening crack of fireworks filled the air, and everyone gasped at the sight of exploding gold stars in the sky.

"What the hell?" Maggie exclaimed, grabbing for her clipboard behind the podium. "They weren't supposed to start the fireworks until nine."

"Oh, it's alright," Ruby shouted over the boom. "It makes for a nice show while we eat this delicious cake."

Maggie made a face but then shrugged when James offered her a slice. They all dug in and ate in happy silence as they watched the show, a magical display of light that popped and cracked and sizzled around them.

"I still can't believe this is our life," Eleanor said, her face lit up in blue as another firework exploded. She turned to her family and pressed a hand to her chest. "That the end of the story turned out to be all of us here, together."

Vera reached out for her daughter's hands—first the youngest, then the oldest—and then smiled up at the sky, her expression one of joy coming to life.

"Whoever said that this was the end?"

Acknowledgements

Anyone who writes books knows that many hands make light work. While this story is the result of my own imagination, it would not exist on paper if it weren't for some truly wonderful people in my life.

First, I want to thank my husband, Pierce, for sixteen years of generous encouragement and steadfast love. You are, as I like to say, the kindest and best of men. I wouldn't be the writer I am today without the story of our life together.

To my daughter, Lucy, who saved the entire operation when you helped me fix a major plot hole halfway through the edits. Talking books with you is my favorite thing.

To Theo, my Sweet T, for the best cuddles a mama could ask for. I hope you never run out of those tender, healing hugs.

To my incredible parents, who taught me to read and then gave me as many books as I wanted. This is all your fault, honestly.

To my siblings—Beth, Tommy, and Kati—who buy my books and send me pics from the store as proof. Thank you for being my very best friends.

To Lolo, who has walked alongside me since before I even knew I'd be a writer. Your friendship (and all those beautiful cross-stitches!) are a deep well of inspiration.

To Rosalie, a champion of my work and a brilliant artist in your own right. I'm so glad to know you, friend.

To Mary Beth, who never fails to have an encouraging word for the people she loves. You've always been my biggest cheerleader. Aren't I lucky?

To Jillian, whose Snapchats make me laugh until my stomach hurts and whose clear-eyed optimism has moved me since that very first day of band camp. I'll come and sit by you any day.

To Peyton, a writing partner, sounding board, and friend of the very best kind. I'm so thankful our husbands met each other!

To all my friends and family, for reading my stories and telling other people about them. You make this whole thing possible.

Finally, and most importantly, to my Father in heaven, for the story He is writing in me. I hope my words always point readers to You.

About the Author

Wendi Nunnery is the author of a young adult duology and a best-selling spiritual memoir. Her work has appeared in *The Huffington Post* and she writes regularly on her Substack, The Nook. Wendi lives outside Atlanta, Georgia with her husband of sixteen years and their two wild, wonderful children. *The Bluestockings* is her third novel.